'HA!' GAXAR BARKED out his laughter. 'Now it's my turn to kill you, Konrad. But when you die, you die forever!'

'What about the shield?' said Konrad.

'What?' asked Gaxar. 'The shield?'

'Where does that shield come from?'

For a moment, Gaxar gazed down at the battered shield he held. 'How should I know?' he growled. 'Let us fight!'

'Why?'

'Why? Why! Because I want to kill you, Konrad, that's why, that's why! I now possess Fenbrod's brutal strength, and I still have my own magical skills. I intend to destroy you. No one kills me and gets away with it!'

More Warhammer from the Black Library

· THE KONRAD TRILOGY ·

KONRAD by David Ferring

SHADOWBREED by David Ferring

WARBLADE by David Ferring

· GOTREK & FELIX ·

TROLLSLAYER by William King

SKAVENSLAYER by William King

DAEMONSLAYER by William King

DRAGONSLAYER by William King

BEASTSLAYER by William King

VAMPIRESLAYER by William King

· THE GENEVIEVE NOVELS ·

DRACHENFELS by Jack Yeovil

GENEVIEVE UNDEAD by Jack Yeovil

· WARHAMMER NOVELS ·

ZARAGOZ by Brian Craig

ZAVANT by Gordon Rennie

HAMMERS OF ULRIC by Dan Abnett, Nik Vincent & James Wallis

GILEAD'S BLOOD by Dan Abnett & Nik Vincent

THE WINE OF DREAMS by Brian Craig

· WARHAMMER FANTASY STORIES ·

REALM OF CHAOS
eds. Marc Gascoigne & Andy Jones

LORDS OF VALOUR
eds. Marc Gascoigne & Christian Dunn

A WARHAMMER NOVEL

Book 3 of the Konrad Trilogy
WARBLADE

By David Ferring

A BLACK LIBRARY PUBLICATION

First published in 1993

This edition published in Great Britain in 2002 by
Games Workshop Publishing,
Willow Road, Lenton, Nottingham, NG7 2WS, UK

10 9 8 7 6 5 4 3 2 1

Cover illustration by Karl Kopinski

Copyright © 1993, 2002 Games Workshop Ltd. All rights reserved.

Games Workshop, the Games Workshop logo and Warhammer are trademarks of Games Workshop Ltd., registered in the UK and other countries around the world. The Black Library and the Black Library logo are trademarks of Games Workshop Ltd.

A CIP record for this book
is available from the British Library

ISBN 1 84154 233 4

Set in ITC Giovanni

Printed and bound in Great Britain by
Cox & Wyman Ltd, Cardiff Rd, Reading, Berkshire RG1 8EX, UK

No part of this publication may be reproduced, stored in a retrieval system, or transmitted in any form or by any means, electronic, mechanical, photocopying, recording or otherwise, without the prior permission of the publishers.

This book is sold subject to the condition that it shall not, by way of trade or otherwise, be lent, re-sold, hired out or otherwise circulated without the publisher's prior consent in any form of binding or cover other than that in which it is published and without a similar condition including this condition being imposed on the subsequent purchaser.

See the Black Library on the Internet at
www.blacklibrary.co.uk

Find out more about Games Workshop
and the world of Warhammer at
www.games-workshop.com

CHAPTER ONE

'KONRAD!' HISSED THE skaven. 'We've been waiting for you...'

Gaxar had adopted his human guise, and he stood in the cave into which the narrow tunnel opened. The cavern was illuminated by phosphorescence from the subterranean rocks, a ghostly light which cast no shadows.

Konrad and the Altdorf officer gazed at the terrible scene which confronted them.

Litzenreich and Ustnar were nailed by their hands and feet to the ground, their limbs outspread. Blood dripped from these raw wounds, and also from the other injuries inflicted to their naked bodies. They writhed in agony, but were unable to voice their pain because they had been gagged.

Human and dwarf lay eight feet apart. Between them was room for another crucifixion, and four iron nails marked where the third victim's palms and ankles would be hammered to the rock – and Konrad was the intended sacrifice, his flesh to be ripped and his bones splintered by the cruel metal spikes.

Gaxar had known that he would come in search of his comrades.

There was another skaven in the chamber, but this giant rodent had not taken on human form. It was Silver Eye. Konrad had given the creature that name when he had been a prisoner in the ratbeasts' lair deep below Middenheim, and named him because of the shimmering piece of warpstone that had replaced his missing left eye. Silver Eye had been one of Gaxar's bodyguards and had escaped with his master when their domain had been assaulted and overwhelmed by the military forces from the City of the White Wolf. Now, here beneath Altdorf, the warrior skaven still carried the black shield with its mysterious golden emblem of mailed fist and crossed arrows.

Recognizing Konrad, the rodent almost grinned, and its tongue curled from its mouth, lapping at its jowls. Konrad remembered the loathsome feel of the creature's rasping tongue when it had licked blood from his face. The next time there was blood between them, he vowed, it would be Silver Eye's...

Konrad had always hated skaven, but clustered around the two supine prisoners were dozens of creatures even more repulsive than the rat-things. They seemed half human, almost like infants. As pale as maggots, their naked flesh displayed their lack of true humanity. They were more like ghouls, drained of all life; their only colour was the red of their eyes.

With their huge and deformed heads, scaly bodies and stunted tails, twisted limbs and three-clawed paws, the troglodyte mutants wailed and cried as they fought each other in their obscene blood lust. It was they who had caused most of the wounds to the supine sacrificial offerings.

These were the victims and torturers; but they were not the only creatures within the underground chamber. There was also an audience to the barbaric scene of torment and mutilation. They stood in the darkness beyond the river, high upon a ledge on the far side of the cavern, a handful of shadowy shapes hidden behind the stalactites that hung from the damp roof of the cavern.

Konrad absorbed all these details in the instant it took him to step from the twisting tunnel. At the same time, he switched his sword from his right hand to his left, then reached behind his back. Beneath his cloak lay the holster which held the weapon to which he had devoted so much practice time over the preceding days. He drew it; he aimed; he fired.

As the trigger released the taut wire, the six inch bolt hurtled from the device. The weapon was a precision mechanism of brass wheels and steel cogs: a one-handed crossbow.

Gaxar was a grey seer, powerful in the dark arts, but he could not defend himself from such swift retribution. The arrow flew straight and true, sinking into his right eye and deep into his skull, its impact knocking him backwards. He attempted to grasp the steel bolt with his right hand, in a vain attempt to pull it free – but he had no right hand. As a skaven, his paw was missing; as a human, his hand was gone. Litzenreich claimed that it was he who had deprived Gaxar of that part of his anatomy.

The skaven dropped, slowly and silently, and lay unmoving on the ground.

The inhuman infants had been wailing and screaming out their hunger for flesh, but now came a shriek which drowned out all their feral sounds, a chilling cry that momentarily froze Konrad. It was Silver Eye, mourning the death of his master. He raised his sword and hurtled towards Konrad in his quest for vengeance. But the Altdorf officer leapt forwards, blocking the skaven's route. Their swords rang as they clashed together.

Konrad sprang to the aid of the captives, flinging his crossbow aside. The pale hordes scurried towards him, and his sword swept at the first of the vermin. Its ugly head flew from its stunted body – but kept on hideously screeching as it arced across the cavern. More of the deformed swarm scuttled towards Konrad, and more of them died.

They tried to drag him down by sheer weight of numbers, clutching at him with their talons, leaping up and tearing at his flesh. Their claws and teeth were their only weapons, and blood soon flowed from his wounds; but far more blood poured from his assailants. Immune to his own pain, Konrad stabbed and hacked at his enemies, punching and kicking, trampling them beneath the metal studs of his boots. Their flesh was carved and squashed, their bones snapped and crushed.

No longer did the mutants gibber with primitive delight as they lapped at human blood; now they gasped as their own lifeblood ebbed away. The sound of their dying was more repulsive than that of their feasting.

A score dead, the same number hideously mutilated and breathing their last, and still they came at Konrad as he hacked his way through them to Litzenreich. He leaned down, ripping away the gag from the wizard's mouth.

More of the verminous things sprang at him, and he nearly fell. His sword swung, despatching yet more of the predators. But there was still far too many of them. If he slipped on the gore which oozed treacherously over the rocks, he would never rise. Down on their level, the pygmy army would overwhelm him in seconds.

'Magic!' Konrad yelled. 'A spell!'

'Free my hand,' Litzenreich managed to say.

Konrad spun around, hurling away the cold bodies which clung to him. His sword flashed, and heads flew, blood spurting. He tried to pull the nail free from Litzenreich's right hand, but it was too firmly embedded in the rock.

'Pull the hand, pull the hand!' ordered the wizard – and Konrad obeyed.

Litzenreich's arm came up, and most of his hand with it, but shards of broken bone and chunks of red flesh stayed fixed to the iron nail. The wizard screamed in agony, clenching what was left of his fist. But then he stretched out his arm, pointed with his hand, and his scream became transformed into a spell. A thunderbolt shot from his ruined fingers, a jagged streak of lightning which impaled one of his erstwhile tormentors, searing through its warped torso, instantly turning it from deathly white to charred black.

The creature screeched as it was roasted alive. It was still burning, still howling, when the next one burst into flames. Then another erupted in a blaze of red and yellow. The cavern grew brighter, the sounds of death became louder, and the stink of death was almost overpowering.

Litzenreich burned them up; Konrad cleaved them apart. Either way: they died.

Konrad reached Ustnar, sliding his sword below the head of one of the nails which restrained the dwarf's hands, using the blade as a lever to draw the nail upwards. Ustnar's right hand came free, and he immediately grabbed the throat of one of the brutes which was trying to bite through his shoulder. He raised it high, squeezed until its neck broke, then cast it aside. By then, Konrad had released his other hand.

There were very few of the stunted monsters left, and yet they attacked with unabated frenzy. Ustnar grabbed one with each hand, and smashed their skulls together, again and again until their heads were reduced to a gory mess. Meanwhile, Konrad released the dwarf's feet. As the final nail came free, his sword snapped in two. He drove the broken blade into the belly of another mutant, right up to the hilt. The screeching thing lurched away, taking the weapon with it.

Litzenreich must have used a spell to free himself, because by now he was on his feet, surrounded by burning carcasses. The troglodytes were all dead or dying.

The Altdorf officer was also dead, but there was no trace of Silver Eye. He had gone, and he had taken Gaxar's body with him. Nor was there any sign of the figures Konrad had noticed earlier, the ones who had seemed to be spectators on the ledge beyond the stream.

Litzenreich and Ustnar and Konrad looked at one another. The first two were almost totally red with blood, most of it their own. Although he had been protected by his clothing, Konrad had been clawed and bitten in many places.

Then they heard a sound from one of the passages that led from the cavern, and they all turned. The ominous sound was growing louder, coming closer, the sound of more enemies rushing towards them. And like the creatures they had just slaughtered, these enemies were not human. There must have been scores of them, their bestial warcries echoing through the tunnels – and this Chaos horde would not be midgets, would not be unarmed, would not be defeated with such relative ease.

'The river!' yelled Konrad. 'It's our only chance of getting out!'

This was how he had originally planned to escape from Altdorf, but he had thought they would only be fleeing from the jail where Litzenreich and Ustnar had been incarcerated – not from a whole legion of the damned.

They made their way quickly to the water's edge, the magician and the dwarf both limping. The river flowed through a channel worn away in the ancient rock, then disappeared into a tunnel at the edge of the cavern.

'I hate water!' said Ustnar, staring down into the swirling foam. Then he jumped in and disappeared. By the time he broke surface, he was halfway to the arch where the river flowed beneath the rock.

Litzenreich did not move, however, not until Konrad shouldered him. The wizard cried out as he fell, and became silent as he went under. His head appeared for a few seconds before he was carried away into the culvert.

By then, Konrad had begun to strip off his heavy outfit. His helmet, his cloak, his cuirass and one boot were gone by the time he saw the first glint of feral eyes in the darkness of the passageway from which the menacing sounds echoed louder and louder every moment.

He leapt down into the icy waters of the subterranean stream. After a few seconds he came up, taking a deep gulp of air, not knowing when he would next be able to breathe.

As he gazed upwards, he saw that the ledge on the far side of the cavern had not been totally deserted. Two dark shapes still stood there, and because he was closer Konrad could see them quite well.

One of them was Skullface!

There was no mistaking the preternaturally thin body, the bald head which seemed to have no flesh on the bone.

And Konrad also recognized the figure by Skullface's side.

It was Elyssa.

Then Konrad was swept into the darkness of the tunnel, lost within the rushing waters of the torrent, and all he could do was remember...

HE REMEMBERED.

For over five years he had believed that Elyssa was dead, that she had been murdered when their village had been attacked and totally destroyed by a ravaging army of beastmen. Until now, Konrad had thought that he was the only survivor.

The assault had occurred on the first day of summer, on Sigmar's holy day. The previous day Konrad had attempted to leave the village, but he had been unable to pass through the ranks of marauders who encircled the valley. Disguising himself in the hide of a beastman he had slain, he had been forced back by a trio of skaven, made to witness the total annihilation of the only home he had ever known.

Making his way through the mayhem and destruction, he had reached the manor, hoping that he might save Elyssa. But the Kastring family house was ablaze; no one could have survived within. No one human.

But an inhuman figure had emerged unscathed from the fierce flames, the skeletal shape that Konrad had come to think of as Skullface. Konrad had taken aim with his bow and sent one of his black arrows deep into Skullface's heart. Had he been human, the gaunt figure would have died. Instead, he had pulled the arrow free from his bare chest – but there had been no blood, not even a sign of a wound.

Konrad had turned and fled, and he had managed to escape from the holocaust.

No one else could possibly have survived, so he had always believed.

Elyssa...

Elyssa who was Konrad's first love, and still his only true love.

Elyssa who had named him.

Elyssa who had changed his life.

Elyssa who had given him the quiver, the bow, the arrows, all of which had been marked with the enigmatic heraldic device – the device emblazoned upon the shield now carried by Silver Eye.

Skullface must have captured the girl, keeping her alive so long for some unknown diabolic purposes of his own.

Having failed five years ago, it seemed Konrad had been given another chance to save her.

He had ventured into the labyrinths beneath Altdorf in order to rescue Litzenreich and Ustnar from the cells in which they had been imprisoned by the city authorities; he owed the latter a debt, if not the former. The dwarf was the only survivor of those who had freed him from Gaxar's clutches, a period of incarceration which had been caused by the wizard's devious machinations in his quest for skaven warpstone. But by the time Konrad had reached Litzenreich and Ustnar, it was too late; it was their turn to fall into the grey seer's power.

Konrad was certain that Gaxar was no more; but Silver Eye had escaped, taking with him the shield which had made Konrad pursue the two skaven from Middenheim to the Imperial capital.

Yet that was of no importance, not now, and neither were Litzenreich and Ustnar. All that mattered was Elyssa.

Konrad wanted to return, to swim back to the chamber where he had seen the girl, but the force of the water was too powerful and carried him inexorably through the narrow culvert. It was Elyssa who had taught him to swim, he remembered.

She had given him so much of his life that it was difficult to remember anything before the day they had met. It was as if he had not been truly born until then. She was the daughter of the lord of the manor, he the peasant boy who worked in the inn. He had saved her life, slaying the beastman which had attacked her at the edge of the forest. In return, she had given him an identity – but he still did not know who he really was or where he came from.

The raging stream did not totally fill the tunnel, and as he broke surface, Konrad was careful to keep his mouth shut and breathe only through his nose. Some of the sewers and drains from the capital emptied into the underground river, but these were by no means the most foul waters Konrad had ever found himself in.

He could see nothing in the darkness and spent most of his time beneath the surface, buffeted against the rocks on either side, judging that injuries to his limbs were preferable to having his head cracked open if the roof of the passage should suddenly become lower.

When he came up for air the third time, he noticed that the darkness ahead was not so total. It was night, and this could be where the river emerged from beneath the city. If it was, then the exit would be blocked by a portcullis, some kind of device designed to allow the water to flow freely but stop intruders using the drainage system as a way of entering the city. There might also be regular sentries on duty at the sluice gate.

When Konrad and the officer had discovered that the two cells beneath the army garrison were empty, the latter had sent orders that Litzenreich and Ustnar should be prevented from escaping via the underground river. By now, there would almost certainly be guards waiting for whoever reached the end of the tunnel.

For the first time, instead of letting himself be carried by the force of the stream, Konrad tried to delay his progress. The waters were far too strong for him to swim against, but that did not prevent him trying. His pace barely slowed. He reached out blindly, hoping to grab an outcropping rock and halt himself. If not, he would soon come to an immediate stop, smashed against the railings or whatever obstructed the end of the culvert.

The blackness ahead had become grey, and he thought he could make out the shape of the opening. Where were Litzenreich and Ustnar? Had the force of the water crushed them against the heavy mesh, knocked them unconscious? Had they sunk below the surface and drowned?

Closer and closer came the paler darkness, faster and faster did Konrad seem to be propelled. Then he saw a distant light. The end of the tunnel was either illuminated on the outside, or else it was the torches of the waiting troops. He turned his back, bracing himself for the inevitable impact against the maze of metal bars which must form part of the capital's defences.

And then, suddenly, he was out of the tunnel. The maze of spikes at the end of the subterranean stream had been snapped and twisted aside. That could only have been the work of Litzenreich's wizardry.

He found himself in a much wider, deeper river. It must have been the Reik. He was out of Altdorf, downstream from the city walls.

He saw lanterns close to the outlet, could make out shadowy figures holding them, heard the sound of voices – and a sudden shout.

'There! Another one!'

He ducked down below the surface, and an arrow hit the water by the side of his face. Deflected by the impact against the river, it missed his shoulder by an inch. Another shaft sliced past his chest. Konrad dived deeper, kicked around and began swimming up the Reik, towards the city. The troops would not expect that, he hoped. The current was not as strong as it had been in the tunnel. Forced into the confines of the culvert, the stream had seemed more powerful than the Reik, the greatest river in the Old World.

He wondered who the soldiers thought they were firing at, but he was in no position to argue with them.

His original idea had been to release Litzenreich and Ustnar from their cells, then escape from the city with them. He had had no reason to stay in Altdorf – it had seemed unlikely that Silver Eye was here – and helping the other two to flee meant he could not remain.

But now he had to return, had to get back into the Imperial capital, into the underground city where Skullface held Elyssa captive.

He ceased swimming and rolled over onto his back, cautiously lifting his face above the surface in order to breathe, poised to dive below again. He saw the lights some forty yards downstream, on the far bank of the river. For the moment he was safe, and the same must have been true of the magician and the dwarf.

Evading a handful of militia would be simple for Litzenreich. Although wounded and naked and unarmed, now that they were beyond the city the other two were more than a match for any of the dangers they might encounter in this region.

Konrad would have liked to have them both with him. They would be very useful companions when he ventured into the unknown network of passages beneath the city, Ustnar for his tunnelling and fighting skills, Litzenreich for his wizardry. But there was no reason why they should have wished to accompany him, even if he could have found them.

As so often in the past, he was on his own. And that was how he preferred it. Litzenreich could not be trusted. Wolf had been right about sorcerers.

For a moment, he wondered about Wolf and where he might be. Was he still in Kislev, on the border? Was there still a border, or had the northern hordes overrun the land? But if things were that bad, news would have reached Altdorf and Sergeant Taungar would surely have made reference to the campaign when he had recruited Konrad into the Imperial guard.

He swam up river, slowly. That seemed the best way to enter the capital, but the city walls were far away and apparently coming no nearer. Although not as powerful as the underground current, the tide was very strong, and Konrad found himself growing more weary, as though fighting against a remorseless adversary. There was a boom across the river, he remembered, a floating barrier to prevent vessels proceeding further up the Reik without permission – and without paying river dues.

The river was always blocked at night, and he could see that the area was well lit. It would also be under constant surveillance, particularly as the alarm had been sounded. He would do better finding another way in, and he began searching for a place to come ashore.

This was no ordinary riverside, where the ground sloped down to the water's edge. Even beyond the city walls, the Reik was lined with high quays for the ships and boats waiting to enter the capital. He made his way across to the northern bank, which seemed a little less crowded.

Despite all that had happened, he realized that it could only have been an hour since he arrived at the army barracks. The night was still young, and there was plenty of activity aboard the vessels berthed along the river. He had to be careful that he was not seen or heard by the men on watch on board all the ships and boats.

There was a gap of thirty yards between a sea-going merchant craft and a humble river barge, and Konrad swam to a point midway between the two. It was ten feet to the top of the quay, and he grabbed hold of a frayed rope dangling from a bollard above.

He stayed there for several minutes, only his head above the water while he leaned against the wooden piling and regained his breath, and he kept gazing around and above for signs of observation. It was a dark night; neither moon had yet risen.

Finally, he began hauling himself up out of the water. Under most circumstances, he could have shinned up such a rope in two or three seconds; but he was exhausted, the rope was wet and slippery, and it took twice as long to reach the halfway point.

He heard voices above and looked up, seeing two faces staring down. They may not have noticed him in the shadows, and he froze. But then the rope swayed slightly and started to rise. They were pulling him up. He was about to let go and drop back into the safety of the water when one of the two men called down to him.

'Hold on, mate! We'll get ya outa there.'

Their accent was unfamiliar; they were not Altdorf soldiers. They must have been sailors from some other part of the Empire, and they must have believed Konrad had fallen into the river from one of the boats upstream.

He had lost his other boot in the culvert, and the only other things he wore which could betray his current profession were his sword belt and scabbard. Without a sword, they had no function.

One-handedly, Konrad swiftly unbuckled the military belt and let it fall.

'Ya doing fine, mate. Soon havya up.'

The two mariners hauled him up, and both reached down to grab his arms. He accepted the grip of one, not wanting to risk both of them seizing him in case this was a trap.

A second or two later, he was up on the dockside. The sailor released his grip, and the two men laughed as they stared at him.

'Thanks,' he said, deliberately swaying to one side, then pretending to regain his balance. 'Can't get used to the ground not moving, you know.'

'Yeah,' agreed the one whose hand he had taken, and he laughed again, 'we know. Where's your ship?'

Konrad jerked his thumb upriver, towards the city. 'Just there. I'll be fine. Thanks. Be fine. Or you want a drink? Maybe we should go for a drink, huh?'

'Some other time, mate,' said the second sailor. 'Looks like ya've had enough. Don't want ta end up in the drink again, do ya?'

Konrad shook his head, and kept on shaking it. 'No,' he said. 'No. No.' He backed away, staggering a little. 'But next time, next time, the drinks are on me. Right?'

'Right.'

'Right.'

He waved to his rescuers, then turned and made his way slowly along the quay. He could tell they were still watching him, making sure that he did not veer to one side and plummet back into the Reik. He reached the barge, turned and waved to them both, then kept on going. Next time he looked back, they were out of sight.

He straightened up, wiped the water from his face, and wondered how to get back inside the city.

Altdorf was the Imperial capital. It did not bar all its gates at dusk. Its citizens did not hide away in terror until dawn, dreading the creatures that prowled the night. The hours of darkness were not lost to the city, as they were in so many villages and towns throughout the Empire. Altdorf felt itself secure, that there were enough troops in the city to protect it against any danger.

It was true that Altdorf need not fear what lay beyond the city walls – but Konrad had discovered that the greatest threat was what lay beneath the capital.

He made his way along the quayside towards the white walls of the city, where the last massive tower seemed to grow out of the depths of the river. Under normal circumstances, it would have been easy to pass through the gate on the inner side of the tower. For a few pence, a bribe to the watch, sailors whose vessels were berthed downriver were allowed in and out of Altdorf no matter what the hour. Their most frequent destination was the Street of a Hundred Inns, but they could also take advantage of the other nocturnal attractions which the Empire's greatest city had to offer to both its citizens and its visitors.

Cautiously, keeping to the shadows, Konrad approached the entrance. It appeared that there was more security at the river gate than seemed appropriate. The area was well lit, and through the opening he could see that several troops were on guard, as well as members of the watch. A number of sailors from different lands were arguing and shouting, trying to leave the city, but each of them was being interrogated and checked before they were allowed out.

A handful of men passed through in the other direction without any such difficulty. The militia were only inspecting those who wanted to leave. They would be under orders to find a wizard and dwarf. The latter should present no difficulty, even to the watch, assuming that one should attempt to pass through. But Konrad wondered how they were expected to trap a magician. Perhaps there was another sorcerer in the guard house, and he could detect when a fellow practitioner was in the vicinity.

If he were not soaking wet and had a few coins on him, Konrad would have been able to pass into the capital quite easily; but he was soaking wet and he had no coins. The golden crown Taungar had given him when he enlisted had been in his tunic before the battle, but it was gone. His clothes would never dry, not at this hour, not now that winter was nigh. Already he was shivering with cold, and he must shed his sodden garments soon.

Konrad watched as the sailors passed out of the city. Most of them were in groups. He needed only one, because what he had to do must be done quickly and silently, and the one he wanted had to be about the right size. He waited. Finally, a lone figure who was suitable emerged from the gatehouse. He was walking very slowly, trying to hold himself straight, but staggering slightly.

'Bastards,' he muttered under his breath. 'Altdorf bastards.' He glanced back at the city and spat over his shoulder.

'Yer right there, mate,' agreed Konrad, stepping towards him from the darkness.

'Yeah,' grumbled the drunken sailor. 'Take all our money, then won't let us out of the damned place.'

'Same here,' said Konrad, and he put his arm around the man's shoulder.

'You're all wet,' he complained, trying to evade Konrad's grip.

Konrad raised his arm, cupping the man's mouth to silence him, then dragged him back into the darkness. The sailor tried to struggle, but it was no use. A swift blow to the back of his head with Konrad's clenched fist, and he became still. A second later, he was lying on the ground. Another half a minute and his outer garments had been stripped off. Konrad tore off all his own clothes and pulled on the sailor's shirt and jacket, his breeches and boots.

The man had told the truth, Konrad discovered. Altdorf had taken all his money. Konrad fastened the sailor's belt buckle and examined the dagger that he had carried. It was a short narrow blade, probably used for gutting fish. He cut the metal buttons from his new coat. They might pass as coins long enough for him to enter the city. The guard would hardly chase after him for a few pence, he hoped. If they did, it would be too bad for them.

'Thanks, mate,' he whispered to the supine sailor. 'We're all bastards in Altdorf.'

He pulled the man's cap down over his wet hair and walked towards the city gate, clutching the three shiny buttons in his left hand. The clothes were a reasonable fit, although the boots were a little loose and rubbed at his ankles.

The watchman at the entrance barely glanced at Konrad as he waved him through.

'Your boys aren't making much tonight, Harald,' he heard one of the soldiers say to one of the watch.

'Wish you lads could be here every night,' came the reply from a tall figure wearing a copper badge. 'But I suppose if they were, your troops would also start taking a cut.'

And then Konrad was past the two officers and back within the walls of Altdorf.

CHAPTER TWO

THE ONLY WAY Konrad knew of to return to the underground cave where he had seen Elyssa and Skullface was to retrace his previous route. Even if he could find his way back down into the cavern, they would probably be long gone, but he must make the attempt.

That meant going back into the army headquarters, then down through the military prison. He expected that the barracks would be in a state of confusion; perhaps the beastmen he had heard charging to attack through the tunnel had even tried to break out into the capital.

When he reached the entrance, he stood watching from the shadows. Everything appeared as quiet as it had been when he originally arrived. Two infantrymen were guarding the open gates, but they were leaning against the wall and talking quietly to each other. It seemed no one realized the full significance of what had happened.

Two prisoners had escaped, and the officer who had discovered the jailbreak had gone in search of them after ordering that all the exits from the city should be checked.

But the officer was dead, and his death might not yet be known. It might still be thought that he was in pursuit of the fugitives, following them through the labyrinthine levels deep below Altdorf. Or if his corpse had been discovered, and there was no sign of any beast creatures, it would be believed that he had been slain by Litzenreich and Ustnar.

If it were known that the officer was the victim of the skaven, that there was a horde of Chaos marauders so very close, then the barracks would have been on full alert and every force in Altdorf would be preparing to join the expedition against the insidious invaders.

The infiltration was still secret and silent. It seemed that Konrad was the only one who knew. Maybe that was for the best, and he stood a better chance of finding Elyssa if he were alone. An army of extermination would inevitably give too much advance warning of its arrival, and the girl's captor would have time to escape with his hostage.

Konrad had to make his way under the city via the military dungeon; the base would also provide him with the weapons and armour which he needed. He had encountered no difficulty entering the barracks earlier, clad in his Imperial guard uniform and wearing the purple plume of an officer. Now, however, he was dressed in the unimpressive garb of a civilian.

He pulled off the cap and stuffed it into his pocket. His hair was so short that it was dry by now, and its cropped style was in keeping with the ascetic look adopted by the officer class of the Altdorf regiments. Konrad had made his way stealthily towards the militia headquarters. Now he backed further away until he was out of sight of the entrance, straightened himself then marched towards the gates, bringing his heels down as hard as he could.

'Ten–' he ordered, '–shun!'

The two sentries sprang to attention in immediate obedience to the order, just as Konrad came in view.

'Eyes front!' he commanded, emerging from the shadows.

They gazed past him, their halberds held out at the precise angle by their rigid arms. Konrad marched between them, through the entrance and across the courtyard, making for the brick guardhouse.

Another sentry stood on guard at the entrance, watching warily as Konrad strode confidently towards him.

'Who goes there?' he demanded, his hand on his sword hilt.

'"Sir"!' snapped Konrad. 'Call me "sir", or I'll have you on a charge for impertinence.'

'Sir!' echoed the guard, clicking his heels together. He glanced back towards the guardhouse.

It was the same man who had been on duty when Konrad first arrived. He did not want him to call for assistance from the officer of the watch.

'At ease,' said Konrad, his voice more casual. 'Your commanding officer is expecting me.' He kept walking and drew level with the sentry, who turned as he began to go past.

'I know you!' said the guard.

He was very observant, recognizing Konrad in the dim light even though he was wearing completely different clothes, and despite the fact that his face had been partly covered by his helmet the first time.

His sword was half out of its scabbard, but Konrad already held the sailor's dagger in his hand. The guard's torso was protected by his armour and chainmail. Konrad's arm thrust forwards and up, stabbing the soldier in the throat.

There was no time not to kill him. He died because he was alert, because he was good at his appointed duty – and because he was not fast enough.

Konrad clasped his hand over the sentry's mouth to silence his fatal scream, supporting his body as it dropped towards the ground, then taking his sword from his death grip. A blade in either hand, he hurried towards the entrance.

'Gunther? What's going on?'

Konrad could see an armoured figure within the building, moving towards the doorway, and then another. He knew he could probably dispose of them both before they realized what was happening, but how many more soldiers were inside? He had wanted to sneak in silently, to make his way unseen through the military quarters and down to the tunnels below. Even if he were able to fight his way through against so many troops, he would become the hunted instead of the hunter. This was already a lost cause; it was time to withdraw.

He slashed with the sword, severing the rope which held the oil lamp over the entrance. As the lantern dropped, he kicked out, smashing it and sending the pieces flying into the guardhouse. Burning oil splashed the ground and the walls, and in seconds the single flame had grown into a raging blaze.

Konrad turned and sprinted towards the main gates. The two sentries had begun to look around.

'Fire!' yelled Konrad, dashing towards them. 'Fire!'

The sentries started to run towards the blaze. Then one stopped and called to the other, who also hesitated.

'Stay at your posts!' Konrad shouted. 'I'll sound the alarm!'

But before they could return to their positions, before they could decide what to do and before they could block his exit, Konrad was past them and out into the square beyond the gates. He did not stop running until he was several streets away, when he leaned against the wall of a bakery and glanced back. There was no sign of pursuit, but he could see a cloud of thick black smoke rising slowly into the dark sky.

He wondered what to do.

He had to stay in Altdorf, because this was where Elyssa was. The only place he knew in the capital was the Imperial Palace. He would have to return and resume his role as a member of the Emperor's elite troops, pretending that the events of the past few hours had never occurred.

Konrad began making his way back to the Imperial guard barracks, taking the longer way around, and headed across Karl-Franz Bridge to reach the southern part of the city. He was still clutching the sentry's sword in his hand. It was possession of another dead soldier's sword which had led to him into this predicament, he realized.

When he had taken part in the assault on the skaven stronghold deep below Middenheim, he had fought with the blade which had belonged to one of the fortress city's troopers – which he had taken from a soldier he had killed. Gaxar and Silver Eye had escaped from their subterranean lair, and with them had been a human prisoner. That captive, Litzenreich had claimed, was the exact double of the Emperor himself!

Konrad knew that Gaxar could construct unliving creatures in the image of other humans, because he had fought a duel with his own mirror image, a doppelganger created by the grey seer. If Gaxar had fabricated a replica of Karl-Franz, it could only be for one reason: in order to replace him upon the throne of the Empire...

In that case, said Litzenreich, Gaxar must have headed for Altdorf via the skaven underworld, the maze of passages which linked all of mankind's towns and cities which had been infested by the ratbeings. That, then, was the direction which Konrad wanted to take. But it was not Gaxar for whom he was searching, it was his bodyguard. Silver Eye had carried a shield which bore the same crest that had been on the bow, the quiver and the arrows which Elyssa had given him a decade earlier. Konrad was convinced that the enigmatic gold emblem, the mailed fist between two crossed arrows, was of untold significance. If he could discover something about the military accoutrements, perhaps even find out the identity of their previous owner, he was sure it would help him in the quest for his own mysterious origins.

Because of what had happened in Middenheim, Litzenreich could no longer remain in the City of the White Wolf. He said he would also travel to Altdorf, where he could continue his researches into the use of warpstone. And so Konrad, Litzenreich and Ustnar, the only survivor of the dwarfs who served the wizard, arrived in Altdorf on board the same stagecoach – whereupon the dwarf and the sorcerer were immediately placed under arrest for breach of Imperial law.

Use of warpstone was illegal, unless in the service of the Empire. The penalty was death, and a message had been sent from Middenheim warning that two such desperate criminals were on the loose.

There was no warrant for Konrad's arrest, because no one knew that he had been with Litzenreich, or no one who had survived the battle in Gaxar's warpstone refinery. But Sergeant Taungar of the Imperial guard noticed that Konrad was carrying a sword with a wolf's head emblem, which meant that the blade belonged to a Middenheim regiment.

Taungar recognized Konrad from the time when they had both fought in Kislev, at the Siege of Praag. He knew what an expert warrior Konrad was, and he wanted to recruit him as an instructor in the Imperial guard. If Konrad joined up, he said, then the matter of the Middenheim sword could be easily dealt with.

That suited Konrad perfectly. He needed to be in Altdorf, but he did not plan on being in the Imperial guard for very long.

Now, it seemed, he would have to remain a member of the Emperor's personal army a while longer.

The sentry's sword was a functional blade, a little too heavy and not very well balanced. It was no replacement for the one he had used beneath Middenheim, nor for the Imperial guard sword which had snapped when he levered the final nail which had pinned Ustnar to the ground.

The bridge was deserted, and Konrad leaned over the parapet and dropped the sentry's blade down into the murky waters of the River Reik. He hated to be without a weapon, but he had no need of the sailor's knife, and it followed the sword into the depths. He pulled the hat from the coat pocket and put it on. It might serve to mask his identity if he were spotted.

As he tugged the woollen cap down almost to his eyes, he noticed blood on his right hand and arm. It was that of the sentry. He removed the coat and wiped his skin as best he could with the sleeve, spitting on the back of his hand to wash away the blood which had already dried, then threw the garment over the side of the bridge. The loose boots made too much noise, and they also ended up in the river.

The cobbles felt like ice, and his breath condensed in front of him as he resumed his journey towards the palace. The huge building was a black shadow against the darkness of the sky, the towering silhouette of its pinnacle outlined by the surrounding stars.

Entering the barracks where he served would be far more difficult than gaining admission to army headquarters had been. He could easily have gone inside if he did not mind being observed, but then he would have to invent a story explaining what had happened to his uniform. When he left a few hours ago, he had no intention of returning; but now it had to appear as though he had never been away. Because he had not had permission to be beyond the palace walls, there was no reason for anyone to believe that he had gone. The sentries had seen him leave, however, not suspecting that he was not allowed out. There was no reason why they should mention it, and with luck they would not be questioned.

Barefoot, Konrad felt almost as though he had reverted to the role he had lived before Elyssa entered his life and changed his whole existence. Becoming a shadow amongst shadows still came naturally, moving about silently and invisibly so that whatever he did went undetected by the innkeeper who had been his master. To this, he had added the skills he had learned working for Wolf for five years, all the tricks of subterfuge and camouflage needed for survival in Kislev, on the frontier between the human and inhuman.

Often Konrad had infiltrated enemy positions, and although these enemies had been subhuman their senses were frequently more than human. They may have been called beastmen, which meant they had none of the nobler attributes of men, but they possessed the awareness of beasts. They could see more clearly in the dark, they could hear the almost inaudible, they could detect the faintest scent of a human adversary. The only way to mask the odour of a human was to overlay it with another smell, and more than once Konrad had hidden his humanity beneath the olfactory disguise of bestial blood.

Tonight, he would not be up against anyone or anything with such an array of keen senses. The palace guards were only human, and they were his own comrades. But that would make no difference if he should make a slight error and be seen. The only challenge made to any intruder was a crossbow bolt.

One of the first things he had done when he found himself within the walls of the fort was to check all the defences, in case it became necessary to leave in a hurry. He knew all the sentry posts, all the turrets, all the observation points. The times of the patrols were frequently altered, and the changing of the guards took place at irregular intervals. He had left the palace by his own unofficial exits on a few occasions while exploring Altdorf. That was somewhat different, because the sentries were watching for intruders trying to enter, not for anyone attempting to leave.

Nothing must happen tonight to disturb the regular pattern of security within the citadel walls, nothing which would make anyone suspicious. He could create no diversions, the night's routine must remain exactly that – routine.

He kept the main entrance under observation for a time, watching while a liveried coach drew up for inspection. There was very little traffic at present, because the Emperor was away on an Imperial visit to Talabheim. Under normal circumstances, Konrad had learned, there would be conveyances entering and leaving until the early hours of the morning, with ambassadors and courtiers and aristocrats and merchants and servants and functionaries going about their duties and their pleasures.

The sentries spoke to both the driver and postilion, opened each of the carriage doors, saluted, and checked the occupants. One of them examined the underside of the coach before it was allowed access to the courtyard, and Konrad deleted this as a possible means of admittance.

But there were more ways of entering the inner fortress than through the entrances.

It was all a matter of climbing and leaping, of timing and creeping. And so Konrad climbed, scaling the outside of the palace wall midway between two observation towers, where the angle of vision gave him the best chance of being unobserved. He went up slowly, feeling for every fingerhold, every toegrip. Then the slowness turned to swiftness as he sprang across the parapet and jumped onto the roof of the stables below. That was where he had to wait, lying prone across the slates until the guards had patrolled from one end of the battlements to the next. After that came the slow squirming over the other roofs, up and down the gables, around the chimneys, then finally down and through the embrasure into the barrack room where he was billeted.

Although of an equal rank to the other recruits, Konrad had been granted an alcove to himself because of his role as a combat instructor and in deference to his military experience. He had made it back unobserved, but still he could not rest. He had lost his sword, his helmet, his armour, his uniform, and now he went about making good those losses.

'IN ALL MY years in the Imperial guard, I have never seen a parade like this!'

Taungar strode up and down, staring in disbelief at the enlisted men lined up for morning inspection in the palace courtyard.

'I've had men lose their helmets; I've had men lose their tunics; I've had men lose their leggings; I've had men lose their spurs. At one time or another, I've had men lose just about everything. Swords, lances, daggers, gauntlets, boots, breastplates, shields, horses. But never, *never* have I had so many men lose so much at one time! The equivalent of a complete uniform is missing. Did it simply walk away? Is this Jape Day? No, it is not. And even if it was, the Imperial guard is no place for practical jokes. I am not laughing. And no one who has lost so much as a single thread of braid will be laughing for a month! You will all be confined to barracks, work extra duties, and lose a month's pay – you're good at losing things – in addition to making good the cost of those items which you have misplaced. How can you be expected to protect the Emperor when you can't even look after the Emperor's uniforms which he so graciously permits you to wear? You useless bunch of incompetent idiots! Why any of you were ever allowed to enlist in the guard, I have no idea. You aren't even clever enough to join the army. You aren't even clever enough to join the watch!'

Clad in his new uniform, Konrad stared impassively ahead as Taungar strode past him, berating over half of the men under his command. There had been no opportunity to reach the quartermaster's stores and replace his missing garments and equipment from there. Instead, he had had to requisition what was required from the other troops in the barrack room: a pair of boots from one, a belt from another, and so on until he had a complete outfit. It had taken a long time to make sure that everything fitted properly. If they had been more alert, Konrad would not have succeeded and they would not have been punished. Military justice was arbitrary and harsh; it should be expected by anyone who had enlisted. Maybe they would learn a useful lesson: they should never feel safe, no matter where they might be, and they should never trust anyone.

They all stood in formation, at attention without breastplate or breeches or whatever item they had lost. There had been much confusion in the barracks when they began to dress in the darkness before dawn. Those who were first to notice their losses tried to find replacements from their comrades who were not so swift, and a number of fights had broken out. Searches had taken place, but nothing had been found. There was nothing to be found, Konrad was wearing it all.

'The army set fire to their own guardroom last night,' Taungar continued. 'If it had been you lot, I suppose you would have burned down the whole palace! Two of their prisoners escaped, and they have a sentry dead, an officer missing.'

Taungar halted in front of Konrad. 'They claim that a member of the Imperial guard was responsible for all of that.' Konrad's helmet could not hide all the fresh bites and scratches on his face. The sergeant looked directly at Konrad as he added: 'But of course they are lying to cover up their own incompetence.'

The dead officer had not been found, and there was no word about skaven or any other of the hell-spawned bestiary which infested the netherworld beneath Altdorf. Even the capital of the Empire was not safe from such benighted creatures. Or perhaps it was because it was the capital that Altdorf had become a centre of Chaos activity.

This had been Sigmar's capital after he had united the eight warring human tribes two and a half thousand years ago, although its original name had been Reikdorf. It was still the heart of the Empire, and the fastest way to destroy most beings was to strike at the heart – and that meant striking at the Emperor himself, at Karl-Franz of the house of the Second Wilhelm.

There could be no immediate threat, not with the Emperor away from the capital. If it had been Gaxar's plan to replace Karl-Franz with a necromantic duplicate, such a scheme would probably have to be abandoned now that the grey seer was dead. Gaxar must have been the only one who could control his creation, and with him gone surely the doppelganger had lost its own semblance of vitality.

Litzenreich would have known if this were the case. At one time, the wizard had claimed that he intended to defeat Gaxar's scheme to usurp the throne by use of a resurrected impostor. The sorcerer and the grey seer were old enemies.

The sentry Konrad had killed was the only trooper who could have identified him. The guards at the gate, and the one who had accompanied him and the officer down into the dungeon had not had the time or opportunity to get a proper look at him. In any case, it seemed that the Imperial guard gave no credence to the army's claims. There was little love lost between the two military forces.

But from the way he had looked at him, Taungar seemed to suspect that Konrad had something to do with the events of the previous night...

'Those of you who are fully dressed,' announced Taungar, as he began walking up and down once more, 'one step forward!'

Konrad and seven others obeyed.

'You, you, you, follow me, at the double!'

Konrad and two others followed the sergeant, and they found themselves becoming part of the escort which climbed two hundred feet to the penultimate level of the palace, the final rampart where the Imperial ensigns were unfurled every dawn, high above the city, above the Empire. One of the flagpoles had always remained empty in the days that Konrad had served here. This was the gilded staff where the Emperor's personal flag was raised whenever he was in residence.

From this vantage point, second only in height to the observation turret in the tower, the city lay spread out below. Konrad could see the army barracks, although there was no longer any sign of the fire. He could make out the Reik, and the gate in the white city walls by which he had re-entered Altdorf. He gazed beyond the red tiled roofs of the walls, and he wondered for a moment how far Litzenreich and Ustnar had managed to get in the hours since their escape.

He felt that he could almost have leaned down and picked up some of the buildings below, raising them like toys, and that underneath he would be able to see where Skullface had hidden Elyssa.

When the ceremony ended, and the last notes of the herald's bugle still echoed from the nearby dome of the Cathedral of Sigmar, the captain of the guard led his troopers back down the narrow spiral staircase towards the lower levels.

Taungar and Konrad were the last to begin the long descent, and the sergeant said: 'I will be at the Wayfarers Rest tonight.'

CHAPTER THREE

TAUNGAR'S WORDS WERE not a casual social invitation. Sergeants and enlisted men did not fraternise, and the Wayfarers was not a regular haunt of the Imperial guard. Konrad wore the clothes in which he had arrived in Altdorf, and he had a pass allowing him out of barracks for the evening. He took a long detour to the inn, going by way of Sigmar Bridge and Oswald the Hero Bridge. While he crossed the former, he jettisoned the rest of the sailor's clothing which he had kept hidden under his straw mattress since arriving back at the barracks. And finally he reached the tavern.

The place was no different from a thousand other inns, crowded and noisy, full of voices talking and laughing and arguing. The walls and ceiling were black with decades of soot, and the atmosphere was thick with the smell of ale, old and new: the sour reek of stale beer which had been spilled over the years and saturated the floor, and the heady aroma of hops from the fresh beer still being brewed behind the taproom.

At first he did not notice Taungar and thought he had not yet arrived, but he was sitting alone in the far corner. Even when he saw him, Konrad was uncertain for a moment that it really was the sergeant. Some men appeared smaller without their armour, but not Taungar. He was not a tall man, but he was well-built and muscular. His civilian clothes seemed oddly inappropriate to his physique and his battle-scarred face. He should have been dressed like a stevedore or a labourer, but he looked more like a wealthy merchant. He was clad in a well-cut light brown felt jacket and matching trousers, blue satin shirt, and a yellow silk scarf was around his neck, fastened by a gold pin of some elaborate design. Although almost as short as Konrad's, his grey hair had been neatly combed. The scabbard for a dagger hung at his hip, and it seemed to be the maximum blade length that a civilian was permitted to carry. Its handle appeared to be silver.

He was smoking a pipe, and there was an almost full goblet of wine on the table in front of him. Konrad nodded in recognition and was about to turn towards the barrels at the other end of the room, but Taungar gestured for him to join him.

'Girl!' he bellowed, as though he were drilling a parade.

Konrad sat down opposite the sergeant, and a few seconds later a young girl weaved her way through the crush. She was holding a tray of full beer tankards, which she could hardly lift, and she set it down on the table.

She could only have been about twelve years old, her hair was almost white, and there was something about her which reminded Konrad of a person he had tried not to remember. Placing one of the tankards in front of Konrad, her soft brown eyes noticed him watching her and she smiled at him. Taungar paid, and she picked up the tray again and moved off.

Her smile was identical to Krysten's: warm and honest but also mischievous.

Krysten who Konrad had almost loved. Krysten who he abandoned when he had left the mine in search of a lost dwarf temple. Krysten who had been captured by the swarms of degenerate northern invaders when the mining camp was overrun and totally annihilated. Krysten who must have been dead by now. Krysten who he hoped had died quickly and painlessly. Krysten who, he now realized, he had loved.

Konrad raised his beer stein and swallowed half the contents in a single gulp.

Taungar had been watching him, and now he said, 'Do you want to tell me what happened?'

Konrad shrugged.

'You don't have to, but maybe I can help.'

Konrad looked at him. Taungar was a veteran of many campaigns; he had survived much more than Konrad could ever know: he had served throughout the Empire, he had fought and conquered every type of adversary, human and otherwise. Konrad looked around, at all the people in the inn, some of whom were within hearing distance.

'The best place to talk secretly is where there is plenty of noise,' said Taungar. 'The best place to be unnoticed is where there are many people. So...?'

Konrad drank more of his beer. 'Chaos,' he said quietly, and Taungar nodded wisely.

It was a word that many used but few understood, and even Konrad was uncertain of its true meaning. For the majority of the population, the foul power of Chaos was completely unknown. They went about their daily affairs never suspecting its existence, never knowing the effect that it had upon their lives and how it influenced the world in which they lived.

'It's here,' Konrad added, 'in Altdorf.'

Taungar sucked on his pipe and blew smoke from between his teeth. 'I know,' he said.

'How long have you known? Since Praag?'

'Before, and I recognized the malign forces that were controlling the siege. I almost died. I'm like you, I'm a warrior. We both live on the edge of death. I was part of the relief army, and I came within a moment of dying.

Sometimes I imagine that I did die, that I have been a ghost ever since.' Taungar smiled at the idea and took a sip of his wine. 'Growing older makes us more conscious of our mortality, Konrad. When I was younger, I took so many risks, fought without a care for my own existence.' He took another sip from his goblet, then set it down.

'I know about Chaos,' he continued. 'About twenty years ago, I was one of those who went into Castle Drachenfels to clear up the mess. I'd enlisted in the Imperial guard to fight for the Emperor – this was in the days of Luitpold – to defend him and the Empire. I was young and innocent, but I grew out of both. All my ideas about the world were turned upside down when we rode into the Grey Mountains and discovered the impossible creatures that lived in the fortress of the Great Enchanter. We tortured them, hung them, burned them, but we couldn't wipe them from our memories. They were more than monstrous, more than bestial, more than evil. They were the exact opposite of everything human. They were corrupted by Chaos.'

'And they are here in Altdorf,' said Konrad, 'plotting against the Emperor.'

'There are always plots against the Emperor,' said Taungar, very calmly.

'The skaven are going to replace him with a double.'

'He can't be any worse than Karl-Franz.'

Konrad stared at Taungar in astonishment. This was not the reaction he had expected from a member of the Imperial guard. He had only mentioned Gaxar's conspiracy because he needed Taungar's assistance, and that assistance would have little to do with protecting Karl-Franz; but by focusing on this aspect, he had believed that Taungar would help him. What he needed was someone who knew Altdorf, someone who would know how to locate the hidden passages beneath the city.

'What has the Emperor ever done for me?' asked Taungar, noticing Konrad's bewildered expression. 'I have loyally served the Empire for a quarter of a century, but I am still only a sergeant. The cobalt plume is all I shall ever wear because I was not born into the right family. It took me a long time to realize, Konrad, but the only person to serve is yourself. I owe allegiance to no one but myself. Whatever I do in the future, it will only be in my own best interests.'

'But... what if the Empire is engulfed by the legions of Chaos... if we all become slaves of darkness?'

'We are all slaves without knowing it. Is one master worse than another?'

'We can't allow the triumph of Chaos!'

'That's all a myth spread by our rulers to make us obey them. We live in fear while they live in luxury.'

'What about Praag? That was no myth. You said you almost died! And what about all the foul creatures that you slew at Castle Drachenfels?'

'Fighting for a so-called just cause has given me nothing but pain and torment. Why should I care what happens to the Emperor or the Empire? While I still live, and whatever happens, more than half my life is already over, I want the best for me.'

Taungar's words resonated in Konrad's mind, because they were so similar to his own recent thoughts. His priority was to rescue Elyssa, and he wondered what price he was prepared to pay for her safety. If it were a case of the Emperor's life for the girl's, then there was no question but that he would choose Elyssa. It seemed almost like heresy to admit it, but there would be another Emperor after Karl-Franz, someone else to act as a symbolic head of the Empire. There was, however, only one Elyssa.

Such thoughts were no mere speculation. Gaxar had been plotting against the Emperor – and Elyssa had been in the same subterranean chamber as the grey seer.

'I'm telling you this,' Taungar continued, 'because I don't want you to waste as much of your life as I have mine.'

Konrad shook his head. 'No, no. We must be able to do both, to fight against Chaos and to further our own aims. The two are not opposite ambitions.'

'You don't understand. You are so like me, Konrad, so like the way I was.' Taungar stared intently at Konrad as he spoke, and he gripped both the younger man's wrists with his hands. 'You must let me prove to you what I am saying. Once you have seen the evidence, you will be convinced.'

This was not what Konrad had expected, and he realized he would get no help from Taungar. He was alone – as always. There was only one person who knew of Elyssa or cared about her, and that was himself. Whatever must be done, he was the only one who could and would make the attempt.

Konrad shook his hands free and stood up. 'I'm going back,' he said.

'It would be best if you came with me,' said Taungar. There was no need for him to add any more. Konrad was aware that the sergeant knew he must have been involved in yesterday's prison break, and that he could betray Konrad if he chose.

Reaching for his tankard and draining it, Konrad knew that he had little choice. He was unarmed, but if necessary he was confident that he could take care of Taungar; but another death would only add to his difficulties.

'The gentleman we shall visit also happens to be on good terms with Matthias, who is the advisor to the Grand Theogonist,' said Taungar. 'If you wish, you can tell him your story about this impostor, and it will be passed on through the usual channels. That is the only way to get a hearing, because who would believe a trooper or even a sergeant in the Imperial guard?'

He took a final sip of his wine, then stood up, and Konrad could at last make out the design on his gold tiepin: it showed two naked women embracing one another. Taungar smiled and added, 'But I think we will be able to persuade you that your true interests lie elsewhere. Shall we go?'

They made their way through the crowd. Taungar went first, and he looked around to make sure that Konrad was following. As he did so, he collided with the blonde girl carrying the tray. She slipped and the tray fell from her hands, the pewter tankards spilling their contents over the floor. There was silence in the taproom for a moment, as people glanced around, and then the conversations, the laughter, the disagreements continued.

Taungar swore and wiped at the drops of ale which had splattered across his trousers, then stepped around the girl, who was kneeling on the ground and picking up the empty tankards.

Konrad stopped and looked down at the girl. Now it was not Krysten who he was reminded of, but himself. He remembered all the years he had worked in Brandenheimer's tavern, when he had been no more than a slave, when he had been beaten and kicked for every little thing that went wrong – and even when things did not go wrong.

'Trudi!' shouted a stocky, balding man who hurried from the other end of the inn. 'Now what have you done?'

He was the landlord, and Konrad knew that the girl would be in for a thrashing. He stepped forward. Tonight it would be the landlord's turn for a beating.

'I'm sorry, Herr Runze,' she said.

'So am I,' said the man. 'Ah well, it was only the slops. This lot can't tell the difference by this time of night.'

Runze turned and headed back the way he had come, and Konrad unclenched his fists. Trudi glanced up at him and she smiled once more, and for a moment she looked exactly like Krysten – the hair, the face, the eyes, the expression.

Konrad glanced away, then followed Taungar out of the door and into the night.

KONRAD WONDERED IF he should simply slip away from Taungar and quit the Imperial guard, but realized that would leave him in a worse situation than ever. If he did not return to the palace, he would have no base from which to operate. He would be unable to remain in the city because he would be hunted down by the Imperial guard as a deserter. He would have nowhere to go, no contacts, no money, no weapons, and without any of these his chances of ever finding Elyssa became more remote.

The fact that Taungar was not a loyal member of the guard might prove to be to Konrad's advantage. From the way the sergeant had spoken, he must have been engaged in some form of criminal activity. That was surely what he meant when he had claimed that from now on he would only be acting in his own best interests. Altdorf was a port, so perhaps he was involved with smuggling. Imperial duties on certain kinds of imported goods were very high, and fortunes could be made by those able to supply such luxuries at reduced prices. And members of a smuggling gang were more likely to know about the secret subterranean city beneath Altdorf than the Imperial guard.

Taungar must be taking him to meet his other employer, the head of the illicit organization for which he worked. It would make sense that such a man would know the adviser to the Grand Theogonist of the Cult of Sigmar, because the most wealthy and influential people frequently had far less respect for the law than the lower orders. Konrad remembered how Litzenreich had said that laws were made by such people for their own benefit. Konrad was inclined to agree. Even should prominent citizens happen to be discovered breaking the law, at worst they would be judged by their equals and punished in the most lenient fashion. Not so a member of the more numerous, less prosperous part of society. No matter how minor their transgression, they would be dealt with very severely – probably painfully, and possibly even fatally.

As a member of the Imperial guard, Konrad's pay was very little, and he would receive none of it until he had served for a month. Whatever happened, he doubted he would still be in Altdorf by then, and he was not averse to earning a few crowns now. The mercenaries on the northern frontier were always dreaming of ways to earn their fortunes. Even Wolf had not been immune to such financial ambition, with his expedition to discover ancient dwarf gold and gems in a lost temple in the mountains of Kislev. Wolf and Konrad and Anvila had indeed found such a forgotten temple, but there had been no buried hoard of priceless treasure – only a horde of cave-dwelling goblins.

It was over five years since Elyssa had been taken prisoner. Konrad tried not to consider the horrendous ordeals she must inevitably have endured during that time. Now that he knew she was still alive, all his senses told him not to waste a moment in finding and releasing her. But when he considered the position logically, he realized that compared to all the tortures that the girl had already suffered, an extra few days could make very little difference.

The only problem might be that Skullface had left the city since last night, taking his captive with him. If so, Konrad was already too late. Otherwise, during the coming days, he would have time to think more clearly of what he should do and make his plans accordingly. If he did succeed in tracking down the creature he had named Skullface, how could he kill such a being, one that could pull an arrow from its heart and show not a trace of a wound...?

He remembered the preternaturally thin figure, apparently the only human who had taken part in the massacre and destruction of Konrad's village. So human, yet so alien. When he had drawn the black arrow from his bloodless chest, he had examined the crest before snapping the shaft. It was as if he had recognized the gold crest. Wolf, too, seemed to know the design when he had seen it on Konrad's quiver.

Konrad yawned as he walked by Taungar's side through the city. He had not slept properly since the night before last and he felt exhausted. He was not as fit as he had been on the frontier, his strength having being sapped during his weeks of capture by Kastring's band of raiders, and then his vitality had been almost drained by the bronze armour in which he had been imprisoned. It was less than two weeks since he had arrived in Altdorf, and while he had been in the guard he had done his best to rebuild his muscles and restore his stamina.

The wounds he had suffered during the underground battle with the pygmy beast creatures had been superficial, only bites and scratches. Such apparently innocuous injuries could often prove the most dangerous, however. The saliva from an enemy's bite might be venomous, a lethal poison which could kill very slowly and extremely painfully. But the teeth and talons of the flesh-eaters Konrad had defeated last night seemed to have borne no such deadly toxins; the injuries to his right arm and hand were well on their way towards healing. Early during his time in Kislev, Konrad had almost lost that arm as a result of a severe wound which had started to turn gangrenous. The limb had been saved by an elf with magical healing skills, and ever since then Konrad's right arm had recovered from its wounds faster than the rest of his body.

Elyssa, too, had possessed latent powers of healing. She had soothed the wounds he had suffered when slaying the beastman which attacked her. Perhaps, somehow, it was her own magical talents which had kept her alive when the village had been overrun by the feral forces of Chaos.

Konrad did not like being in towns and cities, the way they were so enclosed. Altdorf's fortifications seemed to be there to keep its inhabitants inside, not to exclude enemies. He felt that almost anyone he encountered could be an enemy, and there was no way of telling who. Out on the frontier it was easy to distinguish one's foe; not so in a city. There were no beastmen, at least not on the surface, there were only humans – but humans were the most treacherous, most deadly adversaries of all.

Because of its wealth, Altdorf had more than its share of thieves and robbers. The main streets were wide, kept lit throughout the night, and regularly patrolled, but Konrad kept listening for the sound of footsteps on the cobbles behind them. Any villains who fancied their chances would get far more than they could have expected if they tried to attack him and Taungar, although it would take a gang of footpads to attempt an assault on two men who were so obviously fit and so obviously sober. But criminals did not necessarily have much sense, and Konrad kept glancing all around and keeping wide of every alley that they passed on their journey. They remained within the northern sector of the city, making for the mercantile area, and at last their destination came in sight.

The house stood at the top of a hill some two hundred yards from the city boundary, lying behind its own white walls, which were a replica of those of the city. There was also a moat and a drawbridge, although the moat lay inside the walls, and the bridge was only crossed once access had been gained through the heavy wooden gate. Taungar had made their presence there known by using the heavy iron knocker, which was fashioned in the shape of Sigmar's legendary warhammer, Ghal-maraz.

A slim boy, perhaps fifteen or sixteen years old, immediately opened the door, bowing low to admit them. He was clad all in white – slippers, tight breeches, loose tunic, a round cap – and he led the way to a building in the centre of the walled garden. The grounds were lit by a series of lanterns, all of them in the pattern of the fabled double-tailed comet which had lit the night sky above the Old World at the time of Sigmar's birth. Twin beams of light shone from each of the lamps, illuminating the impressive gardens.

There were several fountains, and at their centres were various grotesque replicas of dying orcs and goblins. Water sprayed from different parts of these statues, in imitation of geysers of blood spurting from terrible wounds. They were evidently representations of the goblinoid swarms who had fallen victim to Sigmar's vengeful hammer at the battle of Black Fire Pass. The fountains fed a number of streams which meandered through the grounds, and these were crossed by bridges each of which was a miniature of one of Altdorf's six bridges.

Between these tiny streams, which flowed into the inner moat, lay islands of exotic trees and bushes. Although it was winter, some of these still bore ripe fruit upon their branches.

The house lay in the centre of the gardens, white walled and red roofed. The walls were built of bricks, each of which was embossed with a twin-tailed comet motif; each of the tiles was in the shape of a double hammerhead; the windows were shaped like eight-pointed stars. Another small bridge had to be crossed before the house was reached. The servant opened the door, bowed, and gestured for Taungar and Konrad to enter the hallway.

'May I take your coats, gentlemen?' said another servant, who was waiting in the entrance hall.

Konrad realized this one was a girl, identically clad and of a similar age to the other servant, her hair tucked beneath her white cap. She hung their coats on an elaborate stand, and led them along a wide passageway which was panelled in dark wood, hung with tapestries and paintings depicting the various triumphs of Sigmar. Several crystal chandeliers hung from the ceiling, the candle flames flickering.

She knocked at a door near the end, pushed it open, then bowed for Konrad and Taungar to enter. They went into a large room, the walls of which were lined with fancy cabinets, carved chests and various kinds of elaborately decorated furniture.

'Rolf! How wonderful to see you!'

Taungar was greeted by a man who hurried towards him. He was of average height, but far more than average girth. It seemed he was trying to disguise his width behind the loose pale blue robe that he wore, but without much success. He must have been about fifty, and his fat cheeks were a web of broken veins. His hair was grey and thinning, tied back behind his head with a ribbon which matched his robe.

He carried a ruby-studded silver goblet in one ring-laden hand.

He threw his arms around Taungar, hugging him close and kissing him on both cheeks. Konrad wondered if he could be from Bretonnia, where that was the kind of thing men did to other men.

'Hello, Werner,' said Taungar. 'This is Konrad, the man I spoke to you about.' He turned to Konrad. 'This is Werner Zuntermein,' he said.

'Ah, Konrad!' said Zuntermein, moving towards him. 'Delighted to make your acquaintance.'

Konrad moved back in order to avoid an embrace, but instead Zuntermein raised his free hand and stroked Konrad's face.

'What has happened? Have you been fighting?' He sighed and shook his head. 'Boys will be boys.' He stood gazing at Konrad. 'How handsome. And your eyes, how remarkable!'

Konrad's eyes were different colours. They both appeared to be green, but on closer inspection the left one was gold. At one time, it was more than merely the colours which had been different. His left eye had given him warning of danger, because frequently he could *see* what was going to happen and act accordingly. The gift of foresight had grown more erratic over the years and he had finally lost the talent when Litzenreich had extracted him from the suit of bronze armour.

Konrad leaned back out of Zuntermein's reach.

'A pity about the scars,' Zuntermein added, 'but nothing in life is perfect, alas. Do be seated. A drink?' Without waiting for a reply, he snapped his fingers and yet another servant filled two bejewelled goblets which were identical to the one which he held.

Konrad sat down, as far away from Zuntermein as possible. The servant handed him a goblet, which was probably worth as much as he could earn in five years as an Imperial guard. Whatever it was that Zuntermein did, it was certainly a lucrative profession. The servant was dressed in the same style as the other two, but Konrad could not work out whether the third one was male or female.

'Rolf has told me that you could be one of us,' said Zuntermein, as he settled down on a couch which could have seated two people of normal dimensions.

'A follower of Sigmar?' said Konrad.

'Not,' replied Zuntermein, 'exactly.'

Konrad raised his drink to his lips, and the spicy aroma which assailed his nostrils made him hesitate. He could tell that the pale liqueur was very strong, but this was a time when he needed to keep all his wits. He held the silver to his mouth for a second, as if drinking, then lowered it. Taungar had not even finished his wine in the tavern, but now he was swallowing the exotic drink as though he were dying of thirst.

'You know the advisor to the Grand Theogonist?' said Konrad, deciding that it was time for him to take the initiative.

'Matthias? Yes, I do. But he is away at present, with the Emperor.'

'The skaven are planning to kill the Emperor and replace him with a doppelganger.'

Zuntermein said nothing for a few seconds. He sipped at his wine. 'Really?'

'Is that all you have to say? We must warn the Emperor!'

'If you know of this scheme, Konrad, and if it is not merely wild rumour as so many of these stories are, I am sure that those who protect dear Karl-Franz are equally aware of what is happening. If there aren't at least a dozen threats to the Emperor every week, then it's a very dull eight days. Never fear, he is the most heavily guarded man in the Old World.'

If those who defended the Emperor were as concerned for his safety as Taungar and Zuntermein, then Karl-Franz was in deep trouble, thought Konrad. But he said nothing else; he had more important matters to think about than the fate of the Emperor. He took a mouthful of his wine, and it was as strong as he had suspected. He swallowed it slowly, feeling the warmth trickle down his throat and radiate throughout his body. Taungar, he noticed, was holding out his empty goblet for the servant to refill.

'You served in Kislev, I believe?' said Zuntermein. 'You were there during the Praag siege?'

Konrad nodded, twice.

'You have experienced more of the world already than most people do in a lifetime,' Zuntermein continued. 'The real world, that is. We know what it's like, what is happening and what will happen. We–' his idle gesture took in Konrad, Taungar and himself, '*know*. And we can take advantage of what we know.'

'And what's that?'

'Chaos,' said Zuntermein.

Konrad made no response.

'The Chaos Wastes,' said Zuntermein, swirling around the contents of his goblet and staring into them. 'What did you think you were doing there, Konrad? Maintaining the frontier against the northern invaders? Keeping Chaos at bay? But Chaos can't be held back by force of arms. It knows no boundaries. It's like the air we breathe. It's everywhere. It's here in the Empire, here in Altdorf.' He looked up, meeting Konrad's gaze. 'Here in this room.'

Konrad glanced at Taungar, who said nothing. All he did was smile and sup at his spiced wine.

'The air we breathe,' repeated Zuntermein. 'Just as we need air to live, so we need Chaos. We are one and the same.'

Konrad put down his goblet on the enamelled table by his side and started to rise, then decided against leaving. It would be a futile gesture, because he had nowhere to go. He had decided to accompany Taungar, and now he must stay and listen to what Zuntermein had to say even though – as in the tavern earlier – this was not what he had expected to hear. He felt calm, relaxed and was under no threat; he might as well stay to finish his drink.

Zuntermein said, 'Some believe that mankind is a creation of Chaos, and that is why humans make its best servants. But Chaos can also serve us, and the rewards are not insignificant.'

Konrad laughed briefly, contemptuously.

'Do not mock, Konrad,' said Zuntermein, calmly. 'You have already been touched by Chaos.'

'What do you mean?' Konrad demanded – but he knew the answer.

And Zuntermein knew that he knew. He smiled at Konrad, then sipped at his wine.

'You can't fight it, Konrad. You are part of Chaos, it is part of you.'

'What do you want?'

'We can help each other, Konrad. Join us. There has been much pain in your life. It is time that was balanced out. It is a time for enjoyment, for pleasure.'

'No,' said Konrad, and he did stand up. 'I don't think that we have anything further to discuss, Herr Zuntermein.'

'Werner, call me Werner.' He also stood up. 'I hoped that we could be good friends, Konrad.'

'You hoped wrong.'

'At least let us not part as enemies.'

Zuntermein thrust out his right hand. Konrad accepted it automatically, and they shook in military fashion, palms gripping wrists. Zuntermein's hand felt warm, very warm, and it was growing warmer while Konrad's wrist started to become cooler. He tried to pull free, but could not. His whole arm had been rendered immobile and was being drained of all vitality.

Zuntermein was a sorcerer...

'I know where she is,' he said, and he released his grip.

Konrad staggered back, rubbing at his icy right arm with his left, trying to restore it to life.

'Who?' asked Konrad, knowing there could be but one answer.

'The one you have been thinking of.'

'Where is she? Take me to her!'

'It is not so simple as that, Konrad.' Zuntermein closed his eyes and touched the fingertips of his right hand to his forehead. 'Something might be arranged, however.' He opened his eyes, and he smiled. 'In fact, you shall meet her – if you promise to come to one of our social gatherings and give serious consideration to joining us.'

'I'll do whatever you say, whatever you want.'

'I'm glad,' said Zuntermein. 'Take Konrad back now, Rolf. I will send a message in a few days.'

Taungar rose and walked towards the door, and the servant opened it for him. Konrad followed him out into the hallway. He kept rubbing at his forearm, and the numbness was gradually retreating. He had so much to ask, but he did not know where to begin.

'A few days,' whispered Zuntermein, and he kissed him on his left cheek – but Konrad stepped back in time to avoid a second kiss on his other cheek.

CHAPTER FOUR

ANOTHER DAWN, ANOTHER unfurling of the Imperial ensigns high above the palace, the capital, the Empire, and Konrad gazed over to the north where he could just make out the red roof of Zuntermein's home.

Never trust a sorcerer...

But he had no real alternative. He could never hope to find Elyssa alone.

He had only once mentioned the girl to anyone, when Wolf had examined the black quiver and Konrad told him that Elyssa had given it to him.

When he had touched Konrad, Zuntermein discovered what had been foremost in his mind – and that was Elyssa. The sorcerer was certainly using what he had found to his own advantage, in order to persuade Konrad to join him, and he could so easily be lying. How could he have known where Elyssa was? But Konrad would only return to Zuntermein's house if she was there. If she was not, he would leave – but not before he had taken revenge for the wizard's mendacity.

A few days, Zuntermein had said, in a few days he would know.

Konrad glanced at Taungar, who stood to attention, saluting the embroidered standards as they were unfurled. The sergeant had enlisted him in the Imperial guard, and now he wanted to recruit him as a Chaos cultist...

Could Zuntermein really be a Chaos worshipper? Konrad doubted it. He remembered Kastring and his pagan warband, and he had seen countless other cultists over the years. He knew the price of their blasphemous creed. It cost them everything. They were transformed, becoming part-human, part-animal, until they were no more than the beastmen who were the original creations of Chaos, twisted and mis-shapen in mind as well as in body.

Behind his respectable facade, with his house disguised by the holy symbols of Sigmar Heldenhammer, Werner Zuntermein was playing at being an acolyte of Chaos. It was probably the latest fashion in Altdorf amongst the indolent rich. Somehow Taungar had become involved in the charade, probably because there was a way he could make money out of it.

'I want some money,' Konrad told the sergeant, as again they were the last two to leave the ramparts. 'I also need a pass; I have to go into the city today.'

Taungar looked at him. After what Zuntermein had said – although he could not have been aware who the wizard had meant by 'she' – he knew that Konrad would return to the palace. He nodded.

'Five crowns enough?' he asked. 'I can excuse you from this afternoon's duties.'

It was Konrad's turn to nod, and after a morning spent teaching axe combat techniques he left the palace. Like the previous evening, he was clad in civilian clothes because he was not on official duties. He headed across Altdorf, and he felt as uneasy as he had done last night. He wished he could be somewhere else, anywhere except the largest city in the Empire.

The only other city in which he had spent much time was Praag, and that had been under very different circumstances. After it had first been captured and occupied by the regiments of Chaos two hundred years ago, then retaken, Praag had been razed to the ground and completely rebuilt, which meant that most of the buildings in Altdorf were far older. The streets of the capital followed a pattern laid down thousands of years ago, and some of the houses were on sites which had been in constant habitation since the days of Sigmar.

Yet it was not the buildings, no matter how old, which affected Konrad, nor the streets and alleys that paved the ancient earth which had not seen the light of day for centuries. The whole weight of history was like a miasma which he found overwhelmingly oppressive. He felt as if he could move nowhere without bumping into someone; and even when there was nobody close, the ghosts of so many millennia seemed to impede his progress. Even the desolate winter plains of Kislev seemed far more inviting by comparison.

It could only have been the concentration of people that was so disturbing, and he remembered what Zuntermein had said, that humans were a creation of Chaos...

Could that be true? If so, then this was the greatest concentration of Chaos energy he had ever encountered, and perhaps it explained his reaction.

Because Konrad was now himself a creature of Chaos, and like repelled like – or so Litzenreich had once said. Was that not why the forces of Chaos were so divided and forever fighting amongst themselves, the legions of each benighted god in eternal war with the battalions of the other dark deities? They feuded incessantly, one evil army against another.

Litzenreich had also claimed that evil was not a synonym for Chaos. Chaos simply existed, it was mankind who interpreted that existence. Litzenreich had compared Chaos to water; and Zuntermein had compared it to air; and Konrad believed neither of them.

He had become trapped inside a suit of bronze armour – of Chaos armour. That meant he had been contaminated by Chaos. Litzenreich had freed him from his metal prison, but he had used warpstone to do so... and later revealed that the enigmatic substance originally came from the wastelands and was believed to be the cause of all mutations, to have created the beastmen.

Konrad was doubly damned.

And Zuntermein had detected this.

He had used his thaumaturgical senses to do so – Konrad was convinced. It was not that the sorcerer recognized someone who was as infected as himself. Zuntermein had made his fortune through the application of his magical abilities, not through Chaos worship, because such corruption would surely have taken its toll upon his physical form. It was his wizardry which had enabled him to delve into Konrad's thoughts, and it was the same talent which had led him to locate Elyssa so swiftly – if indeed he had done so.

Having attempted not to think of the girl and what might happen in the next few days, although without much success, Konrad was now trying to concentrate on another matter. He had originally come to Altdorf for one reason, because of the shield that Silver Eye had carried when they fought beneath Middenheim. Konrad wanted to know where the skaven had found the shield, and he also hoped to discover something about its gold emblem. This was a subject which had intrigued him for over a decade, ever since Elyssa had first given him the bow, the ten arrows, the quiver of rippled black hide. Now, at last, here was his opportunity...

EXCEPT FOR THE Imperial Palace and the Cathedral of Sigmar, the College of Heraldry was the oldest building that Konrad had ever seen. It was hidden away in a back street, which must once have been been much wider, and he missed the turning at first and had to retrace his steps and walk down a winding side road. All the other buildings nearby had been built and rebuilt many times, but the ancient college was half-sunken beneath the ground as if it recognized its age and was trying to bury itself. The road outside had risen over the centuries, so that the lower floors of the college had become basements, as the rubbish and debris of the city piled up and the level of the surface had risen. The roof was covered in slates and tiles, every one of which appeared to be of a different colour and size, their variety demonstrating how many times it had been repaired. All the walls and arches and gables were out of true. The whole building was bent with antiquity, like a cripple who somehow managed to survive despite all his deformities.

Konrad climbed down the worn stone steps and knocked on the door. There was at least one other level below, and he noticed that the doorframe was set in what had once been a window. The wood crumbled beneath his knuckles. There was no reply. He pushed on the ancient door, it creaked back on its rusty hinges, and he stepped into the gloom.

It was both dusty and damp inside, and Konrad waited a few seconds for his eyes to adjust to the darkness. He could see a glimmer of light ahead in the distance, and he made his way along the narrow passageway. The floor was uneven, the walls crooked. As he became more used to the lack of illumination, he noticed that the corridor was lined with plaques, some round, some in the shape of a stylized shield, and each of them had a different pattern painted upon it. They were all coats of arms, he realized, hundreds upon hundreds of them; judging by the way the paint had faded or peeled away they must have been very old. There were a number of gaps on the walls, where the shields had fallen off and not been replaced.

As he was gazing at the display, he trod on something which broke under his weight. He stopped to inspect the object. It was one of the missing shields, decorated with a silver cross on a red background, with some type of hunting bird silhouetted in black in one quarter. The other three designs could not be made out because the paint had come off when he stepped on it. He set the two broken pieces of the rusty plaque down in the corner and kept on walking towards the light.

The corridor opened up into a larger chamber, the walls of which were lined with books, thousands upon thousands of them. They were arrayed on shelves which stretched from floor to ceiling. The shelves were packed solid, and more volumes lay upon the ground, stacks and stacks of them piled high on each other. Nothing was straight. All the shelves were tilted at various angles; and even the piles of books on the floor were not vertical but leaned one way or another. Everything was covered in dust and cobwebs, as though nothing had been touched for aeons.

Yet in the very centre of the room, at a desk which was laden with heaps of manuscripts and documents which spilled over onto the floor, sat two men. There was a lantern between the pair, and they were so engrossed in their studies that they seemed unaware of their visitor. They were each poring over different volumes, making notations on the parchments before them.

'Good afternoon,' said Konrad, his voice sounding very loud in the unnatural silence of the library.

Neither man took any notice for several seconds, and then the younger one looked up. He was only younger when compared to his colleague, being about sixty years old, his hair grey as if with dust. His companion appeared to be at least half as old again, his skin as wrinkled and thin as ancient parchment, and he kept on with what he was doing.

'Have you come about the drains?' asked the younger librarian.

'No,' answered Konrad. 'I've come about a coat of arms.'

The man sighed, pushing his spectacles to the end of his nose and rubbing at his eyes. 'What a pity. There are three feet of water in the lowest level, you know, and it can only get worse. Some of the material we have lost is priceless, priceless. None of it can be replaced, you know.'

'The coat of arms?' Konrad reminded him.

'You have come to the wrong place. These are the archives. If you wish to buy a coat of arms, you must go to the new building.'

'I've been there; they sent me here.'

The 'new building' had been at least two hundred years old. It was in a much better state of repair, and with more people working there. The clerk at the first desk had shaken his head when he heard Konrad's request, then directed him to the original building, and charged him a crown for doing so.

'What for?' asked the archivist, sliding his spectacles back into place.

'I've seen an emblem,' said Konrad, 'and I want you to identify it. You can do that for me?'

'You will have to pay, you know. We are obliged to make a charge for our expertise.'

'I can pay,' said Konrad, jingling the four crowns in his hand.

The archivist selected a sheet of paper, then beckoned for Konrad to come nearer. The older scribe had still not looked up. He remained hunched over the single desk, parchment in front of him, his body leaning across to the massive book next to it.

'Can you describe the crest to me? You have to be absolutely accurate, you know, in every detail. Some coats of arms are so similar to others than only a specialist can detect the difference.'

'It's a very simple design.'

'What seems simple to a layman may be very complex to an expert.'

Konrad glanced at the scribe, but his face remained expressionless.

'Let us start with the *tinctures*.'

'What?'

'The colours, you know.' The man gestured to the row of quills in front of him, and Konrad realized that they must all be dipped in different coloured pots of ink.

'There were only two,' said Konrad, 'gold and black.'

'*Or* and *sable*, that is what we call them.'

'And the design is of a pair of crossed arrows—'

'*Fleche en croix*, you mean.'

'With a mailed fist in between.'

'*Poing maille*.'

'The arrows and the fist are in gold. The rest is in black. Or that's the way it is usually.'

'Usually?'

'The pattern was reversed on the set of arrows. The arrows were of black wood, with a narrow band of gold near the flights, and the emblem was carved into the gold to show the wood beneath.'

'So it was *sable dans or* on the *fleches*, instead of *or dans sable*?'

'If you say so.'

'Where else have you seen this coat of arms? On an *ecusson*?'

'What?'

'A shield.'

'Yes. Gold on black. Also on a bow and a quiver.'

'An *archet* and a *carquois*.' The man made another note, then began asking more questions: 'At what angle are the arrows? Do the arrows point up or down? Are the arrowheads very large in proportion to the shafts? Are the flights very large in proportion to the shafts? Which hand is the fist, *dexter* or *sinister*? Can you see the fingers? On which side is the thumb? Where is the base of the fist in relation to the tips of the arrows? What size is the fist relative to the lengths of the arrows?'

Konrad answered all the questions as best he could, while the scribe made a notation on the paper at each reply.

He wondered how long the process would have taken if the pattern were more elaborate.

'Good.' The man chose another sheet of paper and took another feathered pen from the row of inkpots in the stand in front of him. A minute later he said: 'Like this?'

He gestured for Konrad to look at what he had been doing. He had drawn the arrow and fist design, using black ink upon bleached paper, and it was exactly as Konrad remembered.

'That's it.'

'It is probably quite old. Later crests have tended to become more complicated, partly for aesthetic reasons, partly because all of the more basic designs have been claimed.'

'There is no such coat of arms.'

It was the old man who had spoken. He had set down his quill, gathered up the book he was studying, wearily risen from his seat and glanced at his companion's illustration. His body was as hunched as if he were still bowed over his work, his torso leaning to one side, and not under the weight of the heavy volume.

It was almost as if he had contorted himself to fit in with the configurations of the library; or perhaps he had studied here for so long that his whole shape had become stooped and curved whilst the pillars and bricks of the college had been similarly twisted and distorted by the remorseless pressure of time.

'But I've seen it,' said Konrad.

'You may have seen the same pattern on various weaponry,' replied the younger man, watching as his colleague slowly shuffled across the chamber, 'but that does not mean they are part of a coat of arms.'

'Can't you check? Look it up in one of your books?'

'There is no need. Herr Renemann is an encyclopedia of heraldry. If he says there is no such coat of arms, then there is no such coat of arms.'

'He can't know them all.'

'He does.'

'But it could be an old crest, one which no longer exists.'

'They always exist. The family may die out, you know, but their coat of arm remains. We have it in our files. Somewhere.'

'Then it's from outside the Empire.'

'No. Our records cover the Old World, from Albion to the Border Princes, from Kislev to the Estalian Kingdoms. We do not want to risk bestowing the same crest in Altdorf that might already belong to a noble house in Magritta, for example. Although that is not our department any more.' The man shook his head sadly. 'The coat of arms which you have described does not exist. If you wish, however, you could take the necessary steps to bring it into existence. We could have such a crest assigned to you and your descendants. We can still do that here, you know.' He brightened up at the thought, nodding in approval of his own scheme.

Renemann was wrong, of that Konrad was absolutely certain. The mailed fist and crossed arrow pattern was more than a mere design on a few armaments.

'I don't think so,' he said. 'How much do I owe you?'

'Two crowns?'

Konrad dropped two coins from his right hand to his left. 'You mentioned families dying out. Do you keep records of the families who have a coat of arms?'

'Yes.'

'I want to know about a family called Kastring,' he said.

'Where are they from?'

'A village in Ostland, near a town called Ferlangen.'

It was his own village, the village where he had lived for as long as he could remember – although he never felt as if he had truly belonged there. If the village had a name, Konrad never knew it. And he himself had no name until Elyssa gave him one. Elyssa, whose family name was Kastring...

The scribe pushed his spectacles to the end of his nose, gazing over them as he began slowly surveying the shelves of the library. He rose from his seat for the first time and took a single pace towards the nearest line of shelves. He gazed up and down and across for several seconds, then turned towards the end of the room by the entrance. He was much too far away to read what was written on the spines of those books which still had visible lettering. It was almost as if he expected to find the correct reference work without moving.

'Ah-ha!' he said, and it seemed that he did know precisely which volume contained the Kastring lineage. He started towards the distant shelves, waving for Konrad to follow him.

'There,' said the man, as they reached the overflowing ranks of books. 'Five rows up from this one, seven, eight, nine books along from the upside down one with red leather binding. You see it?'

'The one called *Chron Ost XXXVI, Jud-Kel*?'

The man glanced up at Konrad, and he nodded. 'Get it down, will you? You are probably more agile than me.'

None of the other volumes nearby had titles which were even remotely similar. It seemed that the books were distributed at random throughout the library. The one that the scribe had specified was too high to reach, and Konrad looked around for a ladder. There must be one, because that was the only way access could ever be gained to the upper shelves.

'Use these,' said the man, tapping the pile of books on the floor next to him.

'If you say so.'

Konrad climbed up onto one of the lower stacks of books, then onto a higher one, using the crumbling ancient volumes as a flight of stairs. Even standing on the tallest pile, he could not quite reach what he wanted, and so he put one foot on top of the books on the nearest shelf, stretched up and managed to slide his fingertips under the spine of the necessary volume. He eased the book out inch by inch, caught it as it fell, then jumped down to the floor.

'We only keep duplicates of the more recent material,' said the scribe, as he put the register on top of a bundle of decaying books and opened the first page. 'The originals are in the new building. This seems to need updating, but that is no real surprise. We are somewhat understaffed, as you may have noticed.'

He began leafing through the volume. 'Here – Kastring.'

At the top of the page was inscribed the crest which Konrad recognized, a blue diagonal band separating the two halves. The upper left of the shield showed two towers linked by a crenellated wall, red upon white; the lower right showed a signet ring, silver upon purple, and the crest on the ring was that of the Kastring coat of arms.

'A castle and a ring,' commented the librarian, and he shook his head. 'I do like the way that the design must become forever smaller and smaller within the ring, however. But what did you want to know?'

Konrad was at his side and already reading the last entry, which finished halfway down the page. The volume did need updating: there was nothing about the Kastring manor house being burned down, the family destroyed.

'According to this,' said Konrad, 'Kastring had three sons – Wilhelm, Sigismund and Friedrich. What about his daughter?'

'Let me see.' The man's fingers traced the family tree. 'Sir Wilhelm Kastring. Married Ulrica Augenhaus of Middenheim. Eldest son named after his father, you notice, as was his father before him. Two other sons.'

'Why isn't the daughter mentioned? Because she was the youngest and her name hasn't been registered yet?'

'Possibly, although I doubt it. In a genealogical sense, you know, daughters are not very important. The only role of a woman is to produce sons. It is through the sons that the family name passes and the line continues. Daughters are frequently regarded as an unnecessary expense, from the time of birth right up until their wedding day, when a dowry has to be paid to the groom's family in order to secure the marriage. But even if there were a daughter to this Kastring family, she should be registered for the sake of accuracy. Is that all?'

Konrad nodded, and the man closed the book and put his hand on it.

'Leave it. It needs bringing up to date. Perhaps someday...' He shrugged.

Konrad started counting out coins again. The librarian rubbed his hands together to wipe off the dust and dirt. Konrad gave him the four crowns. Having paid for it, he considered asking for the illustration of the mysterious crest, but he had no need of such a reminder.

'Thank you,' said the man, tucking the coins into his tunic pocket. 'If there is ever anything else we can do for you, please do not hesitate to ask.'

The visit had been totally pointless. Konrad had been informed that Elyssa did not exist and neither did the coat of arms – both of which he knew to be untrue.

'You are absolutely certain that there is no such crest?'

'If there is,' said the librarian, 'then it is not human.'

NOT HUMAN...

The words echoed in Konrad's mind over the next two days. The librarian must have been referring to the banners and standards which were borne by the warriors of Chaos; but in Konrad's experience, all such flags and emblems also contained the blasphemous symbol of whatever unholy entity the berserk troops worshipped. The crossed arrows and mailed fist device was not tainted by such depraved idolatry.

When Konrad had returned to his native village soon after the onslaught, the only signs of habitation that had remained were the outlines of the houses and buildings burned into the ground. Sir Wilhelm and Lady Ulrica must have died in the inferno that had devoured the manor house, and until the day before yesterday Konrad believed Elyssa had perished with her parents.

Her brothers had long before left the valley to make their way in the world – and one of them was to become Konrad's tormentor during the long and arduous trek from Kislev into the Empire.

Konrad had been hostage to a band of Khorne acolytes, followers of the Blood God whose campaign of mayhem and murder had taken them far across the border. Gaxar was to blame for his capture. In his human disguise, the grey seer had deceived Konrad, then knocked him unconscious. When he regained his senses, he found himself a sacrificial offering to the huntsman of souls. But the leader of the feral band still wore the Kastring crest upon his accoutrements, which Konrad had recognized. That had saved his life – for a while.

Whether it was Wilhelm or Sigismund or Friedrich, he had already begun to pay the high price of his obscene devotion. Kastring's face and body had become changed, with horns growing from his skull, fur from his flesh, and teeth that were now fangs.

His marauding horde was a bestial rabble, yet it was Konrad who was treated as the caged animal, to be tortured and abused. In the end he had taken his savage revenge, slaying dozens of the dog-faced mutants in a bloody battle that rivalled their own gory ceremonies. And the last one to die had been Kastring himself, impaled upon Konrad's lance – the bronze knight's lance...

Before then, Kastring had spoken of Elyssa, and he had claimed that she was not his true sister. Although Elyssa had been unaware of this, it seemed there was some question over her legitimacy. Kastring himself was not sure of the exact details, but he had maintained that Elyssa's parentage was different from his and his brothers; she was only his half-sister – if that. Perhaps he was correct, and this might explain why her name was not recorded in the Kastring chronology.

Elyssa had found the bow and arrows deep in the cellars of the manor house, and Konrad asked Kastring if he knew of the mailed fist and crossed arrow emblem.

An elf? Kastring had ventured. *Some connection with an elf, could it be?*

Were they elven implements that Konrad had seen? Was it an elven shield which Silver Eye now used? Elves were as tall as humans, and so it could have been an elven bow with which Konrad had taught himself archery.

Humans and elves could interbreed, he had once been told, so was it possible that Elyssa's father had been an elf?

Nothing human...
The words echoed in Konrad's mind over the next two days – and then came Zuntermein's summons.

CHAPTER FIVE

THE HOUSE WAS completely different.

The exterior was exactly the same as it had been three nights ago. Konrad and Taungar were admitted within the outer walls by the same white-clad servant, who led them through the illuminated gardens, across the miniature bridges over the winding streams, and to the door of the house.

It was the interior which had been totally transformed.

The other young servant was waiting in the hallway for them, and this time she was instantly recognizable as female. The white uniform had gone, replaced by a pink silk robe which bared her right breast. Without a cap, her hair was also pink; it had been dyed and hung halfway down her back. She reminded Konrad of someone, or something, although he was unable to recall what it was.

'May I take your clothes, gentlemen?' she said.

The house had been very quiet a few days ago, but now it was filled with noise. From along the passageway came the sounds of laughter and talking, the beat of a heavy drum seeming to shake the whole building to its foundations. A strange sweet smell filled the air, which was cloudy with faint trails of differently coloured smoke. There could be no doubt that this was one of Zuntermein's social gatherings. The number of guests could be judged by the way that the clothes stand was so heavily laden. Even the floor was piled with all kinds of garments, and not merely cloaks.

Konrad had removed his jerkin and handed it to the servant, who casually threw it onto the ground. Then he noticed that Taungar had not stopped once his coat was off. He continued discarding his clothes.

'Everything,' he said, gesturing for Konrad to strip off.

He was naked by now, except for the jewellery which he must always have worn, even beneath his uniform. There were two silver bracelets above his elbows, with an intricate insignia repeatedly etched into their surfaces, and from the gold chain around his neck hung a pendant wrought into the same shape. It was a circle with what could almost be the hilt of a sword projecting to the upper right, its pommel a smaller circle. Konrad had encountered the emblem on pennants and banners carried by many of the legions whose diabolic warriors he had fought and killed on the frontier...

The servant girl handed Taungar a robe similar to the one that she wore. It was pastel blue, and he pulled it over his head. 'Come on,' he told Konrad, 'don't be shy!'

The reason Konrad was reluctant to undress was because it would mean surrendering the dagger he had hidden in his right boot – and also the one tucked inside the waistband of his trousers.

He was almost certain that Zuntermein had lured him here under false pretences. The likelihood that Elyssa would be in this mansion tonight was extremely remote. But if she was, what Konrad must do was obvious: escape with her. How that could be achieved was less obvious as yet, but weapons were surely essential.

And if Elyssa were here, it could only be by permission of Skullface – who would probably also be present.

Konrad had tried not to consider this possibility until now, because the image of Skullface still chilled him to the very bone. Konrad had witnessed many dreadful sights the day that his village had been destroyed by the rapacious horde of mutant marauders, but the vision of the skeletal figure of Skullface, walking unharmed through the flames of the Kastring manor house, had been the most frightening of all.

In the years since then, Konrad had observed many far more appalling feats of endurance. He had seen creatures so badly hacked apart that they could only crawl on the gory stumps of their legs or tentacles, but still they refused to die; he had seen severed limbs take on lives of their own, becoming new recruits to the enemy swarms; he had seen the dead rise and return to battle against the living, although they were infested by worms and maggots, and rotting flesh fell off their bones as they shambled into the fray.

Yet despite all this, Konrad was still haunted by the memory of Skullface. He had often been scared by what he saw and encountered. Fear gave a warrior a certain edge in combat, sharpening his senses and perceptions. The feral invaders seemed to know neither fear nor terror, but that was because they were immune to such human feelings. They were never scared, and they were never brave. All they seemed to live for was to fight and to die, to kill and be killed. Often it seemed it did not matter who suffered so long as the battle produced victims. Ally or enemy, the invaders would kill either without favour, and they did not even care if it was they themselves who were slaughtered.

Konrad would rather face a whole legion of such berserkers than encounter Skullface once more...

Elyssa had been the most important person in his life. Without her, he would have been nothing. Without her, he would probably have been dead – because he would not have escaped when the whole village was massacred. Skullface was the most terrifying being he had ever seen.

To imagine Elyssa being his hostage for so long was almost too repulsive to contemplate.

It was also because of Elyssa's captor that Konrad was carrying the two hidden knives. He had little hope of using the blades effectively, but he must make the attempt. If Skullface could survive an arrow in the heart, a knife thrust would be as harmless as a flea bite to a dragon.

There was no alternative except to do as Taungar instructed. Konrad removed his clothes, slipping the second dagger into his left boot, exchanging his garments for a long silk robe. His was vivid yellow, and – as with Taungar and the servant girl – it was tailored so that the right side of his chest was bared. He felt a fool dressed in such a way, but that was of no consequence. What he had said to Zuntermein three nights ago was the truth: for Elyssa, he would do anything.

Tonight the candles in the chandeliers were red, casting a spectral hue across the corridor as the girl led them along. The tapestries and paintings on the panelled walls were also different from before. Instead of the triumphs of Sigmar, mankind's greatest hero, they displayed the obscene depths to which humanity could descend.

Konrad had never seen so many repulsive images, hardly believed that such vile perversions could ever have been considered let alone performed. Men, women, animals, all indulging in the most corrupt of fornications, each depraved scene was more disgusting than the previous one. The pictures seemed to illustrate the manner in which the repulsive race known as beastmen had been created, that they were indeed the bastard offspring of the debauched matings between the human and the inhuman, between man and beast, and beast and woman.

'Rolf! Konrad! So delighted that you accepted my invitation.'

It was Zuntermein, but Konrad hardly recognised him. He was wearing a flimsy saffron robe, and his right breast was bare. It was a female breast. There could be no doubt that the rest of him was male, however, even though his lips had been rouged, and the broken veins on his cheeks were similarly hidden. Long earrings dangled from each lobe, their pattern the same as Taungar's pendant. Fat and gaudy, his grey hair covered by a yellow wig, he was a parody of the slender servant girl. She remained in the room, closing the door behind her.

Zuntermein hugged Taungar and kissed both his cheeks. Konrad stepped back, out of reach, and quickly surveyed the room.

'Now we are six,' said Zuntermein, and he waved his arm to encompass the other occupants. 'Six times six.' The rings on his fingers sparkled in the candlelight, and wine slopped over the rim of his crystal glass.

'Is she here?' asked Konrad.

'Have patience, my dear boy. The night is yet young. Let us eat, let us drink, let us make merry. And if you're good, if you're very good, then...' Zuntermein smiled and turned away, his arm still around Taungar's shoulder.

Everyone in the room was clad in the same type of garment, but the different colours were hard to distinguish in the scarlet light. There seemed to be equal numbers of men and women, although they were also difficult to distinguish.

The young servant who had given him the spiced wine on his previous visit offered him an ornate goblet from a laden tray. Konrad could still not decide whether the servant was male or female. The right breast was bare, and was male. But the blue hair was long and curled, the face powdered and rouged. Konrad was about to refuse the drink, then decided it would be best if he appeared to join in the festivities. He accepted the goblet and tilted it to his lips, but kept his mouth closed and drank none of the contents.

This was the same room he had been in before, but it was no longer recognizable. The elegant furniture had gone, replaced by satin cushions which covered the floor, while long velvet drapes hung across the walls. The pounding sound came from a pair of drums which were being played bare-handed by a huge bald man. In the corner with him sat a small woman who plucked at the strings of her harp. The instrument seemed ill-suited to such raucous accompaniment, and yet the rhythm of the strange duet was hypnotically powerful.

There were sounds, there were scents, there were sights. Without indulging in what was on offer, Konrad's senses were almost overwhelmed by what was happening all around him. The air was thick with the fragrance of various exotic substances. He recognized weirdroot, and there were many more other forbidden aromas in the room. He began to feel intoxicated simply by breathing in the atmosphere.

Everyone else seemed to be talking or laughing, dancing or kissing, while he remained but an observer. He moved around the room to make his lack of participation less apparent, pretending to drink. He did not even need to taste what the goblet contained to know how strong it was, the heady bouquet told him that.

Meanwhile, the sounds became louder, the scents became stronger, the sights became more indecent.

'Konrad!' said one of the inebriated revellers, slapping him on the back. 'This is the life, hey!'

He stared at the grinning face a few inches in front of his, a face that seemed familiar. He tried to imagine it beneath an Imperial guard helmet – and he recognized Captain Holwald, the officer in charge of raising the Imperial standards above the palace every morning. Konrad wondered how many others from the Imperial guard were here.

'Yes, sir,' he agreed, 'it is.'

'Sir? Sir!' Holwald laughed, and wine dribbled down his beard. 'We're all equals here, Konrad. Call me Manfred. But what's your first name, Konrad?'

'That is my first name. And my second name. It's my only name.'

'This is Sybille,' said Holwald, gesturing to the woman by his side. 'Say hello to Konrad. Konrad, Sybille.'

Tall and fair and definitely female, her bare breast was tattooed with the same runic device that everyone except

Konrad wore. She was nowhere near as intoxicated as her companion. After looking Konrad up and down with undisguised admiration, her eyes met his and she smiled.

'Get me another drink, Manfred,' she said, not looking at her escort.

Holwald staggered away, and Sybille moved closer to Konrad. 'Werner knows how to throw a good party,' she said.

Konrad nodded. A party – that was exactly what this was. The occasion was rapidly developing into an evening of decadence, what passed for a bizarre orgy amongst the rich and bored inhabitants of the capital, but it had nothing to do with Chaos. They were simply indulging their own baser instincts, taking whatever hedonistic pleasures were available tonight, because later they would have to put their clothes on again and return to their normal respectable roles within Altdorf society.

What else could he have expected? He raised the goblet to his lips and this time he took a drink. The liquid was thick and creamy, as potent as he had guessed, and its minty taste warmed his mouth and throat as he swallowed.

'Have you tried these?' asked Sybille, taking his hand and guiding him across the room. 'They're delicious. I must ask Werner's chef for the recipe.' She gestured to the silver tray on the table, scooping a handful of the contents into her mouth.

'No thanks,' said Konrad, recognizing the dish.

Its main ingredient was a type of mushroom which certain troops on the frontier eagerly consumed before going into combat, claiming the substance rendered them immune to wounds. Perhaps it did, because few who ate such a meal were ever wounded; they were usually killed. The mushrooms altered their perceptions, some argued, heightening their awareness of danger. Konrad believed that the opposite was true: their senses were so dulled that they did not care whether they were killed or not. It must almost have been like being a beastman.

'You don't seem very relaxed, Konrad,' said Sybille, who had not released her grip on him.

She was extremely good looking, despite her green hair, and Konrad recognized that under different circumstances he might have been attracted to her. Sybille must have noticed the way he was watching her, because she suddenly leaned forward and kissed him. Konrad felt the warmth of her naked breast against his own bare flesh, and he did not resist – not until a few seconds later, when she tried to feed him some of the mushrooms from her mouth to his...

He drew back, taking another sip of wine. He held the goblet between them, as if it were a shield and Sybille an enemy to be held at bay.

'Give me some of your wine,' she said, and he offered her his goblet. 'Not like that.' She pushed it back towards him. 'You drink first. I want to taste it from your lips.'

He shook his head and finally freed his hand from hers, not wanting even to touch her.

'You're amongst friends here,' said Sybille. 'We're all friends.' She glanced around. 'Why don't we join the festivities?'

Konrad noticed that he and Sybille were almost the only ones still standing. By now, there was near silence in the room and everyone else was otherwise engaged. It did not matter who with, or how many of them. The drummer and the harpist were no longer playing their instruments, they were doing something quite different together; the third servant was involved with someone else of equally indeterminate sex; Taungar was proving that the pink-haired servant girl could do more than lead guests through the mansion; even Captain Holwald had found himself other partners in the brief time he had been away from Sybille. But there was no sign of Zuntermein, who should have been easy to locate. His absence made Konrad feel uneasy.

Sybille's hands began to rove across Konrad's body, and he pushed her away, gently at first, then more forcefully.

She shrugged and turned around, and it did not take her long to discover a welcome elsewhere.

Wizard or not, it was time to find Zuntermein and confront him. Konrad started across the room, to where the door was hidden behind the velvet draperies.

That was when the curtain at the other side of the room fell away. A wall had stood there on Konrad's first visit, but now that had gone and the hidden chamber beyond was revealed.

There was Zuntermein. He stood upon a raised platform in front of a giant effigy of his perverted god, and with him was a girl, helpless and naked.

She was not Elyssa.

Elyssa had been tall and slim and long-legged, and this girl was not. Elyssa's long hair had been thick and straight and jet black, but hers was short and blonde, fine and wavy. Elyssa's face had been oval, whereas hers was round. Elyssa's nose was firm and straight, not small and upturned. Elyssa's eyes had been the blackest of black, the pupil and iris almost as one, not soft brown.

She was not Elyssa.

She was Krysten!

A MOMENT LATER, before Konrad could react to the tableau which had suddenly opened up before him, he was seized from behind by several strong arms which held him rigid and immobile.

The huge idol was half male, half female; the left side of its humanoid body displayed masculine attributes, while the right side showed its feminine physique. Two pairs of horns rose out of its skull, protruding from its long golden hair. Clad in pale velvet, over which was worn a shirt of chain mail, the figure carried a jade sceptre in its right hand and a small dagger in its left.

'Slaanesh! Slaanesh! Slaanesh! Slaanesh! Slaanesh!'

Konrad gazed up at the monstrous effigy, almost mesmerized by its different aspects – it was repulsively ugly, yet paradoxically beautiful.

'Slaanesh! Slaanesh! Slaanesh! Slaanesh! Slaanesh!'

All of those who had been indulging their orgiastic lusts only seconds previously had now risen to their knees, and they chanted out the two syllables of their revered lord's name, making it into a profane prayer. It was they who composed the sacrilegious congregation; this was their blasphemous church; Zuntermein was their heathen priest.

The wizard was still wearing the same garment, but he no longer looked ridiculous. He had been transformed into a tribal shaman, dressed in his sacred robes. His ornaments had become talismanic emblems, his facial decorations were now warpaint, his wig was the same colour as his master's golden mane and a symbol of his ritual authority.

'Slaanesh! Slaanesh! Slaanesh! Slaanesh! Slaanesh!'

Slaanesh...

One of the most powerful of the Chaos pantheon, Slaanesh was the lord of pleasure, the god of hedonism and carnal lust.

'Slaanesh! Slaanesh! Slaanesh! Slaanesh! Slaanesh!'

Konrad knew the name, and now he remembered the symbol of the bisexual deity was composed from a union of the ancient sign for a male and that for a female: a circle with an arrow pointing to the upper right, a circle with a cross rising above it. That was the motif which all the worshippers wore as jewellery or carried permanently as tattoos.

'Slaanesh! Slaanesh! Slaanesh! Slaanesh! Slaanesh!'

The altar to the god of decadence and depravity towered over Zuntermein and loomed menacingly above his defenceless hostage.

Krysten stood with her head bowed, facing the chanting crowd. There was a chain around her neck, and Zuntermein held the other end as if she were some kind of wild animal that he had tamed.

'Slaanesh! Slaanesh! Slaanesh! Slaanesh! Slaanesh!'

Zuntermein raised his other hand, and the chanting ceased.

'I have kept my promise,' he said, staring down at Konrad. 'I knew how disappointed you would be if I hadn't.'

Konrad had believed that Krysten was dead, just as he had thought Elyssa had died five years before her, five years to the very day; he had thought both had been slain on Sigmarzeit, the first day of summer. But it had been Elyssa he had hoped he might see tonight. Now he knew that they both lived – for a while...

'I observed that you didn't seem to have been enjoying our hospitality.' Zuntermein spoke as though he and Konrad were totally alone and simply making conversation. 'Perhaps there was nothing we had to offer which was to your liking. I can understand that. We all have different tastes, some more refined than others. But we do like to provide our guests with whatever pleasure they most desire. You have no excuse now, Konrad. We have the very thing to tempt you.'

At the sound of Konrad's name, Krysten moved for the first time. She raised her head slightly and looked in front of her. When she saw Konrad, her eyes widened, and she took a step forward. That was as far as she could go, because the chain kept her back. She held out her arms towards him.

'Konrad,' she whispered. 'Konrad,' she begged. 'Konrad...'

'Let her go!' yelled Konrad, and for the first time he began to struggle against the arms which gripped his limbs and neck. He could hardly move, it was almost as if his whole body were in chains. His captors were experts in restraint. Taungar was one of them, Holwald another.

'Don't be so foolish,' replied Zuntermein. 'I have gone to a lot of trouble on your behalf, Konrad. You should be very appreciative, although I suppose gratitude is too much to expect. But aren't you pleased to see your ladyfriend again?'

'Are you all right?' said Konrad, speaking to Krysten instead of answering the sorcerer priest. He knew that was also a foolish thing to say, but he could think of nothing else.

Krysten shook her head, in confusion rather than in reply.

'I thought,' she said, 'I thought...' Silent tears dripped down her cheeks as she gazed at Konrad, and she wiped her face with her fingertips.

'Let her go!' he shouted again. That was all that he wanted, he realized, and so it was not a foolish demand.

'I can imagine how overjoyed you are to find your beautiful friend is safe, Konrad. You have not seen her for a long while, I believe? That means you have so much lost time to make up. It will be wonderful to kiss her again, to hold her. Think how much *pleasure* you will both have. To thank us for bringing you together, I think you ought to show us exactly how much you have missed her.'

Konrad stared up at him, knowing exactly what the wizard meant. He was expecting them to behave in the uninhibited manner that everyone else had been doing a few minutes ago. Konrad had vowed to do anything to save Elyssa, and the same was true for Krysten. He would obey every command the sorcerer gave him – yet he was well aware that no matter how he and Krysten might abase themselves, Zuntermein did not intend allowing them to live to see another dawn.

Konrad lowered his gaze and nodded his head. 'Whatever you say,' he said quietly.

'I knew you would see things my way,' said Zuntermein. 'Bring him up here.'

As Konrad was manhandled towards the steps which led up to the dais he remembered that while he had been a prisoner of Kastring's raiding band, they had captured a small group of marauders whose misfortune it was to honour another deity. Konrad's hosts were adherents of Khorne; the others obeyed Slaanesh. The followers of the god of blood and those who bowed down to the god of pleasure were the greatest of enemies, so implicitly opposed were they in the extremes of their beliefs.

Kastring had prepared a very special death for the Slaaneshi cultists, ensuring that they died far more slowly and much more painfully than any other of the sacrifices his acolytes so regularly made to the huntsman of souls. The worshippers of the two powers hated and despised each other – and the gods themselves were forever in conflict, two rival deities battling for superiority within the realms of Chaos.

Zuntermein had difficulty in pulling Krysten away to the far side of the altar. She had slipped her hands between the chain and her neck so that the metal links did not bite into her throat. It took three pairs of arms to keep Konrad at the other edge of the shrine.

'Hold her,' Zuntermein ordered, and one of those restraining Konrad released his grip and went to take the end of Krysten's chain.

'Are you sincere?' said the magician, walking slowly towards Konrad. 'Are you really going to demonstrate your affection for her... for us?'

The one idea in Konrad's head had been of how to kill Zuntermein, and now he tried desperately to think of something else – to imagine that he and Krysten were obeying the wizard's perverted demands.

Zuntermein put his hand on Konrad's bare chest, and the touch was like ice. He felt the warmth of his body draining away, but that was not important. What mattered was what the sorcerer was stealing from his mind.

'You should not have tried to deceive me,' sighed Zuntermein, stepping back. 'As for wishing me harm...' He shook his head sadly. 'What a shame. When we first met, I hoped that we could be such good friends. Alas, it was not to be. So if you will not do what is required–'

'No!' yelled Konrad.

'Yes,' smiled Zuntermein.

Konrad began to struggle again. There were only two of them holding him now, but he felt much weaker, as though the wizard's freezing touch had also depleted his strength.

He watched helplessly as Zuntermein strolled back across the dais towards Krysten. Krysten tried to evade him, but the man holding the metal leash would not allow her to back away. She struck out at the wizard, but he ignored the blows and reached forward to stroke the side of her face. At his touch, her frantic movements slowed. Her arms were still in motion, but at a fraction of the previous rate.

Zuntermein looked at Konrad. 'There is pleasure in pleasure,' he said. 'And there is pleasure–'

He reached up to the huge effigy's left hand and took the blade from its grip. The knife no longer looked so small in the wizard's hand, because it had been made for a human. It was an Imperial guard dagger, and Konrad knew it must have been one of those he had brought here.

'In pain!'

'*No!*' Konrad's cry was a tortured scream.

'Slaanesh. Slaanesh.' The audience took up the name of their foul deity again, softly at first, then building up to an even greater crescendo than before. 'Slaanesh! Slaanesh! Slaanesh!! Slaanesh!! *Slaanesh!! Slaanesh!!!*'

Zuntermein stepped towards Krysten, whose arms were still slowly trying to fend him off. He nodded to the other man, who removed the chain from her neck and stepped aside. The wizard priest leaned towards the girl, and he whispered in her ear. Then he kissed both her cheeks – and gave her the knife...

'Slaanesh! Slaanesh! Slaanesh! Slaanesh! Slaanesh!'

For a moment Konrad did not realize what was happening. He had expected Zuntermein to use the blade upon Krysten's naked body, to begin slowly torturing her. Instead, Krysten now had the dagger. Her eyes gazed at Konrad, her empty eyes, her possessed eyes, and slowly she walked towards him, raising the knife as she did so.

She was under Zuntermein's command, and the wizard's command must have been to slay Konrad!

'Krysten!' he yelled. 'Krysten!'

But he knew that his shouts would not be enough to break the hypnotic spell which had captured the girl. He renewed his attempts to break free, but he was as powerless as Krysten. They were both Zuntermein's hostages.

Konrad's body was no longer his own, while Krysten's mind belonged to the witch priest.

'Slaanesh! Slaanesh! Slaanesh! Slaanesh! Slaanesh!'

Krysten moved closer to Konrad, every slow step bringing his death nearer. There could be no death more cruel than to be executed by a lover.

This was why he had been drawn here, he realized: so that he could be slain, sacrificed to the lord of pleasure.

'Slaanesh! Slaanesh! Slaanesh! Slaanesh! Slaanesh!'

The girl halted a yard away from him, the point of her blade half that distance from his throat. Her staring eyes were focused beyond him, her face was without expression.

'Krysten!' he shouted again.

She blinked, and the hand which was holding the knife trembled.

She whispered something, and Konrad thought that it was his name, but the word was lost in the depraved ritual chanting.

'Slaanesh! Slaanesh! Slaanesh! Slaanesh! Slaanesh!'

'Krysten!'

Then suddenly she regained full control of herself. Her limbs lost their rigidity, and for a moment she smiled. She repeated what she had said, but far louder, screaming out the word – and simultaneously thrusting the knife towards Konrad's chest.

'*KHORNE!*'

CHAPTER SIX

'KHORNE!'

The point of the blade slashed across Konrad's chest, leaving a line of blood.

As the loathed name of their revered god's hated rival echoed through the room, it shocked the fevered chorus of acolytes into sudden silence and Konrad felt his human bonds briefly slacken – and he burst free.

He drove his left elbow into Taungar's face, feeling the sergeant's nose crumple under the blow. Taungar cried out in agony and stepped back over the edge of the dais and dropped into the crowd beneath him.

Holwald maintained his grip upon his prisoner's right arm slightly longer, until Konrad swung around and smashed his fist into his throat, crushing it with a single powerful blow. With such a terrible injury, Holwald could not even whisper his pain. Konrad thrust the heel of his hand up against the captain's chin, jerking it swiftly back. There was a sharp sickening snap as Holwald's neck broke, and he was dead before he hit the ground.

The man who had held Krysten's chain now rushed towards her, his face contorted with hatred, his fingers held out like claws. The girl had not moved since slicing at Konrad, but now she turned. She dodged aside as the man lunged at her, then drove the dagger into his belly. He grunted in surprise and pain, and toppled to the ground, taking the blade with him.

Krysten had dispatched the cultist exactly as Konrad had taught her to deal with an assailant. He glanced at the girl, but did not recognize her expression. Her features had become malevolent, devoid of all innocence. Free from Zuntermein's spell, she was in thrall to a far more dominant power.

Although blood was pouring from his chest, Konrad felt no pain. He had suffered many wounds which were far worse. If she had meant to kill him, Krysten could have done so with a swift and accurate strike deep into his heart. That was something else he had taught her.

But it was not Konrad's death that she wanted – it was his blood...

'Khorne!' she shouted once again, raising her arms as she prayed to the god of blood.

Konrad saw a movement above him, and he looked up. The effigy of Slaanesh seemed to shimmer, its outlines melting, its features dissolving into a different image, and Konrad could see another vast idol in its place upon the dais. It wore brass armour, sat upon a throne mounted over the bones of its victims, carried a mighty waraxe and a shield which bore an X-shaped emblem.

He remembered the last time he had stood before such a shrine, when he had been with the beast-girl called Silk, and how she had carved that same runic cross into the chest of one of Kastring's captives...

He touched his own chest, feeling the wet warmth which flowed from the wound, and it was as if this were Konrad's own offering to the lord of death and of pain.

Time seemed frozen, stretching to eternity. Krysten gazed at Konrad, and their eyes finally met. The girl's pupils seemed to glow red. And through them Khorne himself appeared to be offering Konrad the opportunity of swearing blood allegiance – that the only way of escaping the Slaaneshi cultists was for Konrad to join their most hated enemy.

His pulse raced, his heart pounded, and more blood oozed from his wound.

Krysten had become one of Khorne's acolytes. All of Konrad's desires were reawakened as he remembered the passions they had shared.

He wanted to be with her again, no matter what the price; and he wanted to flee the Slaaneshi temple, whatever the price.

Yet a part of him held back, aware of how high that price would be. It would cost him far more than his own life, he realized.

Krysten smiled, beckoning to him.

Then she screamed.

But this was no scream of devotion as she called upon the foul deity that she worshipped. It was a scream of ultimate pain. Her whole body shook in an agonized spasm, and she dropped to the ground, still twitching.

It was Zuntermein's doing. Only a second or two had passed, and now the magician had turned his thaumaturgical talents upon the girl.

Khorne was banished, the altar to Slaanesh was back in view again, and in a moment Zuntermein would direct a spell against Konrad. Against such magical attacks he had no defence.

Already Konrad had acted. He had no weapon, but did not wish to touch the wizard with his bare hands for fear of what spell could flow from flesh to flesh. He sprang up to the effigy of Slaanesh, up towards the the jade sceptre which the figure clutched in its left hand. The wand was an elaborately carved green staff, the deity's emblem wrought into its upper end. Konrad pulled it free and he leapt down at Zuntermein, who had raised his arms to cast another spell.

Before the wizard could utter a single syllable of his fiendish chant, Konrad rammed the lower end of the sceptre into his mouth, silencing him, then drove it down into his throat, choking him.

Konrad forced the jade sceptre even deeper – and discovered that it was as easy to slay a sorcerer as it was to kill anyone else. They were mortal, they could die.

And Zuntermein died.

The sudden unwelcome sound of the enemy deity's name had both silenced and stilled the congregation of the damned, but by now they had all regained their voices and their volition. The heathens were swarming up to the dais, screaming out their demented blood lust. Konrad rolled Zuntermein's corpse towards the steps, knocking the first few of the horde back.

He drew the knife from the belly of Krysten's victim and dashed forward, striking out at the first two men who made it to the top of the steps. One fell back, his throat sliced open, fountains of red spraying from his severed blood vessels. The second dragged the knife from Konrad's grip, the blade embedded in his heart as he dropped.

Even though none of his opponents was armed, Konrad realized that there were too many of them to fight. Such odds had seldom stopped him before, but there was more on his mind than combat: he had to get Krysten away from here.

He glanced up at the chandelier above his head, at all the candles, at all the red flames, and he noticed the velvet curtains which covered the walls of the secret temple.

Turning back to the altar, once more Konrad leapt at the giant effigy. But this time he kept a grip on the figure of Slaanesh, hauling himself up, using the image's limbs as his stepping stones, climbing to the deity's horned head, then reaching out towards the elaborate lamp. It was a yard beyond his reach, and he launched himself through the air, grabbing hold of the lower edge – but the supporting chain was torn out of the ceiling by his weight and the whole thing fell. So did Konrad. He dropped onto the acolytes below, dragging the heavy chandelier down on those around him. More blood was spilled where the crystal shards struck.

Most of the candles had been extinguished by the fall, but a few were still alight. Konrad kicked and punched himself free, and pulled two of the guttering candles from the sconces. Holding them upright, he hurried to one side of the room, touching the flames to the drapes. The fabric immediately caught fire, erupting vividly in a matter of moments.

Ripping off a piece of velvet from another curtain, Konrad wadded it into a ball and ignited it from the blaze. The fabric unravelled as it flew across the room, like a barrel of burning pitch hurled from a ballista, and the draperies on the far side also began to blaze.

The screams of venomous hatred quickly turned to cries of desperate fear, and instead of trying to attack Konrad the cultists were now attempting to escape the incendiary assault. But some did not move aside swiftly enough, and Konrad used his bare hands as his weapons. Men or women, it made no difference, all became Konrad's victims as he forced his way back to the dais and to Krysten's side.

She lay on her back, her eyes open and unblinking. Zuntermein's unseen assault had left no sign of injury, and she was still alive.

'Konrad,' she breathed, as he knelt next to her. 'I thought you were dead...'

'Not me,' he told her, sliding one arm under her knees and the other beneath her back. 'And not you,' he promised.

Krysten gasped in pain as Konrad picked her up. He carried her past the shrine, down the steps, through the swirling smoke and towards the flames. By now, it was not only the velvet curtains which were blazing; everything was becoming engulfed by the inferno. There was absolute mayhem within the temple. A crazed cultist rushed past, his hair turned to fire. Others were frenziedly tearing at their robes which were ablaze, their flesh blistering in the raging heat.

The door to the passage beyond was visible now that the curtains masking it had burned away, and a number of acolytes were gathered near the exit, but it seemed they could not make their way through to safety because of the intensity of the heat. They pushed forward, but then withdrew hastily towards the centre of the room, which was the only part not yet ablaze.

The conflagration had engulfed all the walls, and tongues of fire were licking hungrily across the floor and over the ceiling.

The temple was full of smoke and screams, the roar of vivid flames and the stench of burning flesh.

A few more seconds, and the conflagration would have destroyed everything.

Konrad carried Krysten through the fire, and the flames seemed to part for a moment wherever they passed. It was as if there were a route through the incandescence, a pathway which only he could sense and which was not part of the room, not part of Altdorf, perhaps not even part of the world...

He walked between the blackened bodies of his tortured enemies, towards the refuge offered by the only area of the room still untouched by fire. When he reached the door, he kicked it open and stepped through into the sanctuary of the corridor beyond.

The door slammed shut behind him. A moment before it did so, Konrad caught sight of the funeral pyre within and witnessed the hideous fate of those who were still alive and trapped by the immolation, the ravenous flames consuming their living flesh.

He realized that the door must have been drawn shut by the severity of the heat, as it sucked in even more air to feed the inferno, but he knew that it was more than merely the blaze which had imprisoned the doomed worshippers. Some sinister force had held them contained within the conflagration, unable to escape, yet it had permitted himself and Krysten to leave. Not even the hair on his arms had been singed, despite the ferocity of the flames.

Within the passageway, suddenly everything was still and silent; there was not even a smell of burning. It was as if the blaze were a thousand miles away. Supporting Krysten with one arm, Konrad reached out to touch the wall – and swiftly drew his hand away. The wooden panel was hot, very hot. It could not contain the raging fire beyond for much longer.

He made his way to the end of the hall, laying the girl upon the pile of clothes on the floor. She winced in pain. Her eyes had been closed, but now she opened them again and she smiled when she saw Konrad.

'I'm glad you aren't dead,' she said softly.

'And I'm glad you aren't,' he told her, and he kissed her forehead.

She raised her face and lifted her hands, pulling him down so that he kissed her lips – and he tasted warm blood. His arms were covered in blood where he had held her.

For a moment he thought it was his own blood, then he realized that it was hers. Earlier, Krysten's eyes had seemed to be red, but now her entire body was suddenly that colour. It was as if she had been flayed alive.

'We have to go,' he said, releasing her and standing up.

He smiled so that she would not notice how concerned he was. He looked around for something to cover her with, and he found a green velvet cloak, then another. They were the kind worn by courtiers at the palace, but their wearers no longer had need of them. Konrad wrapped Krysten in the cloaks.

She opened her lips for another kiss, and he responded. This time there was even more blood.

'Why did you leave me?' Krysten asked, and then she died.

Konrad gazed in disbelief at her corpse. He pulled a loose strand of blonde hair away from Krysten's cheek, wiped the blood from her face, touched his fingertips to her lips one final time, then pulled one of the velvet cloaks higher, over her head, folding it around her as if he were tucking her into bed.

He stood up, found his own clothes and swiftly dressed. The second of his knives was still in his boot.

Krysten was gone. All that remained was her body, and Konrad piled more of the discarded clothes around and on top of her lifeless corpse, reached for a candle from the wall and set fire to the stack of garments. He walked back along the corridor, igniting the tapestries and everything else that was flammable, before opening the outside door and stepping into the night.

The servant boy was waiting for him. He was armed with a spear, which he thrust at Konrad's stomach. Konrad stepped aside, grabbing the shaft as it slid past his hip. He pulled, and the servant was dragged towards him – and onto Konrad's knife.

The boy gasped in agony as the blade slid into his chest, the gasp turning into a long scream of ultimate despair as Konrad killed him.

He killed him slowly; he killed him coldly; he killed him without mercy. He stabbed him over and over again, until his white uniform had become totally red. Only then did Konrad kick the servant into the moat, where the waters turned to blood as his life finally ebbed away.

Konrad made his way across the gardens of Zuntermein's mansion. When he reached the gate he looked back. The blaze was far more spectacular than the one at the army guardhouse had been.

IT WAS AFTER being in a tavern with Taungar that Konrad had first met Zuntermein. The young serving girl had reminded him of Krysten, and that was why it was she who had been foremost in Konrad's thoughts when Zuntermein had probed into his mind.

Then, after so many months apart, and however briefly together, Konrad had been reunited with the girl.

There is no such thing as chance, Wolf had frequently said. Either that was true or the converse: there was too much chance. Too many things had happened for them all to be attributed to random circumstance. So many intertwining events could only have been part of a greater design, but Konrad was too close to see his own place within the pattern.

After returning from the dwarf temple which Wolf and Anvila and he had discovered, Konrad found that the frontier mine was destroyed and everyone within had been killed or taken hostage. There had seemed to be but one survivor, the one-handed man called Heinler – but in reality this was the skaven, Gaxar. The grey seer had taken on human form, masquerading as a miner, and it was he who had destroyed the watch towers so that the invaders could approach the fortified workings unseen.

Unable to find her body amongst the ruins, Konrad had assumed that Krysten was a prisoner of the pagan hordes. While tracking the marauding armies, he had revealed to Gaxar that his motive for pursuit was to locate and rescue the abducted girl.

Having discovered this, Gaxar had knocked him unconscious. When he awoke, Konrad was the captive of a marauding band of Khorne worshippers. Another group of Khorne acolytes must have captured Krysten at the mine – but it was more than her body which they had taken. She had become corrupted, joining them to become a devotee of the Blood God. And then, somehow, she had fallen into Zuntermein's hands.

Konrad had escaped Kastring's warband by dressing in the armour of the bronze warrior, the knight who Wolf said had been his twin brother. This was the same figure Konrad and Elyssa had seen ride through their village the day before the swarms of rampaging beastmen had totally annihilated everyone and everything within the valley.

It was Litzenreich who had saved Konrad from his prison of bronze; it was Litzenreich who was the cause of Gaxar losing his right paw; it was Litzenreich who had convinced

Konrad that Gaxar must have been heading for Altdorf after the skaven sorcerer's subterranean lair had been assailed by the Middenheim troops.

And Gaxar had indeed been in the Imperial capital – as was Elyssa... and Skullface... and Krysten.

There was no such thing as chance...

Konrad felt as if he were enmeshed within a giant web, becoming more and more trapped all the time. The strands of the web seemed to link all the people that he had ever known, his enemies as well as his friends.

Elyssa and Kastring; Kastring and Gaxar; Gaxar and Krysten; Krysten and Zuntermein...

Wolf and the bronze knight; the bronze knight and Litzenreich...

Elyssa and Skullface; Skullface and Gaxar...

Silver Eye and the golden crest; the golden crest and Elyssa...

Chance...

Deep beneath Altdorf so many of them had been together: Litzenreich, Gaxar, Silver Eye, Elyssa, Skullface.

And himself.

There was no one line linking all of these; each was connected by several interlocking links. And everything was circular. Whichever direction Konrad explored, he was brought inevitably back to where he had begun.

Chaos...

He was a pawn of Chaos, cast helplessly whichever way the winds of fate happened to blow him, a piece of driftwood at the mercy of the currents and oceans, washed up on some foreign shore and then carried away again by the next tide. He had believed it was his own decision to come to Altdorf, but that was not so. All he had done was play the role which destiny had assigned to him.

Moreover, he had become a creature of darkness, corrupted by the warpstone within the bronze shackles which had held him for so long, then further infected by more of the evil unearthly substance which Litzenreich had used to extract him from the armour.

Zuntermein had recognized the taint of Chaos which had taken hold of Konrad. It was something that Konrad knew he would never escape. Skaven could even smell the odour of the warpstone which permeated his body.

When Krysten called out the name of the huntsman of souls, had she really summoned up a vision of the Blood God? For a few moments Konrad believed he had seen the image of Khorne upon the altar, and he had felt his allegiance being drawn towards the powers of damnation. Had he been granted some profane strength by the cruel deity which had enabled him to escape?

Unlike the time when he had battled the goblins in the ancient dwarf temple, below the mountains of Kislev, Konrad had been aware of no inhuman power invigorating him. He had felt no different when he had slain Zuntermein and fought against the Slaaneshi cultists. It had been his own hatred which had given him all the energy that he needed to defeat his benighted foes.

He and Krysten had escaped from the doomed church, however, whilst everyone else within had perished. He could not deny that some supernatural force had seemed to help him survive, guiding him unharmed through the deadly flames.

Was it the Blood God who had saved him, then claimed the price of its assistance by taking Krysten as another sacrifice?

Konrad had no way of knowing, and neither did he want to consider any of it, not now, not ever.

He had to get out of Altdorf. The web was drawing tighter and tighter around him, sucking him towards its centre and what must surely be his inevitable nemesis. That was why he must leave the capital.

He was aware that he would be able to escape the city without any difficulty, although he realized that it would have been wisest to have taken some of Zuntermein's valuables before he left – but so far as Konrad was concerned, there had been only one precious thing inside the mansion.

For months he had falsely believed that Krysten was dead; now it was true.

Even as he made his way out of the city, slipping past the watch like a shadow in the night, Konrad knew that he would return.

CHAPTER SEVEN

HE COULD HAVE gone anywhere that he chose, anywhere in the Empire, anywhere beyond – but there was nowhere that he wished to go, nothing that he wished to do.

His only profession was that of a soldier, and he could have sought employment as a mercenary in any land within the known world. There were always wars and battles; there was always fighting to be done, always killing and looting and destroying. He could have returned to Kislev, continued his role in the eternal battle against the incursion of the armies from the northern wastes. At least on the frontier one knew who one's enemies were – unlike in Altdorf. Within the capital, members of the court of Karl-Franz could be Slaaneshi cultists, while the Emperor's own guard might be manned by Chaos worshippers.

Konrad wanted to be as far away as possible from Altdorf and all its treachery and intrigue, but part of him still lay within the Imperial capital.

That was the memory of Elyssa, the brief moment when their eyes had met before he was swept into the culvert and out of the subterranean cavern. The girl had been so much a part of his life for so long that it was impossible to obliterate her from his mind. Even throughout the years when he believed she was dead, she had never been far from his thoughts. Now that he knew she was alive, he spent more and more time thinking of her.

Konrad was exactly the way he had been before he and Elyssa had ever met. All he had owned then were his clothes and his knife. That was all he had now, and all that he needed.

Krysten had died, died in his arms, and Konrad tried to make himself accept that Elyssa was also lost to him. Physically she may still have lived, but her soul must have been ensnared long ago. If Krysten had been corrupted in a few brief months, then Elyssa had surely become one of the damned during the years since she had been captured. She could not have been Skullface's prisoner for so long without being tainted by his benighted influence. By now she must have been his consort and his ally, as much a creature of Chaos as he was.

For Krysten, the ordeal was over; but not for Elyssa.

And there was nothing that Konrad could do except try to forget her – yet that would be the hardest thing of all.

Konrad had gone to Altdorf because of Silver Eye, pursuing the skaven and the mysterious shield which he carried; but now that his master was dead, perhaps the warrior rat had departed from the tunnels below the Imperial city. The conspiracy to replace the Emperor with a doppelganger must have ended with the death of Gaxar.

After escaping from the Imperial capital, Konrad travelled south through the Reikwald Forest. It reminded him of the woodlands where he had spent his early life, and for the first few days he seemed to have returned to that kind of existence, surviving on the animals that he could trap.

There was plenty of wildlife in these woodlands, which was a sure sign that there were few mutated predators in the vicinity. Most of the birds were not carrion eaters, the majority of the animals not scavengers: they did not survive by eating what remained after the beastmen had mutilated and devoured their prey.

The Forest of Shadows had seemed far older, full of ancient trees, many of which were rotten and covered with fungus. Konrad had taken the all-embracing miasma of decomposition for granted at the time, because he knew nothing else. Now he was aware that it was not simply age which had caused the trees to become twisted and decayed – it was the touch of Chaos. In Ostland, the forest was still inhabited by numerous beastmen, the descendants of those who had taken part in the last great Chaos invasion two centuries ago; and the woodlands were themselves still corrupted by the effects of the incursion, as well as by the infection of the ugly creatures who still lurked within the darkest depths.

They existed throughout the known world, but there were fewer such deformities in this part of the Empire, or so close to the capital. When he had been young, Konrad's gift of foresight had saved him from the beastmen on many an occasion. But even without his extra vision, he felt safer in this forest than he had ever done in his native valley. The trees here were more healthy and did not seem threatening. In the Forest of Shadows the rows of trunks often appeared to form impenetrable walls to keep out intruders, or seemed arrayed in maze-like patterns to prevent escape.

Winter was fast approaching, and Konrad had no intention of staying in the forest for an hour longer than necessary. Without a horse he would not be able to travel far, which meant he would have to remain in the first village that he found; but he had no money to pay for a room at the inn.

The village was larger than the one where he had grown up, and was situated at a crossroads. The signpost showed that one highway led to the city-state of Carroburg in one direction, to Grunburg in the other; the second road led to Bogenhafen, whilst the other direction was the route Konrad had followed from Altdorf to bring him here. The largest building was the tavern, which was also a coaching inn. The sign which hung outside bore the name The Grey Stoat, plus an illustration of such an animal.

He needed something to trade, and he wished that he had a bow and quiver of arrows to make his task easier; but he was able to snare a young deer. He bled and gutted the animal, slung it over his shoulders, and headed for the village.

As he did so, Konrad remembered when he had entered Ferlangen. He had been carrying a rabbit which he hoped to sell, but had ended up being sentenced to death for poaching. It was Baron Otto Krieshmier who had condemned him to death, the man who Elyssa was to have married.

Krieshmier and Elyssa – another strand of the web in which Konrad was ensnared.

He had been saved by Wolf, who had fought and killed Krieshmier because the baron had once cheated him out of some money.

Wolf and Krieshmier – yet another strand...

This time Konrad could fight his own battles. He was no longer the frightened youth that he had been five and a half years ago.

No one would dare accuse him of poaching, not without a handful of armed men to back up the charge. But he would be a lot more careful this time, which was why he waited until dark before he entered the Grey Stoat, and why he used the back door, and why he left his prize hidden outside behind a row of barrels.

There was a boy by the kitchen fire, turning a pig on a spit; and there was a man chewing a piece of meat, his feet up on a table, his chair tilted back on two legs. Neither of them noticed as Konrad silently shut the door and walked slowly up behind them. Suddenly the man turned. He saw Konrad and lost his balance, falling to the floor. He lay on his back, his hand clutching for the hilt of his sword. The hilt was embossed with the Imperial crown; it was an Imperial guard sword.

'Don't come any closer,' he warned. 'I'm in the Imperial guard.'

Despite the sword, Konrad very much doubted that. The man's hair was too long and he wore a beard, but his accent was far too common for that of an officer. In any case, despite being of the necessary height, he was too overweight to be a member of the Emperor's elite fighting force.

'Are you the landlord?'

'Why?'

'I'm asking the questions. Are you the landlord?'

'No,' replied the man, as he stood up and backed away. He held the hilt of his sword, but having taken the measure of Konrad he had evidently decided it would be unwise to draw the blade.

'Fetch him,' said Konrad.

'Go get Netzler,' the man told the boy.

'I told you to get him,' said Konrad, picking up the chair and sitting down.

The man stared at him for a few seconds before he opened the inner door and left the kitchen. The boy watched him leave, then he looked at Konrad.

'Dieter is in the Imperial guard,' said the boy, and he laughed as if he had never heard anything so stupid. 'He can't even guard the kitchen,' he added, and he laughed again.

Konrad also laughed. The boy was about eight or nine years old, his face dirty, his clothes ragged, and he was doing exactly the kind of work which Konrad had done a decade and a half ago. In Brandenheimer's tavern, Konrad had to do all the most menial, most boring, most dirty of jobs. That had been the whole of his early life; but unlike this boy, Konrad had never had any occasion to laugh. He had always kept silent, pretending that he could not even speak. Until he met Elyssa, there had been no one that he wished to talk to.

'You'd better start turning the spit before that hog burns,' said Konrad, and the boy did so.

A moment later, the door swung open again and the landlord entered the kitchen. Slimly built, without the expansive beer belly that usually denoted his trade, he looked more like a prosperous merchant. Dieter followed him through the door, and he stood to attention, as though on sentry duty.

'What's going on?' the landlord demanded.

'I have a business proposition which might be to our mutual benefit, Herr Netzler,' said Konrad.'

'That always interests me, Herr...?'

'Taungar,' said Konrad. The sergeant no longer had any use for his name, while Konrad had no reason to reveal his own.

'Bring Herr Taungar a drink, Dieter. What would you like?'

'A beer,' said Konrad.

'A beer,' echoed Netzler, as he sat down opposite Konrad.

'Hans,' Dieter said to the kitchen boy, 'a beer.'

'You fetch it,' Netzler told Dieter. 'Then get to work.' When the door behind him closed, he said to Konrad: 'He's in the Imperial guard.' He smiled, and Hans laughed.

'And he comes here to work while he's off duty?' said Konrad.

'He's always off duty, it seems. But enough of this, what can I do for you?'

'It's more what I can do for you.'

'I thought that's what you were going to say.'

'I have some fresh local produce you might like to buy.'

'What?'

Konrad glanced at the spit. 'Venison,' he said.

'Not the Emperor's venison, I hope.'

'Only if he comes here to eat it.'

'Karl-Franz has dined here, and sampled what else we have to offer.'

Dieter came back, carrying a tankard of ale. He slammed it on the table, slid it towards Konrad, then returned the way he had come.

The stein was only half full.

'Outside, to the left, behind the barrels,' said Konrad, sipping the ale, then swallowing it down in two thirsty gulps.

Netzler went out through the back door, came in again, nodded and asked, 'How much?'

They haggled over the price.

'...and that's my final offer,' said the landlord.

'A deal.'

'And I won't charge you for the tankard of ale.'

'In that case,' said Konrad, nodding to the empty stein, 'I'll have the other half.'

A FEW MORE beers, a meal of bread and pork and turnips, the price of a bed for the night, and half of Konrad's money was already accounted for. Little wonder that Netzler was clad as a wealthy merchant, because that was what he was.

The Grey Stoat was bigger than Konrad had first realized. It was more than a tavern which served the villagers, more than a coaching inn for travellers to spend a night before renewing their journey across the Empire. Upstairs were other private rooms set aside for entertaining the noblemen from Altdorf who rode out from the capital for a night of pleasure. For these, the Grey Stoat provided not only board and lodgings.

Konrad drank slowly, alone in a corner, watching all that was happening around him. He noticed the curtains on the far side which hid the flight of stairs up to the next floor. The clientele on the gallery preferred to drink imported wines and exotic liqueurs rather than local ale; the maids were the youngest and prettiest in the tavern – and they provided more than mere alcoholic refreshment.

Most of all, Konrad kept watching Dieter. It seemed he was employed to keep order throughout the establishment, and he was good at beating up drunks and throwing them out. Konrad looked through the window, and it had begun to snow again. It would cost a deer every two days to stay in the inn, he realized. Or maybe there was an alternative...

Dieter appeared to spend most of his time drinking with two friends. Konrad had noticed that it was he who always collected the fresh tankards of ale, refilling them from one of the huge barrels but never paying. Every now and then, Dieter would walk around the taproom, his hand on his sword hilt as though he were on patrol. Invariably while he was doing this, Netzler would show his face a minute later, looking from one of the doors which led into the drinking hall, or leaning down over the balcony.

'Dieter!' shouted Konrad, as the man began one of his tours of inspection. 'Over here.'

'What you want?' asked Dieter, approaching him.

Konrad waited until he was a yard away, then slid his tankard towards him. 'Get me another beer.'

Dieter stared at him. 'What?'

'You heard: get me another beer.'

'I'm not a sodding serving boy!'

'I've seen you. You've been serving your friends. And without paying. So get me a free beer – or I'll tell Netzler.'

'Don't you sodding threaten me! I'm in the Imperial guard.'

Konrad drew his dagger and put in on the table in front of him. The intricate pattern on the handle marked it as an Imperial guard blade. He spat on Dieter's boots and said: 'You're a liar, you fat slug.'

'Say that again,' warned Dieter, drawing his sword, 'and you're dead!'

'Say what? That you're a liar or a fat slug?'

'Both!'

'You're both a liar and a fat slug.'

By now there was almost complete silence within the tavern. All eyes were focused on Konrad and Dieter, both in the taproom and from the gallery. Netzler was amongst those watching, and he was also the only person moving. He was pushing his way through the hall, towards the antagonists.

'Yaaahhhh!' yelled Dieter, and he thrust his sword at Konrad's chest.

Konrad was still sitting down, and he simply leaned to one side and the point of the blade was driven into the plaster wall where he had sat. He slid away from the table, stood up, punched Dieter in the stomach, then chopped at the back of his neck as the man went down. Dieter collapsed in a heap on the ground. That was enough, but to show everyone that he was serious Konrad kicked him in the ribs a few times, and Dieter began spewing up some of the gallon of beer he had consumed in the previous two hours.

Sheathing his knife and then picking up Dieter's sword, Konrad saw that the blade had once snapped at the hilt and then been badly welded back into place. Exactly how bad a weld was revealed by the ease with which it was broken again. Konrad stabbed the blade into the floorboards, then twisted the hilt. It came away in his hand, and he let it fall.

'He's in the Imperial guard,' he told Netzler, as the landlord reached him. Everywhere else, people were returning to their drinks and conversations.

'What happened?'

'He's a liar and a thief.'

'I know, but I need someone to do the job. His predecessor got himself stabbed a month ago, bled to death out in the courtyard.'

'You need someone better than him.'

'You, you mean?'

'Yes.'

Netzler glanced around to where Dieter's drinking companions sat, then he looked back at Konrad. It was clear that he knew what had been going on. The two men did not seem bothered by what had happened to Dieter.

Konrad made his way to the table where the two men were drinking. He picked up the tankards in front of them and emptied them on the floor.

'You haven't paid for it,' he told them, 'so you don't drink it.'

They argued angrily and tried to rise, but he grabbed each of them by the hair and cracked their heads together.

'And I think you should pay for what you've already drunk. That's one pint. How about the second?' He was still holding them, and he made as if to bang their skulls hard together once again.

'No,' said one, while the other reached for his purse and emptied a handful of coins on the table.

'Thank you, gentlemen,' said Konrad, sweeping up the money. 'Enjoy the rest of your evening.'

'Get rid of him,' said Netzler, when Konrad brought him the payment. He gestured at Dieter. 'Then come and see me.'

Dieter was struggling to rise, and Konrad hauled him to his feet. He slid the broken blade into its scabbard and stuffed the hilt into Dieter's shirt, then half-dragged him to the main entrance and shoved him out of the door and into the snow.

'All you have to do is make sure there's no trouble,' the landlord told him, a minute later. 'If there is, take care of it as you see fit. Do it quietly, discreetly, and I don't want to know about it. Occasionally you may have to help out with the horses, or do whatever else is required.'

'I'm not serving drinks,' said Konrad, 'or clearing tables, or sweeping the floor, or doing any cleaning.' He had done enough of that during the first part of his life.

'You won't have to. You share a room with Hans, you get all your food, a reasonable amount to drink, and whenever the girls upstairs aren't working you're free to make your own arrangements with them.'

'With what? How much do I get paid?'

They haggled again, came to an agreement, and Netzler added, 'And whenever you have free time, I'll buy whatever you bring back from the forest.'

Konrad's only profession was that of a soldier, and he could have sought employment as a mercenary in any land within the known world – but he had become a guard in a tavern.

Working in the coaching house was almost like returning to the start of his life, and at first he kept remembering his time at the inn in his native village. The aroma of the fermenting ale, the myriad daily tasks essential to the running of a tavern, they all reminded him of the past. But now there were plenty of others to do most of the work, and none of them were ever beaten the way that Otto Brandenheimer had whipped Konrad nearly every day.

The Grey Stoat had other compensations, and Konrad found himself spending much of his time with the girls who served drinks in the exclusive gallery, then later served their clients behind the doors which led off it. They and Konrad all worked together at the tavern and were colleagues, and sometimes after the last of the customers had gone home or fallen asleep, they would just talk and joke together, sharing a drink.

But he was sharing far more with Gina and Marcella the night that the riders came for him.

A NEW YEAR had begun, the worst of the winter was over, and both the moons were high and at their brightest. Even though he was distracted, Konrad should have heard the approaching column of horses, but he was aware of nothing until the sound of a scream echoed chillingly through the night.

There were many types of scream, and during his life Konrad had heard them all. He recognized a scream of absolute terror, a scream which ended so abruptly that it could only have been terminated by death. It had been the scream of a man, and Konrad knew that it was Netzler who had just been murdered.

Konrad pushed away the two girls, who by now were holding on to him in fear instead of passion, and grabbed his clothes and his knife as he looked out of the window. That was when he saw the riders in front of the Grey Stoat. The moonlight glinted off their brass helmets and breastplates. Although he could distinguish no colours because of the darkness, Konrad knew they wore scarlet uniforms, decorated with pearl buttons, trimmed with braid, and that their flowing plumes denoted their rank within the force.

They were members of the Imperial guard.

Two of them were below the window, and there were two more riderless horses with them. There was something strange about the dark figures, but Konrad could not work out what it was, and neither did he have the time to wonder. He had to escape, which would not be easy. These were amongst the best troops in the whole Empire, they had the inn surrounded – and there was no doubt that they had come for him.

He now had a bow and full quiver of arrows, but they were down in the room he shared with the kitchen boy. It was evident that some of the guard were already in the tavern, but if he could get to his room before they did, he might be able to despatch a few of the horsemen and even up the odds.

Gina had ventured towards the window and glanced out, and she gasped as she saw the ominous figures waiting in the courtyard below.

'Don't go,' she pleaded. 'Look after us.'

'They won't hurt you,' Konrad assured them both – and as he spoke there was another scream from elsewhere in the inn. This time it was a woman, but it was another death scream.

'Quickly,' he said, beckoning to the girls. 'Into the roof.'

They wrapped themselves in blankets and followed him out into the passage. They pushed open the other doors as they went, signalling for the girls inside to join them. By the time he reached the ladder to the attic, Konrad had all five of them with him.

'Not a sound,' he whispered, as he ushered the girls up the steps. 'A single noise and we're all dead.'

He had already investigated the attic space when examining the whole inn soon after he arrived. It was a vast dusty area, full of forgotten junk which had been stored beneath the rafters over the decades. As the girls climbed up into the loft, Konrad made his way back along the corridor and cautiously peered over the balcony. There were more screams now, more murders. It seemed that the intruders were putting everyone to the sword, acting more like a gang of brigands or invading marauders – but, he supposed, that was what the Imperial guard had become.

Like Taungar and Holwald, these must have been Slaaneshi cultists, and somehow they had tracked Konrad down to his hiding place. They could not be certain he was in the Grey Stoat, but that was of little consequence. Like all creatures of Chaos, they lived only for slaughter and for death. No one would be spared.

All Konrad had was his knife. There seemed little chance of reaching his bow and arrows. A moment later this was confirmed: the next death cry came from Hans. They must have found the boy cowering in his room and put an end to his brief existence. Very soon the killers would have slain everyone on the ground floor and ventured up to the next level. It would be futile for Konrad to sneak up into the attic, hoping to hide away in the darkness.

He might be able to surprise the first of the corrupted guardsmen who reached the gallery, finish him off with the knife, take his sword and hold back the rest of the attackers for a while. The stairs were narrow, and so only one of them could reach him at a time. He made his way back to the foot of the ladder.

'Hey!' he hissed, and Marcella's worried face appeared above him. 'I'm taking away the ladder. Close the hatch and they won't know you're there. Have you got your daggers?'

He saw the flash of blades. The girls all kept knives for their own protection – but they would not protect them from the Imperial guards.

'Cut through the thatch,' Konrad instructed. 'If you have to, get out near the kitchen chimney.'

He lowered the wooden ladder, but could not leave it where it was because its purpose would be only too evident. He made his way back along the passageway and was about to hurl the ladder over the balcony when the first of the guards came into view at the top of the steps. In the dim illumination, Konrad only caught a glimpse of brass armour, but he charged straight at the figure, using the end of the ladder as a battering ram. He caught the guard in the chest and drove him back the way he had come.

He threw the ladder down from the balcony, drew his knife, and ran back into the room from which he had emerged less than two minutes earlier. Closing the door and wedging it shut with a chair, he silently opened the window and climbed onto the narrow ledge outside. The two riders were still below, as were the horses they held for two of those who were carrying out the massacre.

His only chance was to take one of the horses, and he could only do that by killing both guardsmen and escaping before the other riders realized what was happening. It was about twenty feet down to the ground, slightly less to where the armoured figures sat astride their mounts. They were too far apart for him to reach them both.

Konrad leapt down at the nearest rider, feet first, knocking him straight out of his saddle. Rolling over as he hit the ground, he was instantly on his feet and diving at the man he had dismounted – except he was not a man...

That was why the riders had seemed so strange. They were not human. They were beastmen. Beastmen wearing the uniforms of the Imperial guard!

The one Konrad had felled had the head of a bull, and its eyes were round and green, its fur very pale. Recovering from his astonishment, Konrad continued what he had begun, plunging his knife into the neck of the supine creature he held pinned down. Its hot blood spurted from the gaping wound in its throat, and it roared out its fatal agony.

While it was still writhing, Konrad sprang up, and immediately had to duck as the second bullman's sword scythed through the air above his head. He dived forward, his own blade slipping between the leather straps of the bronze cuirass. More evil blood was spilled, and another bestial cry of pain and rage was heard.

There was not time to kill his second opponent, too many precious seconds were passing. The unattended horses were shying away, and Konrad managed to grab the reins of one of them. A moment later his left foot was in the stirrup, and he urged the animal forward even before he was in the saddle.

A sudden shadow appeared in front of the horse. Steel flashed in the moonlight, and then the horse was dropping. Konrad threw himself free before the animal pinned him to the ground with its dead weight.

He twisted his foot as he tried to rise, and he slipped back to the cobbles. Before he could regain his footing he was surrounded by beastmen: three, then four, then five. Their swordpoints touched his body, and he gripped his dagger even tighter. Five Imperial guard swords against one Imperial guard knife. A booted heel came down upon his hand, hard, and he let go of the knife. Another boot kicked the weapon away.

'That's him, that's him!' yelled a very human voice.

Dieter stood behind the shadowy figures of the beastmen. It must have been he who had led the riders here, but that was of little importance now. Konrad was counting the number of beastmen. He had killed one, wounded another, five had surrounded him, and there was another with Dieter.

'See? I am one of you,' claimed Dieter, speaking to the last of the guardsmen. 'I am in the Imperial guard.'

The eighth beastman must have been the leader, and now he finally drew his sword. He beckoned to Dieter, and the man stepped closer. Then with a single sweeping blow, the bull creature severed Dieter's head. The head rolled away into the darkness, and the acephalous corpse slowly collapsed to the ground.

The leader summoned two of the feral warriors, and they withdrew from Konrad. A few seconds later, they made their way back to the tavern once more.

Their inhuman commander walked slowly towards Konrad, limping. Beneath his armour his body must have been even more twisted and deformed than that of the others.

There was a sudden flare of light. The two marauders had lit torches, carrying the burning brands into the inn. In the afterglow Konrad glimpsed their leader's face – and it was even more hideous than those of the bull-headed Slaaneshi beastmen who circled him.

He must once have been human, but he had survived some terrible ordeal. Although almost masked by his helmet, his face was a shapeless mass of blackened, melted flesh. He had no lips, no nose; his right eye seemed huge because the eyelids had been burned away, while the left was nothing but a raw hole in his skull.

He held the point of his sword at Konrad's throat, and Dieter's warm sticky blood dripped from the blade.

It was Taungar – or what was left of him.

CHAPTER EIGHT

THE GREY STOAT was quickly ablaze, its dry wooden frame burning like paper, and in the glare from the vivid flames Konrad gazed up into the horribly mutilated features of Taungar.

His whole body must have been as badly devoured as his face. It seemed impossible for anyone to have survived the inferno which had engulfed Zuntermein's mansion – and it seemed impossible for anyone as monstrously crippled as Taungar to still be alive.

His breathing was hoarse and ragged, as though his lungs were still full of smoke. His teeth were as black as charcoal, like stumps of burned down trees. His lipless mouth became even more twisted when he spoke, his words but a rasping whisper.

'Thiss iss why I wass sspar-ed from fire,' he hissed, taking a short gasp of breath between each syllable. 'To kill you, trait-or.'

'You're the traitor, Taungar,' spat Konrad. 'A traitor to everything human!'

Taungar pushed the tip of his sword into the soft flesh beneath Konrad's chin, and a few drops of Konrad's blood mingled with that of Dieter's.

'You musst hurt like I hurt,' he sighed. 'I sstill hurt, and you hurt for-ever.'

Pressing harder, the drops of blood became a trickle. A fraction harder, and the blade would have been in Konrad's windpipe, but then Taungar withdrew his sword and gestured to the beastmen. Two of them hauled Konrad to his feet, while the third went to examine their fallen comrade. The predator was clearly dead, and the bullbeast strode over to the creature Konrad had wounded, who was sitting on the ground trying to staunch the flow of blood from its wounded side.

The other two were inside the tavern, carrying out their incendiary task. Although the pair who supported Konrad maintained a grip of iron, Taungar had limped back out of reach. He must have remembered how Konrad had burst free when he had been one of those holding him captive in Zuntermein's unholy temple.

'Pray to your god for help,' he taunted. He must have believed that Konrad, like Krysten, was an acolyte of Khorne.

'I need no help to deal with you and your bastard god!'

Taungar issued a guttural command in the mutant tongue, and a blow to the side of Konrad's head almost knocked him unconscious. One of the beastmen had hit him with his fist, and it felt as hard as rock. His head fell forwards, and blood oozed from the wound in his scalp and streamed down the side of his face. Then one of the creatures ripped a strip from Konrad's tunic and wedged it into his mouth to ensure his silence.

He wondered whether the warped guards had human bodies beneath their armour, or whether the fist which hit him had felt so hard because it was a mutated hoof. They stood upright like men, but was their flesh covered in pale fur? Their inhuman heads were oversized, and there were holes in their brass helmets through which their twisted horns protruded. Their breath smelled foul, and they were as hungry for his blood as was Taungar.

Konrad was gagged; he was held as if in shackles from head to foot; he had no weapon; he was surrounded by beastmen – beastmen who seemed to be members of the Empire's elite military battalion; and he could feel the heat from the blazing coaching inn searing his skin. The heat did not seem to bother his captors, protected by their armour and their bestial hides, and it was too late to make any difference to Taungar.

It seemed that Taungar had been the only one to escape from the ruins of Zuntermein's heathen church. Did he plan to take his vengeance in a similar manner, by burning Konrad alive? Was that why he had ordered the tavern to be torched, so that it would be where Konrad's living body was cremated? But Taungar had threatened a slow death, and it was only when they talked of maiming and murder that Chaos cultists were likely to be speaking truthfully.

All Konrad could do was hope that his two captors would slacken their grip for a moment. Each of them was taller and heavier than he, they were armoured and armed. When the other two returned from burning down the tavern, the odds would be insuperable. But he was held so tightly it seemed that if they should grip a fraction harder, his flesh would tear and his bones snap.

'Plann-ed what to do if ev-er found you, Kon-rad,' whispered Taungar. 'Had sso ma-ny i-de-ass...'

Konrad could only see the lower half of Taungar, and he saw him raise his sword, once again placing it under his hostage's chin. He used it as a lever to raise Konrad's head, knowing that he was conscious. They stared at each other, Taungar's one remaining eye gazing out from the ruins of his face.

'Sstart with your eyess,' added Taungar, and his sword-point was suddenly against the lower lid of Konrad's left eye.

Konrad jerked his head back instinctively, and he was able to move it an inch or two before it became locked rigid by the gauntlet of one of the bullmen. The tip of the sword returned towards his left eye, this time aiming straight for the pupil. There was still blood on the sword, the blade glinted in the light from the fire – and Konrad realized that this was the last thing his left eye would ever see.

He tried to lean further back or to turn his head, but it was impossible. He closed both his eyes, tensing himself for the inevitable pain as his eyeball became skewered upon Taungar's sword.

Then suddenly his head snapped back and around, he felt the blade slice across the side of his face, cutting through the flesh, scraping his cheek bone, and he was half-falling...

Only half, because one of his captors was still restraining him – but the other had let go, crying out in agony as he released Konrad.

Konrad opened his eyes and saw Taungar looking past him, but without hesitating he spun around and drove his right fist into the bovine face of the cultist who still clung to his left arm. The other beastman was writhing on the ground, screaming – dying. Under the impact of Konrad's blow, the second one staggered back a pace, and a moment later he also howled in mortal agony as he was attacked from behind.

Dodging aside as Taungar rushed forward, Konrad pulled the gag from his mouth, glanced back and saw the dark shape of an armoured figure behind him. The figure wore black armour, carried a black sword with which he had despatched Konrad's captors, and his black helmet was forged into the shape of an animal's head, the head of a...

Wolf!

'I want him!' Konrad yelled, as the black knight levelled his sword to impale Taungar.

Wolf sidestepped, and Taungar lurched past him. Konrad seized one of the dying beastmen's swords, and Taungar turned to face him. The bull-thing who had been tending the one Konrad had earlier wounded raced at Wolf, and Wolf engaged the creature in combat.

Taungar and Konrad gazed at each other. Taungar raised his sword vertically in front of his face in a duelling salute, and Konrad did the same.

'When did you become a slave to Chaos?' he asked.

Taungar slowly shook his deformed head, and made an ugly choking noise at the back of his throat – it was the nearest sound he could make to a laugh.

'Sslave? Ne-ver! Be-came free in Praag. Thought wass dead, but made rea-lly a-live.'

'You won't be alive for long!'

They lowered their swords, crossing them, and the two Imperial guard blades touched lightly for a moment – and then the battle to the death began.

Konrad pressed hard, wanting to finish off his opponent swiftly. The advantage should have been with him. He was fit, whereas Taungar's body had been twisted and bent by the conflagration. But Taungar was an expert swordsman, making up in experience what he lacked in agility. It was his combat skills which had kept him alive long enough to become a veteran trooper – but it was his allegiance to Chaos which had kept him alive more recently.

Taungar was also wearing armour, and that protected him from most of Konrad's thrusts. Konrad, however, had to spring back out of range whenever the sergeant's blade avoided his defence. If he were hit, he would be done for. Already he was losing blood from his neck, his scalp, his cheek.

The swords rang together, and there were echoing clashes from the blades of the other two combatants several yards away. Then there came an agonized cry, an agonized bestial cry, and Wolf's enemy was down, its ululating howl a mourning lament for its own imminent death. Wolf left his enemy bleeding and kicking and writhing, then went to finish off the beastman that Konrad had earlier wounded. The creature tried to rise, but all it could do was attempt to crawl away. It did not get far.

And still Konrad could not overcome his own opponent. Even with one eye, Taungar was able to accurately judge the strokes which were aimed at him, parrying and then counter-attacking. His senses were more than human, although he had become less than human, and it was the malignant powers within him which granted the sergeant such strength.

Each fought with only a sword, neither carried a shield. The two beastmen that Wolf first slew both had an Imperial guard blade, one of which Konrad now wielded. That meant there was another weapon lying near. He backed towards the corpses, and Taungar drove him so hard that he stumbled against the first of the bodies, almost falling. Taungar's blade sliced through the air, and Konrad avoided decapitation by but a moment. He bent down, seized the other sword, then twisted around and came up facing Taungar once more.

He held the new blade in his left hand, keeping it behind his back, and continued to fight with the one in his right. When Taungar next lunged forward, Konrad caught the sword with his own, and the blade slid down onto his quillons. He forced his enemy's arm away, further and further to one side.

Then he struck with the second sword, driving it straight into Taungar's only eye, through into his brain and out from the back of his skull.

Taungar's jaws opened, but before he could scream his mouth was full of blood, which silenced him forever. Konrad pushed his left hand forward a little more, released the sword hilt, and Taungar fell backwards.

Konrad stared around. All the other beastmen lay stretched out on the ground, their bodies illuminated by the blazing tavern. Wolf had slain them all – if it was Wolf.

It could have been someone else within the black armour. Although he was apparently an ally who had come to Konrad's aid, that meant little. As well as being the enemy of those he had defeated, he may still have been Konrad's foe.

The black figure stabbed his sword into the ground.

'Clean that,' he said – and it was indeed Wolf.

He pulled off his helmet, and Konrad saw the face of the man who had been his master but had become his friend. His white hair and beard were still cropped short, and there could be no changing the sharpened teeth or the black tattoos which made his face look like the animal he was named after.

'There are two more inside,' said Konrad, lowering his own sword and wiping at the blood which covered half his face. He turned towards the burning coach inn. Flames erupted from every window, from each doorway.

'I know,' said Wolf. 'And they won't be coming out.'

They would not be the only ones who did not emerge, Konrad realized, as he moved quickly back to avoid a piece of blazing timber which came crashing down near where he had been standing. The tavern had become a roaring inferno.

The thatched roof was burning fiercely, and suddenly most of it collapsed. Konrad hoped that the girls had escaped through the roof; no one who had remained in the loft space beneath could possibly have survived. The whole inn had become rapidly transformed into one huge mass of burning firewood.

'Clean that,' Wolf repeated. 'You owe me two days.'

'And are you going to demand another five years for saving my life this time?' asked Konrad, as he picked up the black sword.

'If I asked you for five years each time I rescued you, you'd be serving me for all eternity.' Wolf shook his head in mock bewilderment. 'I can't understand how you've survived all these months without me.'

When Wolf had fought and killed Otto Krieshmier and saved Konrad from being hung, Konrad had agreed to serve the mercenary as his squire for exactly five years. That time had almost expired when he left the injured Wolf in Anvila's care and went in search of the bronze warrior. He did not mention that he had saved Wolf's life a short time before that, freeing him from the goblin swarm that had taken him prisoner, because Wolf knew it full well.

'How did you find me?' asked Konrad.

Wolf shrugged. 'Chance,' he said.

'There's no such thing as—' Konrad began, but then he noticed that Wolf was grinning, showing his sharpened teeth.

Konrad wiped the black blade clean on the cloak of one of the beastmen, while Wolf vanished in the darkness. When he returned, he was riding a black steed and leading a packhorse.

The former must have been the replacement for Midnight, his white stallion which had been killed by the goblins who had taken him captive.

'Let's go,' said Wolf, accepting his blade and sheathing it.

Konrad was tempted to ask *Where?* Instead he went in search of a mount for himself.

He had always been warned against touching enemy weapons, because they had absorbed traces of corruption from their previous owners. It was only recently that Konrad had become aware this meant the taint of Chaos – the word had been unfamiliar to him, although its insidious effects were not – but he was already one of the damned and so it was too late.

The first time he had held such a weapon was when he had returned to his village, or where his village had been, soon after the place had been annihilated. A trio of crimson and gold creatures had swooped down upon him and Wolf, and he had forced one of them to drop its sword. When he picked it up, Konrad had felt a surge of power flow through his whole body. He had touched many inhuman weapons since, but never again sensed such latent potency.

The sword with which he had fought Taungar felt like any other sword. He examined it, thinking of the beastman to whom it had belonged. Could that creature really have been a member of the Imperial guard? How many of the elite force had been similarly corrupted by the foul influence of Chaos? How many of them served Slaanesh instead of the Emperor?

And what of all the other military forces within Altdorf? Had they been similarly subverted? From the city watch, up through the Reikland army and all the other Imperial regiments, which of them could be trusted? How many owed their loyalty to the Emperor – and how many to the perverted powers of darkness?

Taungar was a member of the Imperial bodyguard, but he was a traitor, one of the damned. Konrad now realized why the sergeant had been unconcerned to hear of Gaxar's plot to replace Karl-Franz with an impostor. Although he had thought that the threat to the Emperor must have ended with the grey seer's death, that was not necessarily so. Skullface still lived. He had been with Gaxar, and he must have been intimately involved with the diabolic scheme.

Konrad took a scabbard and sheathed the sword. He did not bother with any of the armour – the bronze suit was too close in his memory and he did not wish to be reminded how he had been trapped. He managed to find his own dagger, then approached one of the horses which had not fled very far from the fire, took its reins and climbed into the saddle.

Wolf said nothing about Konrad's steed or his armament. He passed him the packhorse's leading rein, and Konrad followed the mercenary through the dark and silent village.

All the doors were locked, the windows shuttered, the inhabitants hiding away in total terror from the devastating eruption of violence which had invaded their tranquil lives.

As they rode away, Konrad glanced back at the tavern. The flames were no longer so fierce; there was not much left to burn. By dawn, all that remained would be charred embers and a few blackened bones amongst the smouldering ashes.

Wolf also looked over his shoulder at the blaze.

'Pity,' he said. 'That was the only place to get a drink for miles.'

'I SAW THEM on the road halfway between here and Altdorf,' said Wolf. They were next to another fire, but one which Konrad had lit to keep them warm during the last long hours of darkness. 'And I decided to follow and find out what they were up to. Then I saw you.'

'What were you doing on that road?' asked Konrad.

Wolf stared at the fire, and finally he said: 'I was in the capital, then I left. I could have taken any road, but that was the one I chose. Or maybe it was chosen for me.' He kept gazing into the flames, then asked: 'And you, Konrad, what have you been doing since the first day of summer?'

Konrad shrugged, not knowing where to begin, not even knowing how much he wanted to tell Wolf. There was much that he would never reveal to anyone. Apart from Elyssa, Wolf had been the most important person in his life; but so much had happened to Konrad since they had gone their different ways that Wolf seemed almost a stranger.

'I saw the bronze warrior,' said Konrad. 'Did Anvila tell you that?'

Wolf nodded.

'I'd last seen him five years previously, five years exactly. That was the day before my village was wiped out by a horde of beastmen. The day after I saw him in Kislev, the mine was destroyed by an army of outlanders.'

In the gloom, Wolf nodded again. 'Did you find him?'

'He'd gone by the time I was down from the mountains.' That was true, but it was also true that Konrad had found the bronze warrior some time later. He did not mention that yet, and he did not know whether he would. 'You once told me he was your brother, your twin brother, and you said he was worse than dead. A creature of Chaos?'

'That's right.'

'How did it happen?'

Wolf said nothing for a while. He continued staring into the flames of the campfire, and Konrad thought that he was not going to answer, but then he began to speak.

'I was the eldest, by a few minutes. We were physically identical, although my hair was white and Jurgen's was black; but in every other way we were complete opposites. We may have started off alike, but Jurgen became... different. His interest in sorcery and the black arts led to his corruption. He came to believe that he was only half a person, that he would not be complete until he destroyed me and absorbed all of my being. He was convinced that when he killed me, it must be by force of arms, not by magic. He created the bronze armour to wear when we fought. But... it didn't happen like that.'

Wolf became silent once more, and Konrad wondered if he had ever admitted this to anyone else. He was still staring into the flames, but his eyes were focused far away – upon a part of his life which was long gone.

'Betrayed by the person closest to you,' Konrad said softly, remembering something Wolf had said soon after they first met, but Wolf either did not hear or pretended not to.

Konrad wondered about Wolf's own armour, the black metal suit which he had worn for so long. The heavy black sword was the same one he had carried over half a decade ago; the black shield which bore no emblem was the same. Few weapons lasted that long, because the blood of beastmen and their foul allies acted like acid, rusting metal and causing it to weaken and decay. Wolf's sword had caused much blood to flow, but there was still no trace of damage to the blade. Was there some connection between the bronze armour and the black? The former had contained warpstone – but the latter...?

If it had been anyone else but Wolf, Konrad would have suspected that some magical process had been used during the fabrication of the black armour. But Wolf had always hated magic and magicians, and possibly that hatred had originated with his twin brother's treachery.

It was Jurgen von Neuwald who had constructed the bronze armour, and Litzenreich who had dismantled it. Wolf's brother and the Middenheim magician: another strand. The more Konrad knew, the more complex the web which held him became.

The bronze armour must have devoured Jurgen, leeching his lifeforce in exactly the same way that it had begun to consume Konrad. As well as Jurgen and Konrad, the Chaos armour must have had many other wearers, all of whom had been similarly sucked dry. Jurgen was the first, Konrad the last.

Konrad waited for Wolf to continue, but the only sound was the crackle of burning firewood and the distant cry of an owl in the forest. In the silence, he touched the bandage around his neck. The blood was now dry, the wound had begun to close up, and so he loosened the strip of cotton slightly. His scalp and cheek were similarly swathed with pieces of fabric.

At one time, Konrad would have been worried that he might die from the poisoned touch of a marauder's blade. A seemingly harmless cut could lead to an agonizing death, as if bitten by a venomous snake. But he had been wounded so frequently over the years, and always recovered, that by the time he left the frontier he was no longer concerned by such injuries. It was possible that one might die in such a painful fashion, if a minor wound grew worse instead of better, but not probable.

For a moment, Konrad thought of Taungar and what had happened to him. The sergeant had mentioned how he almost died during the Siege of Praag; instead he had become a creature of Chaos. Was that what sometimes happened to warriors who fought against the northern invaders? They became infected by the corruption all around them. Perhaps a wound might not lead to death but instead cause transformation, exactly as the bite of a vampire could kill but also create another such being. This might be one method by which the legions of damnation increased their numbers, recruiting from the very forces who strived to throw them back into the infernal regions whence they had been spawned.

In a few brief sentences, Wolf had revealed more of his early life that he had done during the five years Konrad had served him. He continued gazing into his past, although it seemed that he would say nothing else about his brother, the first warrior in bronze; but Konrad had more questions.

'When we first met,' he said, 'I was carrying a quiver made from rippled black hide. Remember?'

He thought that Wolf had not heard, but after a few seconds he shook his head.

'It bore a golden crest,' Konrad continued. 'A mailed fist between a pair of crossed arrows. I asked if you recognized the emblem. You denied it, but I could tell it seemed familiar to you.'

'Yes,' said Wolf, after a few more seconds, 'I do remember. I had seen the coat of arms before. It was on a shield.'

A shield! The shield which now belonged to the skaven Konrad had named Silver Eye. Yet another strand in the web...

'Whose shield?' Konrad demanded.

There was more silence, until Wolf said: 'An enemy, an enemy who could have slain me but instead spared my life.'

'Who?'

This must have been the person who had originally owned the bow and arrows Elyssa had given to Konrad. And this was yet another strand, he realized, which linked Wolf to Elyssa.

'An elf,' said Wolf.

'An elf?' That would explain what Konrad had been told at the College of Heraldry: the enigmatic coat of arms was not human.

'We were enemies. He could have killed me. He didn't.'

'How long ago?'

'Twenty years.' Wolf nodded slowly, as though counting each of the passing years. 'Or more.'

'Where?'

'Middenheim way.'

Could this indeed be the answer to Elyssa's past? That her father had been an elf? That the weapons she gave to Konrad had unknowingly belonged to her true father?

'Near where we met?' asked Konrad.

'Possibly.'

'What happened to the elf, to his weapons?'

'I don't know. I'd tried to forget all about him – until I saw you with the quiver.'

'What was the elf's name?'

Wolf shrugged.

Konrad leaned back, staring up at the stars. It was a dark night now that Mannslieb had sunk below the horizon. The world's greater moon was named after Manann, god of the seas. 'Beloved of Manann' had been full tonight and would be so again in another twenty-five days. But Morrslieb was still high in the heavens, and its unnatural glow cast very little light upon the world below. Named after the god of death, Morr, its size was irregular and the sequence of its appearance unpredictable. Sometimes it was larger, sometimes smaller, and its shape seemed to change almost every night. One legend claimed that 'Beloved of Morr' consisted entirely of warpstone. This was a common belief amongst Chaos worshippers, who held their blasphemous ceremonies whenever Morrslieb was at its greatest dimension. Kastring's Khorne-worshipping cultists had sacrificed to the blood deity whenever the lesser moon was full. Tonight Morrslieb had been at its maximum, and Taungar's Slaaneshi acolytes had come hunting for Konrad.

'What happened to Anvila?' asked Konrad, because the female dwarf seemed to be the one person who had no connection with anything else in his life.

'She spent days copying down all the runes in the temple we found,' said Wolf. 'The goblins never came back, I'm glad to say. When I'd recovered enough to travel, we headed back down the mountain, found the horses you'd left for us, then returned to the mine. Or what was left of it. That was when we said farewell. Anvila made for the World's Edge Mountains. She was returning to her university in Everpeak, Karaz-a-Karak as the dwarfs call it – "The Eternal Way to the Pinnacle". She wanted to write a book on her discoveries. I rode east, finally arriving in Altdorf. Things had changed since I was there last, and all for the worse. There was nothing for me in the capital, so I left. And here we are.'

The mercenary did not look much different from the day that he and Konrad had first encountered one another, although his face was more marked – both with the lines of age and the scars of combat.

'Was the Emperor back in Altdorf?' asked Konrad.

'He decided to winter in Talabheim, but there were stories of some romantic liaison being the real reason for him staying there. That was why he sent the Empress back to Altdorf, not because he was busy with matters of state. Some say he was having an affair with Arch Lector Aglim's niece, some that it is Duchess Elise Kreiglitz-Untermensch herself who has claimed the Emperor's affections, while others report that he spends every night in the temple of Sigmar – with a different priestess each time.'

Wolf laughed. 'Sometimes I regret not having worn the velvet cloak. I would have made a wonderful courtier, spreading gossip and inventing rumours. But I suppose I would have missed out on so much else in life.' He reached inside his tunic, scratched himself, then drew out his hand. His index finger and thumb were pinched together. 'But you get a better class of flea in the Imperial palace.'

'When he gets back to Altdorf, the Emperor will be killed and an impostor placed upon the Imperial throne.'

Wolf nodded as casually as if he had been told the time of day. He poked at the fire with a branch, then threw a few more sticks onto the blaze.

'How do you know?' he asked. 'You've managed to avoid telling me anything about what has happened to you.'

'I left Kislev,' said Konrad, avoiding all mention of Kastring. 'I went to Middenheim,' he continued, avoiding any reference to the bronze armour and Litzenreich. 'I arrived in Altdorf,' he added, avoiding what he could have said about Gaxar and the skaven. 'And I ended up here,' he concluded, avoiding everything else.

For the first time since they had begun speaking, Wolf looked directly at Konrad, although again it took a while before he spoke.

'You're different,' he said. 'Something has changed you. Despite everything that occurred in Praag, all the atrocities you must have witnessed, all the impossible creatures you must have fought, you weren't like this when you returned from the siege. That can only mean something far, far worse must have happened to you since we parted. There's a darkness to your soul, Konrad.'

Konrad had never heard Wolf use such a phrase. Although he had professed to belong to the cult of Sigmar, and claimed once to have planned joining the Order of the Anvil, Wolf had never seemed very religious. In fact, Konrad had followed Wolf's lead in paying little attention to prayer and worship.

Soldiers on the frontier between humanity and the hellish invaders had no time for religion, they were far more concerned with their own mortal survival than with spiritual existence.

'*Chaos*,' said Konrad. 'That was the very last thing you said to me before I left the dwarf temple. What did you mean by that? It was a warning, but...'

Wolf yawned and stretched out his arms, then said: 'Tomorrow we head for the Wasteland.'

'The Wasteland?'

'You will do as I say,' Wolf told him. 'For the next two days at least. And if you have any sense, you will stay with me as long as necessary. I know now that you're the one.'

'What one?'

'The one I must take. There's someone you must meet, someone who can answer all your questions, someone who can tell what has really happened to you over the past months.'

Konrad stared at Wolf. Someone who could answer all his questions...?

As he gazed across the flickering flames of their campfire, Konrad realized that he and Wolf had more in common than previously. It was Jurgen von Neuwald's armour and the warpstone used to release him from within the bronze prison which had tainted Konrad; but long before then, Wolf had already been corrupted by the seductive kiss of Chaos.

CHAPTER NINE

THE WASTELAND LAY to the west of the Reikwald Forest, and it took much longer than two days for Konrad and Wolf to reach the border. By then, Konrad's five years of service had expired. Neither of them made any mention of the subject.

The Wasteland was barren and inhospitable, a cold wind from the Middle Sea perpetually sweeping across the plains, and so poorly populated that there was only one town in the whole desolate country. That was Marienburg, the largest port in the entire Old World. But that was not where Wolf led Konrad, and neither did they stop at any of the small villages or farms where the rest of the inhabitants dwelled.

Wolf would not reveal their destination or who would be there when they reached it, and Konrad soon gave up asking. This was the reason that Wolf had suddenly appeared out of the night to rescue Konrad from the bull-headed beastmen: so that they would ride together into the Wasteland to meet the mysterious 'someone' who could answer all of Konrad's questions on Chaos.

Or at least he could pretend this was what fate had intended, that there was nothing else he could do but allow himself to be carried along with the course laid out for him. And the further west that he travelled, the more he seemed to escape the web which had threatened to trap him amongst the interwoven strands of his life.

Wolf had also refused to reveal how and when he had become infected by Chaos. Konrad could understand that, because he was unwilling to speak about his time within the bronze armour and what it had done to him. But the fact that Wolf had survived for so long since he must have been affected, and that he was still such an implacable enemy of Chaos, gave Konrad renewed hope. He knew that the touch of warpstone had condemned him to ultimate destruction, but perhaps he could delay the time of his inevitable doom.

For as long as he had known him, Wolf had been fighting against Chaos, although he had never used that word. Wolf had been aware that the battle took on many forms, that the world was in danger upon many fronts. Because he was a warrior, he had chosen to combat the legions of damnation the only way he knew – by force of arms. He used military might to hold back the northern hordes which sought to break through the frontier defences in Kislev, and in this he had proved very successful. The mercenary army he built up had even pushed the barbaric tribes back towards their own benighted realms. But then came the day when the feral invaders had swarmed south, eliminating the mining town and destroying everyone within. Or almost everyone. Krysten had been the final victim.

Konrad and Wolf rode on, day after day, across the wilderness. The Wasteland was aptly named. The grass was parched and withered, the occasional tree was stunted and twisted.

There was hardly enough vegetation to sustain the few wild birds and animals that they saw. Little wonder that the population was so small. It was almost as if the whole land had already been claimed as Chaos territory and then abandoned as being worthless.

There were no roads, because there were not enough people to use them. There were not even rough tracks across the lifeless ground, and Konrad wondered how Wolf could possibly know which direction to take. Where there was nothing, however, it did not matter which compass point was chosen.

Finally, Konrad saw a point of green on the horizon. As the distance reduced, it grew into a clump of woodland. By then it was almost dusk, and they set up camp for the night. The next morning, the woods were identifiable as a small island of vegetation, entirely surrounded by a wide lake. The presence of water could not alone explain the fertility of the land in the centre. It was almost like a castle in the middle of a moat, but with trees instead of stone walls.

'This is where Galea lives,' said Wolf, reining in his horse as they reached the edge of the water.

'Who,' asked Konrad, doubting that he would be given a proper answer, 'is Galea?'

'The wisest person in the world.' Wolf looked at Konrad, then grinned. 'The Old World, at least.'

'He's going to tell me everything I want to know?'

'And plenty you didn't know that you wanted to know.'

'You've been here before?'

'Yes.' Wolf nodded thoughtfully, remembering.

'Then let's go.' Konrad nudged his horse towards the water.

'No!' Wolf stretched out his hand to hold him back. 'You have to go across alone, barefoot, bareheaded, without any weapons, without any armour.'

Konrad stared at him for a few seconds. 'If you say so.' He dismounted, unbuckled his sword belt, dropped his dagger and removed his boots. He looked at the water again. 'You sure about this?'

'Yes. It's not deep. You can wade across.'

It was about fifty yards to the island, which itself was of a similar diameter.

'When you get to the middle,' Wolf added, 'you have to immerse yourself completely. Three times.'

'You sure you're sure?'

'Yes. I've been there once, and no one is allowed to return.'

Konrad stared up at Wolf. He trusted him totally, but he still felt uneasy. It must have been years since Wolf had come here; things might have been different now.

'Everything I want to know?' he said, gazing across the water.

'That's right. And don't eat anything, don't touch anything, don't try to bring anything back, and you must take something as a gift.'

'What?'

'This,' said Wolf, and he gave Konrad a small ivory comb. 'I've had it for a long time, waiting for this day.'

Konrad examined the comb. There seemed nothing special about it, and he tucked it into his tunic pocket. 'Anything else you want to tell me about Galea?'

'You'll find out when you get there. It was a surprise to me, so I don't want to spoil your surprise.'

'This had better be worth it.'

'It will be,' Wolf assured him.

Konrad turned and walked into the water. It was very cold, and within a few paces the level had reached his waist. 'Am I allowed to swim across?' he called.

'I don't know, but make sure you duck completely below the surface three times when you reach the middle.'

Like bowing in a temple, thought Konrad, as he took two more slow steps through the water. The level came up to his chest, but after two more steps he had gone no deeper. He swam the rest of the way, and halfway across he kicked himself below the surface, diving down three times before continuing to the other side.

As he waded ashore, he discovered that the mud above the water line was white. This seemed so odd that he picked up a handful of the stuff and examined it. He noticed that there were pieces of bone mixed in with the white mud – and then he realized that all of it was bone! The entire island was surrounded by a wall of powdered bone, which could only have been washed there by the waters of the lake.

Was this the fate suffered by those who disobeyed the proper etiquette? The ones who wore hats or carried swords or forgot to pay the correct obeisance midway across the lake...?

If so, there must have been many hundreds of them, thousands of them who had perished in the cold waters. Konrad shivered and rubbed his hand on his wet breeches, trying not to think what it was that he was wiping off.

The island seemed larger than it had first appeared, he noticed, much larger; and when he glanced back over the lake to where he had left Wolf, there was nothing in sight but water.

He should have been able to see to the other side, fifty yards away, but it was as if nothing else existed except the lake he had crossed. It appeared as wide as the Sea of Claws, whose shores lay hundreds of miles apart. He was tempted to turn back, but decided that might not be wise, that he would never reach the opposite side, which could now be hundreds of miles away. That was probably another factor which had increased the number of corpses swallowed by the lake, adding to the bleached bones which encircled the verdant island.

As Konrad began making his way within, he realized that it was far warmer than a few minutes ago, and that his clothes were drying rapidly in the heat. The sun was almost directly above, higher than he had ever seen it before; the sky was a rich shade of blue, a colour only seen at the height of summer; and he had never seen trees and plants as exotic as the ones which grew here. He was astonished by what he saw. It was as if he were in another land.

Perhaps he was. This was no mere island he had reached. In crossing the water he seemed to have arrived upon another continent...

He was gazing around in amazement when he heard a savage growl, which immediately brought him to his senses. He automatically reached for his knife; he had carried one for almost as long as he could remember. The first was the wavy-bladed dagger he had stolen from a soldier; the trooper had been part of a force which came to his village to eliminate all the beastmen in that part of the forest. Years later, Wolf had identified the blade as a kris, saying that it had come from the other side of the world. Konrad's most recent knife was the one he had been issued with when he enlisted in the Imperial guard. Now he had no such blade.

The growling grew louder, came closer. There was some kind of ferocious beast stalking towards him through the thick undergrowth, and Konrad quickly looked around for something he could use as a weapon. A tree branch would make a club, and he reached up to snap one free from the nearest trunk. But as he wrapped his hands around the branch, he remembered Wolf's warning: *don't touch anything.*

He hesitated, then let go and stepped back. His only defences were those with which he had been born, but which had served him well when he had no others: his bare hands.

A moment later the creature appeared, striding confidently towards him. It was a huge black cat, a diamond of white fur on its chest. He had expected some kind of preternatural creature, but this was a leopard, its fur sleek and shiny, its fangs long and sharp.

The animal slowed, then halted, its tail slowly twitching, and it opened its huge jaws and roared out its challenge to him.

He would have preferred to confront a beastman, because that kind of creature would have attacked immediately. A wild animal was much less predictable and therefore more dangerous.

'Hello,' said a voice to Konrad's side, and he spun around rapidly.

A young girl stood four or five yards away from him, eating an apple. She was about eight years old, her black hair braided into two plaits. Barefoot, she wore a peasant dress which had been patched and mended many times. Her face was dirty, and there was something strange about her expression, but Konrad could not work out what it was.

'Er... hello,' he replied, and he glanced back at the black leopard.

'He won't hurt you,' said the girl. 'Not unless you're bad. Have you brought me a present?'

Konrad kept watching the animal, which was still quietly growling. 'I've come to see Galea. Do you know where he is?'

'I'm Galea.'

Konrad glanced briefly at the girl again.

'I am,' she said, as she took another bite from her apple. 'Really.'

Konrad stared at her. *The wisest person in the world.* This must have been the surprise that Wolf had mentioned.

'Who led you here?' she asked.

'Wolf. Wolfgang von Neuwald.'

Galea nodded. 'I remember. He brought me a bracelet and I told him I wanted a comb.'

It seemed impossible that Wolf had seen this girl when he visited the island, that she had spoken to him. Even had he been here immediately before leaving for the frontier, a few weeks before he met Konrad, she could only have been two or three years old at the time.

It seemed impossible, but evidently it had happened.

'This is for you,' said Konrad, and he held out the ivory comb.

'Oh, thank you!' Galea said, stepping forward and accepting it. She pulled at one of her plaits, examining the frayed piece of rag with which it was tied. 'I would like some ribbon next time. Silk, I think, and red.'

'Next time?' said Konrad, gazing into her eyes – and realizing what was so strange about her appearance.

Her eyes were like those of a cat. The pupils were narrow ovals of black, but otherwise they were completely gold.

He glanced back at the leopard, which was no longer growling. Its eyes were the same as the girl's. Exactly the same. And her hair was as black as the animal's fur.

Galea walked towards the leopard, reaching out to rub its neck. Its head came to a level with her shoulders, and it began purring as she stroked behind its ears.

'What's your name?' she asked.

'Konrad.'

'Come with me, Konrad,' she said. She turned and walked away through the trees, her pet leopard by her side. Konrad looked back and could still see nothing beyond the shore but water. He followed Galea deeper into the island.

HE TOLD HER. Everything. Things he had never revealed previously, but now could finally unburden from deep within himself.

They sat together on the grass, sheltered from the sun in a glade of trees, while the huge leopard lay by Galea's side. She had not asked him to speak about himself, but as soon as he stared into her wise eyes, her feline eyes, he was aware that was what he should do. Although he had no evidence, Konrad knew he was doing so of his own volition, that she was exerting no supernatural power over him.

He narrated the story of his life, from his early days before he knew Elyssa, right through until when he met up with Wolf again. He remembered all the people he had encountered over the past several years, and how so many of them all seemed to be linked with one or more of the others. He told of the mysterious golden crest, the mailed fist between two crossed arrows. He related his fight with the goblins in the lost dwarf temple, how he had felt a new kind of vitality as he massacred the green fiends, and how he had falsely believed he was wielding a double-headed battle hammer instead of a waraxe. He spoke about his time within the bronze armour and the way he had been corrupted by warpstone. He described the strange visions he had experienced when Litzenreich and his dwarfs had removed the bronze suit and believed him dead, of his apparent travels amongst the stars, of his rebirth in his own body, of memories which were not his own, of confusing the death of Elyssa with that of Evane: she had been Sigmar's first love, murdered by a goblin raiding band, and Konrad originally learned about all of this during his dream, confirming it later from one of the chronicles of Sigmar's life.

Most of his story came out unbidden, as though he had rehearsed it for so long, although occasionally Galea had to prompt him, or ask for clarification or for more specific details. Sometimes he found himself repeating what he had already said, but most of these were aspects which needed emphasis. And finally he was finished with his narrative.

He had completely forgotten that he was apparently addressing a young girl, because he knew that was not what Galea was.

She had sat without moving while Konrad had been talking. Now she unplaited her hair and began running her new ivory comb through it. Her hair reminded Konrad of Elyssa's, and he tried not to think about that. It did not take long for his mind to become overwhelmed by other matters. As Galea combed, she spoke, and it was her turn to talk about everything, while all Konrad could do was to sit and listen and wonder.

'Imagine,' she said, 'that the world is an island, an island surrounded by Chaos. Sometimes the tide rises higher than normal, and the world is threatened because it may be totally swamped. That is what is happening now.

'Mankind evolved millennia ago, when the world was also flooded by Chaos, when its raw essence first solidified into warpstone and warpdust. The elves and dwarfs were not so affected as the new race known as humans. They had their own times of ascendancy before then, times when they were the superior race; but when mankind claimed domination, the world was not as it had been. Mixing warpstone with the substances of our world led to the creation of the Chaos Wastes and of the mutants who originally dwelled there, but which now roam everywhere. Beastmen are the product of Chaos arriving upon this world, as are goblins and orcs and skaven and all manner of foul and perverted beings.

'And humans may also be regarded as the creation of Chaos.

'Within what we call the Old World, the dwarfs had replaced the elves, who had migrated across the Western Ocean, and now it appeared that the dwarfs would lose their lands to the goblinoid races. It seemed that the mutants would become rulers of the lands to the west of the World's Edge Mountains, but then the eight warring human tribes who inhabited that region were united by Sigmar. Sigmar allied himself with the dwarfs, who gave him their sacred warhammer, Ghal-maraz, and together human and dwarf destroyed the goblin armies at the Battle of Black Fire Pass. This was two and a half thousand years ago, and Sigmar Heldenhammer – Hammer of the Goblins – founded the Empire.

'Sigmar is now revered as a god. He has a cathedral in Altdorf, temples throughout the known world, countless worshippers. The inhabitants of the Empire are all Sigmar's children, literally as well as metaphorically; he lived so long ago it seems inevitable that every human is descended from his line. There is some part of Sigmar in everyone.'

Galea paused, gazing at Konrad.

'There is more of Sigmar in you than in most,' she said.

He stared at her suspiciously. From what Konrad had already told Galea, it was easy for her to suggest an association with Sigmar. She knew of Konrad's battle with the goblins, when he had imagined himself wielding a hammer instead of an axe, how he had become imbued with almost supernatural strength. And Konrad had revealed the dream in which he had confused his own past with the life of Sigmar.

'I am not trying to flatter you,' Galea said. 'You already suspect that Sigmar has given you a purpose. And you are correct.'

'What purpose?' demanded Konrad. 'What?'

'I do not know the future, although I knew that when Wolf was here that he would one day lead someone else to me. That is his purpose, Konrad, to guide you as he has done ever since the day you and he first met.'

Konrad said nothing, he was too busy trying to absorb all the implications of Galea's revelations.

'You are important to Sigmar,' she continued, 'and this means that you have many enemies who wish to thwart Sigmar's intentions. There is one in particular who appears to have been manipulating various diverse foes in order to further his own nefarious schemes.'

Konrad knew exactly who Galea meant.

'Skullface! Who is he? What does he want with me?'

It was Galea's turn to say nothing.

'Tell me more about Sigmar,' said Konrad.

Galea said, 'Half a century after becoming Emperor, Sigmar returned to the World's Edge Mountains to take Ghal-maraz back to the dwarfs. He was never seen by human eyes again, and his mortal body is believed to have perished.

'The body is a part of the material world, but the soul is a part of Chaos. In moments of extreme stress, it is possible for a mortal to summon up the inner resources of the soul, thus deriving power directly from Chaos. Upon death, the human spirit returns to Chaos, to join the other souls or to await reincarnation. Few spirits will be reborn, but those that are become more and more powerful through each rebirth.

'Chaos is sometimes known as the Sea of Lost Souls. These souls may combine into a greater whole, a coalescence of energy created by the linking of similar spirits. These centres of energy are thus created by the very essence of life, and they are known as the powers of Chaos. Or the gods of Chaos...

'And thus it can be claimed that men make gods in their own image, while the gods themselves exert their own influence upon mankind. Or is there only one god, and all others but different aspects of the one deity? Is there only one soul which all humans share? Is this one soul part of the one god, or is the one god part of the one soul?

'Good and bad, Law and Chaos. Could one exist without the other? Are they but different aspects of the same belief?

'All I know is what I have learned. I have learned much, and some of what I have said may conflict, but that is all we can rely on: our memories, our trust in the experiences of ourselves and others. Yet human memories are fallible and cannot be totally relied upon. None of this might be true, or only some of it. What you have told me might never have occurred, or was not what you believed. Perhaps the dwarfs never did inhabit the Old World, and the ancient temple you discovered was merely created the previous day. What is recorded in the history books might only have been written an hour ago, and similarly the dust which lies across the worn covers of such volumes was the creation of but a moment past. There is no proof and there can be none.'

Galea had told Konrad this and much more, and then she had said none of it could be trusted. He had already known that what was true one day might be false the next.

'Why have you told me all this?' he asked.

'Because you should know,' she said.

He gazed at her, trying to see beyond the figure of a little girl, past her feline eyes. 'Who are you?'

'I am one who was saved. I was possessed by the darker side of Chaos, many many years ago. I was a daemon, for many many years.'

It was a word Konrad knew, but he could barely imagine its implications.

'But I was released by a far greater force, like the one to which you were being drawn in your vision of the afterlife

– but infinitely more powerful. And that is who I now serve.'

A white dove had landed on Galea's shoulder, and now she took hold of it, stroking its feathers. It began to coo, just as the black leopard had purred when she had stroked its fur.

'What must I do?' asked Konrad.

'You must do whatever you must.'

'Who am I?'

Galea smiled and shook her head. Konrad did not know whether this meant she could not answer or would not answer.

She clutched the bird with one hand and suddenly thrust it towards the leopard. A single bite, a gulp, and the bird was gone down the huge cat's throat.

THE OTHER SIDE of the lake was once more in view as Konrad waded into the cold water and began swimming back. He felt quite content and had been unwilling to leave the island, but there was nothing else that he wished to learn. It was only when he reached the far bank that he realized how little Galea had really told him. There was some history, which might not have been true; but most of it he already knew, whether it was true or not. Galea had explained the nature of Chaos, but her interpretation was not necessarily accurate.

Despite this, he felt reassured by what he had discovered. The world did make sense, and he had a significant part to play in its events; he had no doubt that in this Galea had told him the truth. And beyond the world there was another, a greater realm of existence, and what occurred upon one had a significant effect on events elsewhere.

Everything was connected, just as all the important people in his own life were linked. He was unable yet to comprehend the pattern, but at least he knew there was one; and perhaps eventually he would be able to understand it all.

Konrad had learned nothing of his origins, but that seemed of little consequence compared with what had been revealed of his focal role. The past no longer mattered, because it could no longer affect him. What he did now and in the future was far more important.

Wolf was waiting when he arrived back, and he had a fire lit. It was almost dusk, and Konrad stared at the setting sun.

'I didn't know I was gone that long,' he said, warming himself by the blaze.

'Three days, you mean?'

'Three days!'

'Time is different there – and everything else.'

Konrad looked back to where he had been, and he nodded in agreement.

'Now where?' asked Wolf.

There could be only one answer. Wolf had been his guide until now, but not any longer.

'Altdorf,' replied Konrad.

'Me, too. I headed for the frontier because that was where the enemy was. Now the enemy is in the capital, and it's an enemy I know how to deal with.' Wolf gripped the hilt of his sword, pulling the blade slightly out, then sliding it swiftly back into its oiled black scabbard as if he were thrusting it into an enemy's flesh.

Konrad was still gazing at Galea's island. It looked so small, so dark, but he knew that the sun was still shining down upon its numerous acres.

'I now know that you're the one,' Wolf had said, after their battle with the mutated Imperial guards. 'The one I must take.' Then he had led Konrad here.

Was this the reason that Wolf had made Konrad his squire, so long ago? Had everything which had happened over the subsequent years been nothing more than a prelude to his meeting with Galea?

And, Konrad remembered, it was not until Wolf had seen the black quiver which he held, the one with the enigmatic emblem, that he had offered Konrad the role of squire.

'We can be in Marienburg in a few days,' added Wolf, 'then take a boat up the Reik to Altdorf.'

As he stared at what appeared to be an island in the middle of a lake, Konrad wondered about Wolf's previous visit here, when it had been he who had made the journey through the water. How long ago had it been, and who had led him here? And who was it who had visited Galea previously, when she had asked for the bracelet that Wolf had taken to her?

He did not ask, because he knew Wolf would not answer. But he wondered if some day he would return and stand here while another ventured across the lake. Perhaps he should buy some red silk ribbon at the next opportunity, and carry it with him until it was time for him to guide someone else to the eternal child.

CHAPTER TEN

Less than a century ago, the Wasteland had been part of the Empire; but over the years the burgomeisters of Marienburg had won a number of concessions for their city, which was the gateway to the rest of the world for so much of the Empire. With the backing of Bretonnia, the Wasteland had finally seceded and gained its own independence.

The mouth of the Reik was a mile from one shore to the opposite bank, but there were many islands in the delta, so that the river flowed down to the ocean in a series of narrow tributaries. Marienburg was built upon these islands, the different parts of the city joined by numerous bridges. Only one such waterway was dredged deep enough for the largest ships to pass through; and over this there was but one bridge beneath which the tallest vessels could sail: High Bridge. The major navigable channel was on the south side of Marienburg, which was where the dock facilities had developed.

The city was walled to protect itself from raiding pirates and to assert its independence, and many of the largest houses were themselves fortresses. They belonged to wealthy merchant families, explained Wolf, traders whose ancestors had probably been pirates and corsairs. Konrad had once been very impressed by the port of Erengrad, on the Kislev border, but that was no more than a fishing village when compared with the size and splendour of the greatest port in the Old World.

He and Wolf gazed across at the city, and to where all the vessels rode at anchor in the wide bay beyond, waiting for the tide to turn so that they could enter the harbour. There were ships of every size and description, with pilots and customs officials being ferried between the foreign vessels by a number of small boats flying the emblem of Marienburg: a mermaid holding a sword in her right hand, a bag of coins in her left.

'Let's get a drink,' said Wolf. 'Although now that you're here, there's a chance that every tavern in town will burn down!'

'I thought we were heading for Altdorf.'

'We'll make for one of the dockside inns, that's the best way to find a passage. But while we're there, we might as well refresh ourselves after our journey.'

'How do we pay the boat fare?'

'I have a few funds,' said Wolf, which was probably the most astonishing thing Konrad had ever heard him say.

Throughout the time he had been with Wolf, Konrad's total pay had not amounted to more than a handful of crowns.

Wolf never had any money, even from the very start. When they were heading for the Kislev frontier, he had swapped his packhorse for their passage to Praag along the River Lynsk. Wolf had hoped to make a fortune while working as mercenary in the gold mine, and he had dreamed of untold riches from the lost dwarf temple.

'What about the plot to replace the Emperor with an impostor?' he asked, as they rode towards the Reik.

They both knew this was the reason for returning to Altdorf, but they had not discussed it until now. Although not a direct descendant, Karl-Franz was the latest of Sigmar's heirs – and he had to be protected.

A few months ago, Konrad had felt no concern for the Emperor, but much had happened since then; and now he knew what his mission must be, what Sigmar required of him.

He had originally been reluctant to reveal all that had happened to him during the months since Kislev; and now that he and Wolf were together, comrades again, it no longer seemed important.

'The skaven have made a doppelganger of the Emperor,' he said. 'I've seen it.'

At one time, Konrad had been Gaxar's prisoner deep beneath Middenheim; but during the human invasion of the skaven lair, while Konrad had been fighting against Silver Eye, Gaxar had been seen with another human hostage. Litzenreich had identified the figure as the Emperor. It could not really have been Karl-Franz, and must have been a replica. Konrad had since seen portraits of the Emperor, and the likeness was perfect.

This was not the first duplicate Gaxar had produced. The grey seer had also made a likeness of Konrad – which Konrad had fought and destroyed.

'The only reason the skaven can have for wanting a double of Karl-Franz is so they can assassinate the real Emperor and replace him with a puppet,' said Konrad. 'The Imperial guard must be in on the plot, which is why they tried to kill me when I found out.'

'Maybe.'

'Maybe?'

'The guard seem to have become the minions of Slaanesh, while the god of the skaven is the Horned Rat. It seems unlikely that these two factions would co-operate. Perhaps the skaven would ally themselves with Nurgle's pestilential swarms, but not the servants of the lord of pleasure. They'd be more likely to rip each other apart.'

'But the rival forces of Chaos do operate together on occasion, when it's to their mutual advantage. You know that. And destroying the Emperor, the figurehead of human resistance, would be exactly what they both want.'

And Konrad knew exactly who had forged this alliance of the damned: Skullface.

He had only ever seen Skullface twice, but his skeletal figure had always been in the shadows, manipulating and scheming.

It must have been Skullface who had directed the warrior in bronze, luring Konrad away from the dwarf temple, then ensuring that the suit of armour was there to capture Konrad when he had escaped from Kastring's marauding warband. He had wanted Konrad dead, devoured by the Chaos armour, but Konrad had survived.

It must have been Skullface who had arranged for Krysten to fall into Zuntermein's clutches. Corrupted by the depraved beliefs of Khorne during her unimaginable journey from Kislev to Altdorf, she had become the hostage of a Slaaneshi cult.

Krysten was the lure to entrap Konrad, but once again he had survived.

And it was Skullface who had Elyssa...

'Maybe,' said Wolf, again. 'But what are we going to do about it?'

'We can warn him. Tell him that the Imperial guard are all traitors, that the skaven intend to destroy him.'

'Write him a letter, you mean?'

'No!'

'You're right. The postal system isn't what it was. It would probably arrive too late.'

Konrad stared at Wolf. 'You don't seem to be taking this very seriously.'

Wolf met his eyes. 'And you seem to be taking it too seriously.'

He seemed aware that Konrad had another motive for returning to Altdorf, and until now Konrad had been unwilling to admit this even to himself.

Elyssa had been tainted by Chaos, and Konrad had considered that she was forever doomed. But Galea was once far more damned than Elyssa, and her soul had been redeemed. Perhaps Elyssa, too, could be saved.

'What do you think we should do?' asked Konrad.

'Warn the Emperor, as you said. If he's not back in Altdorf, we keep on the river to Talabheim and find him there.'

'Or we could stop in Altdorf to try and find out what is going on – and stop it.'

'Fight the Imperial guard, fight the skaven, find and destroy the impostor? Just you and me?' Although he had been trying to keep a straight face, Wolf could not help but smile.

'Have you got a better idea?'

'Maybe.'

Konrad waited, and waited. 'What?' he prompted.

'We invade the city.'

'Just you and me?'

'And a few others. We raise an army of mercenaries to attack Altdorf, creating a diversion while we sneak in and discover what's really happening.'

'Attack the Imperial capital? That's quite a diversion. Where do we find this army?'

'Here.' Wolf gestured towards the city beyond them. 'Everyone hates Altdorf and Altdorfers, even me – and I'm from there. They are so arrogant, believing they're far superior to everyone else in the Empire, the Old World, the entire world. We'll loot the city, burn it down!'

Konrad stared at him.

Wolf shrugged. 'Maybe you can burn down a couple of taverns, Konrad. The ones which sell the worst ale.'

'How can we raise an army here?'

'We can find the kind of army we want. One that will make enough noise and call plenty of attention to themselves and waste valuable time while they are all slaughtered – while we do what we have to do.'

On the frontier, Wolf would have no hesitation in allowing a group of his own men to be killed if he deemed it necessary, offering them as bait to draw the Chaos clans into a trap where they could be exterminated. But the ones that he sacrificed were never those he considered true warriors. He regarded most of those who called themselves mercenaries with as much contempt as the benighted battalions they fought. Their only function was to die, and it was a bonus if they happened to kill some of the enemy troops before their own deaths.

Murderers, thieves, bandits, cutpurses, the vermin of the Empire, they all dignified themselves with the name 'mercenary,' believing that the assumed title granted legitimacy to their brutal cowardice.

This was the reason why Wolf had once said he preferred to consider himself a 'soldier of fortune'; he did not wish to be associated with the gutter thugs who gave fighting for reward a bad name.

When Wolf and Konrad first arrived at the gold mine, those were the kind of men who had already been hired as guards. There was little to choose between them and the miners, all of whom were convicted criminals serving out their sentences. The guards had probably fled their native lands in order to avoid being jailed; the miners were the unlucky ones who had been caught.

It was only after Wolf took charge that true soldiers were recruited, men who knew how to fight face to face, instead of relying upon a knife in the back; men who had been trained for years, who accepted discipline and would obey orders – most of the time. The robbers and assassins died, while the real warriors fulfilled their proper function. This was when Wolf's professional army began driving back the invaders, taking the battle to the renegade hordes instead of waiting for the mine to be attacked.

Marienburg stood at the edge of the Old World, and here was where the scum from every land would gather, because this was as far as they could travel. The city was full of fugitives, criminals on the run from all over the world, deserters who had jumped ship as soon as they reached port, desperados who would slit a dozen throats for the price of a drink.

This was the ideal place for recruiting a force of ersatz mercenaries.

'And we find our army in the harbour taverns?' said Konrad.

'That's right. And while we're there, we might as well raise a tankard or two.'

Konrad laughed and shook his head. 'I hope you have plenty of funds. You'll need a fortune to equip this army and get them to Altdorf.'

'We find some backers,' said Wolf. 'They finance the expedition in return for a share of the profits.'

Konrad watched Wolf as he explained, and he began to wonder if Wolf really did intend to sack Altdorf, if that was his own motive for returning to the Imperial capital.

'They'll expect to make a killing,' Wolf concluded. 'And, in a way, they'll be right.' He grinned wickedly, his sharpened teeth gleaming.

'Maybe it would be best if we went to Altdorf alone,' suggested Konrad.

'No, no.' Wolf shook his head. 'They know you weren't killed, so they'll be expecting you back again – but they won't be expecting an invasion. The more the better.'

Konrad had his doubts, but at the moment it seemed futile to argue. They rode on to where the river bank marked the edge of the city. Marienburg proper began on the other side of the channel, but over the years numerous buildings had spread along the southern side of the waterway, and several vessels were berthed there. Wagons and coaches would cross the river by ferry, but people on horse or on foot could make their way to the other side via High Bridge.

It was almost sunset, the sky rapidly darkening, as Konrad gazed up at the structure. It reminded him of the long road which zig-zagged up the mountainside towards the gates of Middenheim. Although the City of the White Wolf was reached by a number of viaducts and along a wider and higher road, the route to Marienburg was in its own way equally spectacular. A huge stone tower was built upon the southern side of the river, with a roadway coiled around and around, steeply circling the tower on the outside.

The main bridge in Erengrad had a longer span, but that was built of wood, and the centre section could be elevated like a drawbridge. The High Bridge, however, was constructed entirely from massive blocks of stone. These were all wedged against one another, forming a wide arch that was held in place by its own weight. At the opposite end, to the north, the bridge abutted a solid rocky cliff where it was anchored by two heavy pillars.

The toll keeper accepted Wolf's coins, but the city guards at the base of the tower barely glanced at him or Konrad before waving them past. The two riders began to climb, their horses slowly circling towards the top, while the pinnacle grew narrower towards its apex. Although he was no longer Wolf's servant, Konrad led the packhorse, as he had done most of the time, and he gazed at the darkening landscape all around.

To the east, the direction from which they had come, was the kind of desolate territory which had given the Wasteland its name. To the north, beyond the gulf, lay the Sea of Claws, its waters grey and ominous. To the south was the River Reik, flowing from Altdorf and deep within the Empire, its tributaries stretching far beyond: to the Black Mountains, Sudenland, Averland, Stirland, the World's Edge Mountains, and as far north as Kislev. And ahead lay Marienburg itself, which was all that was really visible because of its proximity and its lights: its islands and its bridges, its houses and its shops, its stables and its taverns, its markets and its warehouses, its barracks and its temples, its rivers and its ships.

The bridge was narrower than Konrad had expected, its sides marked by low parapets. The wind was fierce at this height, blowing icy gusts, and he was glad that it was not far to the other side.

He was ahead of Wolf as they began to cross the stone span, and he became aware of two riders approaching from the opposite side. He paid little attention at first, trying not to think how close he was to the edge and how far down it was to the river below.

The first rider was short and squat, with a thick red beard: a dwarf. The other was a human, hooded within his black robes, his beard long and greying.

Konrad slowed his horse and edged it to one side, allowing the other riders plenty of room to pass by. That was when he first took a proper look at the dwarf – and recognized him.

At the same time he heard Wolf's angry shout of recognition: 'Litzenreich!'

WOLF DREW HIS sword and urged his mount towards Litzenreich, but Ustnar blocked him off with his own horse. A double-headed fighting axe had been slung over the dwarf's shoulder, and already the weapon was in his hand. Wolf was clad in his armour, but without his helmet, while Ustnar wore thick furs as protection from the cold.

'Out of my way, runt!' snarled Wolf. 'Or you die first!'

'Don't even try!' growled Ustnar, swinging his axe in an arc to keep Wolf at bay.

'What seems to be the problem?' asked Litzenreich.

'Problem? Problem!' yelled Wolf, his sword pointing at the wizard. 'You're the problem, you bastard! But you won't be for long!'

'Wolf!' warned Konrad, urging his horse forward. 'He's a wizard...'

With a single bolt of lightning, Litzenreich could hurl Wolf's burning body over the side of the bridge – and probably Konrad's own blazing corpse, too.

'I know,' hissed Wolf. 'That's one of the reasons he must die!' He thrust his sword towards Ustnar. 'Back!'

The dwarf caught the black blade on the handle of his axe, and they glared at one another. Neither of them had attempted to breach the other's defence, not yet, but within a few seconds the real fighting would begin.

A blast of cold wind blew through Konrad's hair, and he glanced down, seeing the shadow of a ship passing through the narrow channel beneath the bridge. The last rays of the sun were reflected from the surface of the river, which seemed even further down than it had done.

He had no quarrel with Litzenreich and Ustnar, but Wolf was his comrade, and if it came to combat then Konrad would fight side by side with Wolf. Under normal circumstances, even such a ferocious warrior as Ustnar would stand little chance against Wolf. But these were hardly normal circumstances, and a sorcerer was the ideal ally in any battle.

'Back!' repeated Wolf.

This time his sword stroke was faster, more forceful, and Ustnar parried with equal alacrity and strength.

'No!' said Ustnar. 'You get back! Out of our way!' And he swung his axe, quicker, harder, closer.

Konrad looked at Litzenreich. 'Can't we all pass by in peace?'

'No!' retorted Wolf, as his black blade stabbed forward again. By now he was hardly holding back.

'Peace?' said Litzenreich. 'He – that fellow – does not know the word.'

'Fellow! I'm not surprised you've forgotten my name. You thought I was dead, didn't you? You left me to die. But now I'm here to kill you. Wolf! That's who I am. You won't have time to forget, because it's the last thing you'll ever know!'

Another swordstroke, another axesweep.

'I do not understand why you are complaining,' said Litzenreich. 'You did not die. If you had done, you would not now be here.'

Wolf was in no mood for a discussion. He feinted to the left, drew back as Ustnar moved that way to counter the stroke, then leaned forward in his stirrups, jabbing his sword forward. Ustnar dodged aside in time, the blade missed, and it was Wolf's turn to take evasive action as the dwarf axe sliced towards him.

The two antagonists and their horses occupied most of the width of the bridge, and Konrad could do nothing but watch as the conflict escalated. Litzenreich held his mount's reins with his left hand, and Konrad expected him to use his right at any moment, a thunderbolt flashing from his outstretched fingers towards Wolf. But it seemed that the wizard was content to be a spectator. Then Konrad caught a glimpse of his right hand, or where his right hand should have been: it was missing. Bound with a piece of leather, the sorcerer's arm ended at the wrist.

It was Litzenreich who had caused Gaxar to lose his right paw, although Konrad did not know the circumstances. Then when Litzenreich had been the grey seer's prisoner beneath Altdorf, his limbs had been nailed to the ground, and he had ordered Konrad to pull his right hand free so that he could cast spells against the attacking pygmy troglodytes. But magicians were unable to heal their own wounds, and it seemed Litzenreich's mutilated hand had not recovered from being ripped loose from the rock. Gaxar was dead, yet he had gained revenge for his own amputation.

When Konrad had been studying the High Bridge earlier, he had observed a number of figures crossing the stone span. Now he realized that he and Wolf had passed no one descending the steep spiral road while they had been ascending. The only others they had encountered anywhere on the bridge had been Litzenreich and Ustnar. Four riders, five horses, there was still no one else attempting to cross – and that did not seem right to Konrad. The imminent darkness should not have prevented other travellers from crossing from south to north.

Wolf and Ustnar fought in earnest, matching each other blow for blow. Litzenreich appeared to be paying little attention to the combat. He had lowered his hood and his head was tilted to one side, as if listening, and he slowly looked around in the direction from which he and Ustnar had come. The far end of the bridge was embedded in the steep rock face, and the dark granite to either side of the end pillars had been hollowed out to form a passage leading directly onto the bridge.

A dim shape glimmered on the horizon. Morrslieb, the lesser moon which was so important to Chaos cultists, was on the ascendant.

And suddenly there were others on the bridge: menacing figures racing towards the centre...

'Skaven!' yelled Konrad, releasing the packhorse and drawing his own sword.

He glanced back over his shoulder, seeing a second dark band of ratbeasts swarming from the tower at the other end of the bridge. The three humans and the dwarf were under attack from both sides, trapped in the middle by their savage ambushers.

Konrad claimed the first victim, as the rampaging creature leading the charge fell to his blade. He avoided the wild swordsweep and hacked at its furry throat, slicing it open, and a spray of blood cascaded from the wound. A second inhuman attacked, its sword thrusting up at Konrad's waist. He turned the stroke aside with his own weapon, then stabbed the beast between its snarling jaws as its momentum carried it up against Konrad's horse.

Wolf and Ustnar had disengaged and turned away, the dwarf to defend Litzenreich, the mercenary to join Konrad, their blades slashing and slicing into the mutated rats who rushed at them.

Konrad saw flashes of bright light behind him, smelled the stench of roasting flesh, and he knew that Litzenreich was using his thaumaturgical talents against their common foes.

Konrad and Wolf were above the feral horde, but Konrad preferred to fight on foot under such conditions. Trapped on the bridge, with no room to manoeuvre, he was more of a target on horseback and could easily have been dragged down. But before he could dismount, his horse was hacked away beneath him, its legs chopped clean through. He threw himself aside, and Wolf did the same. They fought side by side, sword by sword.

Skaven seldom fought blade against blade. Their tactics were more likely to be of ambush, to attack with overwhelming strength. They dwelled underground, and they preferred to fight in fetid tunnels where their eyesight gave them an advantage in the dark.

Now they had chosen combat in the open, on the High Bridge; but every other factor was in their favour – the ambush, their numerical superiority, the approaching night.

They were armed with jagged swords and curved blades mounted on long poles, and Konrad recognized the emblem which they carried on their shields and banners and which was branded onto their flesh: a circle with a vertical line down the middle, and two more lines from the centre directed down towards the edge of the circle. It was the clan mark of the skaven he had fought beneath Middenheim, the ones commanded by Gaxar...

But these skaven seemed to have no commander. They were tough, they were strong, they were wild – too wild. In battle, more was required than strength; there had to be brains as well as muscle. The predators were so crazed with blood lust that their numerical superiority counted for nothing; they all wanted to attack at once, and so inevitably obstructed each other. Many of the berserker rats were wounded by the frantic sword strokes of their own verminous breed. They growled and spat, hurling themselves forward without regard to their own fate.

At first Konrad and Wolf were protected by the bodies of their dead horses, and soon their defensive ramparts were strengthened by the increasing pile of skaven corpses.

Konrad kept looking for Silver Eye. If he were here, that would explain the sudden attack – Gaxar's bodyguard was taking revenge for the death of his master. But Konrad saw no sign of that particular skaven.

Sword in one hand, dagger in the other, he fought as he had not done for a long time. The night air was filled with the screams of the assault force, and with his own and Wolf's answering battle cries. The rat-things screamed as they attacked, and they screamed as they died. The stones of the bridge became awash with skaven blood, which glistened in Morrslieb's spectral light.

Konrad thrust and swung with his sword, slaying with ruthless efficiency. He severed limbs and cut off heads, ripped out entrails and crushed bones. He used his feet and his knife, kicking at the wounded, stabbing at those who had not been sufficiently damaged to become immobile. Even with legs that were but stumps, with arms that ended at the elbow, they could still crawl, they could still bite. While they could move they were lethal.

Suddenly everything became still. There was no silence, because many of the ugly brutes screamed as the blood spilled from their fatal wounds and they gasped for their final breath of air.

'Just like old times,' Wolf said to Konrad, as he surveyed the carnage and wiped blood from his face with his gauntlet.

During the onslaught, it had seemed that there was a whole legion of inhumans charging from that end of the bridge; but there could have been no more than a score of bodies scattered around them.

Then there was another yell, and one last demented skaven came bounding over the mound of the dead, launching itself towards Konrad and Wolf. They both caught the creature at once, impaling it upon their weapons, one black blade and one Imperial guard sword. The mutated rodent staggered to one side, twitching, screeching.

Wolf pulled his sword free from the dying brute, but Konrad felt his weapon being twisted out of his hand. He tried to retain his grip, but his hand was too slippery with blood.

The final enemy staggered to the side of the bridge, vainly trying to tear Konrad's sword out of its chest; but it only succeeded in severing its own clawed fingers on the blade's edge. Colliding with the low parapet, it swayed and fell backwards. It tumbled down, down, its screech of pain and of death diminishing as it dropped towards the Reik far below.

'You all right?' asked Wolf.

'I think so.' Konrad was covered in blood, sticky and slimy, but not much of it seemed to be his own.

They turned to face Litzenreich and Ustnar, both of whom had also survived. Their horses were slain, and a pile of hideous carcasses lay around them, some bloodied and some blackened. The wizard and the dwarf looked at Konrad and Wolf.

'A truce,' suggested Konrad, and he was speaking to Wolf as well as Litzenreich.

Ustnar was leaning upon his dripping axe; he would do whatever the wizard commanded.

'Very well,' agreed Litzenreich. 'We seem to have a common enemy, which is a good basis for negotiation.'

'This isn't over, Litzenreich,' said Wolf, but he nodded his agreement. Then he added to Konrad: 'But at the moment, the most important thing is to get a drink...'

He started to hand his sword over for the blade to be cleaned, then remembered that Konrad's five years of service had elapsed. Wolf wiped his weapon on his packhorse's blanket, and unloaded what he needed from the dead animal. One of the skaven was still twitching, and he kicked it a couple of times until it became still.

'If they had had any sense,' he said, 'they'd have waited till we killed each other.'

Litzenreich said something to Ustnar, who began to examine the skaven corpses. Having lost his sword, Konrad studied the blades which had been carried by their insane attackers. But there was a difference between taking an Imperial guard sword which had been used by a Chaos cultist and a weapon which had always belonged to one of the creatures of the damned. He let the benighted blades lie where they had fallen.

These creatures must have been the survivors from the assault on their lair beneath Middenheim. The City of the White Wolf lay hundreds of miles away, yet it would be linked to Marienburg by one of the subterranean passages which connected all the centres of skaven habitation. Wherever humans dwelled, there was also likely to be an infestation of skaven.

But why had this clan come to the Wasteland? Konrad guessed there must be one reason – to try and destroy him. Litzenreich had also been instrumental in annihilating the skaven nest deep below Altdorf. The rat beasts also wanted revenge against the sorcerer.

'How do you know Litzenreich?' Konrad asked.

'From Middenheim. It was–' Wolf stopped. 'You know him? Yes, because you knew he was a magician.'

Konrad nodded. 'We've met.'

Wolf waited for more explanation. None was forthcoming, and so he continued: 'When I arrived in Ferlangen and found you, I'd just come from Middenheim. I was almost killed there because of Litzenreich.'

Wolf and Litzenreich...

Yet another link in the web which held Konrad ensnared, its strands becoming ever tighter, like a noose around his throat.

CHAPTER ELEVEN

WOLF AND USTNAR led the way off the bridge, sword and axe at the ready in case of another barbaric assault. They took the northern exit, past the stone pillars and through the passageway carved out of the solid rock, heading for the heart of Marienburg.

The tollkeeper at the entrance to the bridge lay dead, what was left of him; the troops in the guardhouse were also bloody corpses, mutilated by the skaven.

The same must have happened to the men on the other side of the bridge after Konrad and Wolf had begun their ascent.

As the four made their way cautiously down the winding lane from High Bridge, Mannslieb rose in the east, dissolving the darkest shadows where more enemies might have lurked, and illuminating their route to the city. Down below were the lights of houses, voices could be heard, and a few dim shapes were visible in the streets. Nobody was yet aware of what had happened a hundred yards further back, high above their heads.

And no one might ever know. By dawn tomorrow, the bridge would most likely be devoid of dead vermin. Their corpses would have vanished during the night, spirited away by the skaven of Marienburg who had come to collect their kin. All that would remain were the bodies of the guards, mysteriously slain, and the five butchered horses.

Reaching the river near where a slipway angled down into the cold dark waters of the Reik, Konrad waded straight in. He was still holding his dagger in his right hand, and he immersed himself completely to wash away the skaven gore which coated his flesh and his clothes, and to bathe his own wounds. Wolf had been wearing his black armour during the battle, and so the blood and bones and brains of the beasts he had slain would have to be wiped off the metal before it dried to a stinking crust. He bent down at the water's edge, wiping his face clean.

If anything, Ustnar was even more contaminated than Konrad. His beard and hair were matted with skaven slime. Despite this, he was very reluctant to soak himself. He stood watching as Konrad stripped off his clothes, until finally his own hatred of water became secondary to his loathing of the putrid remains which were splattered across him. He tugged off his outer furs, then slowly walked into the river and ducked his head beneath the surface. He kept hold of his battle axe. Konrad and the dwarf stood two yards apart, warily watching each other, but neither of them spoke.

Only Litzenreich had not been touched by the alien blood, and he waited at the top of the slipway. He held his arms out in front of himself, as if studying them, comparing his left hand with where his right should have been.

No matter how much Konrad rubbed at himself and what he wore, he could not remove the fetid stench of rodent death. His body needed to soak in a hot bath and his clothes would have to be destroyed. He climbed up from the river and onto the quayside, wringing out his shirt and then putting it back on. As he did so he shivered, and behind him he heard Ustnar sneeze. He was glad his hair was not as long as the dwarf's, and that his beard had not yet grown to its previous thickness.

'We must find somewhere to stay for the night,' Wolf said to him. 'Where you can get dry and warm, and where I can get clean.'

'We shall join you,' Litzenreich announced.

'Will you?' said Wolf.

'There are various matters we must discuss.'

'I'm not discussing anything with you, you treacherous bastard. Get out of my sight before I–' Wolf gripped the hilt of his sword, and Ustnar hurried up the slipway to step between him and Litzenreich.

'We ought to continue our truce,' said Litzenreich. 'We have much in common. We were on that bridge at exactly the same time, yet going in opposite directions, when those creatures attacked us. For us to have met precisely there and then, was that coincidence?'

'Yes!'

Wolf sensed Konrad watching him, and he shrugged.

Coincidence, chance, luck: Wolf did not believe in any of them.

'All right,' he conceded, 'we'll talk.'

And so they did.

Marienburg's very existence depended upon the sea and the river which flowed into the ocean, and it was a city of water as well as of land. Its bridges were more than merely links between the different districts; they were as much a part of the city as any of its roads. They happened to be built above the water instead of upon land, but the widest of them were like any other street in any part of the Empire; they were lined with houses, shops, taverns.

The four reluctant allies found rooms in one such tavern, the Eight Bells, which was in the centre of one of the bridges across the Tussenkanal, one of the Reik's many tributaries. Konrad's first request was for a hot tub, his second for a change of clothes. The garments had probably come from a guest who had been unable to settle his bill, but they were a lot cleaner than the ones Konrad discarded.

Wolf had requested that their evening meal was served in his room, so that his conversation with Litzenreich could not be overheard. It was too late to hide the fact that they were together. Ustnar said hardly anything all evening, and Litzenreich spoke as though he did not exist. The dwarf sat with his axe by his side, ready to dismember Wolf should he make a move against the wizard. Wolf's black sword belt was slung over the back of the chair where he sat.

Konrad was equally sparing with his words. He had little to say, but there was much to be learned by listening. While they ate, he had great difficulty keeping his eyes open. This was the first time he had been indoors for weeks, and the first time he had been warm during that period. The heat from the fire was making him lethargic, but even before the battle with the rat beasts he was exhausted from the long journey to Marienburg, and he would have preferred sleeping to eating.

'I was crossing the bridge to take a boat to Altdorf,' explained Litzenreich. 'And you?'

Wolf took his time before answering. It seemed that he did not trust what the wizard had told him, which Konrad could well understand, and so he was reluctant to reveal his own intentions. He chewed slowly upon a piece of mutton, and then inspected a lump of gristle he had extracted from his mouth, while deciding his reply.

'We had only just arrived in Marienburg, and we were also planning to head for Altdorf,' he said, truthfully.

'I had been here for some while, but decided it was time to return to the capital.'

'Return?'

'I was a guest of the Altdorf army. It is a long story, but your friend...' Litzenreich gestured with his fork towards Konrad.

'Konrad,' said Wolf.

'Yes, he knows some of it.' The sorcerer rubbed at the stump of his right arm. 'I kept heading downriver, although not in the river. I finally reached Marienburg, which I thought would suit my purposes most admirably.

Being a port, one can find almost every kind of commodity if one knows where to look and who to ask. And if one can pay the price. You know the kind of substance to which I am referring, of course?'

'Warpstone.' Wolf spat out the word, and he glanced from Litzenreich to Konrad, realizing that the enigmatic substance linked the two of them. 'You know what warpstone is?'

Konrad nodded. He knew, or he thought that he did; but he also knew that nothing could be certain.

'Warpstone is the stuff of Chaos,' said Wolf, 'and Chaos is the source of all magic. You know that?'

Konrad nodded again, although he was unaware of when he had discovered this. It may have been one of the things which Galea had told him, or possibly he had gradually grown aware of it during his dealings with Litzenreich.

'Magic and Chaos and evil are one and the same,' Wolf asserted.

Litzenreich laughed, spraying food over the table, then shook his head in disbelief.

Konrad assumed that Wolf was biased because of how he had been adversely affected by sorcery and sorcerers throughout his life, from his brother's treachery right through to whatever Litzenreich had done to him. By now, Konrad no longer believed everything that he heard from Wolf – or anyone else. It was too simplistic to associate magic with evil. Maybe Litzenreich was correct: Chaos did not necessarily mean evil. It was there, it was a part of the world. The effects of Chaos, whether positive or negative, were open to interpretation.

'My life was saved by magic,' said Konrad.

'By science,' Litzenreich said.

But Konrad was not referring to the way he had been extracted from the bronze armour. He held out his right arm.

'That elf,' he said to Wolf. 'Remember?'

Litzenreich glanced at Konrad's right arm, then at his own. 'You were healed by an elf?' he asked, and Konrad nodded. 'A pity I could not find one to help me. I thought elven magic only worked on elves, but that proves how the art is always advancing. And that is why I have to get back to Altdorf. I need more warpstone to continue my research. There is very little in Marienburg.'

'And you think we're going to help you?' said Wolf.

'I believe we are going to help each other, that our interests are the same. Why do you wish to go to Altdorf?'

Wolf looked at Konrad, and he told Litzenreich: 'We weren't doing much, so we thought we'd rescue the Emperor and save the Empire. Konrad tells me that the skaven are up to some kind of mischief, that there's a replica of Karl-Franz waiting to step into his shoes.'

'That is correct. It was constructed by Gaxar.'

'Gaxar!'

'Yes, but he is dead now. He – er – Konrad, he killed him in the catacombs of Altdorf when I escaped.' He glanced at his right arm. 'Or most of me.'

Konrad was watching Wolf, whose teeth were bared in rage, whose eyes were wide in anger, whose fists were clenched in fury, whose muscles were tensed in wrath.

Litzenreich had taken Konrad to Middenheim when he was trapped within the bronze armour; and deep below Middenheim was where Konrad had first encountered Gaxar in his skaven form. But long before that, it was Middenheim where Litzenreich had betrayed Wolf, leaving him to die. Evidently, this treachery had something to do with Gaxar. Was it the grey seer who had almost slain him?

Wolf and Gaxar...

IT SEEMED THAT nothing Konrad had ever done was of his own volition, he had merely been playing out the role assigned to him. No matter what he did, he was always restricted to the confines of the intricate web whose strands linked everyone he had ever known.

And now he sat and watched and listened while Wolf and Litzenreich planned the next part of his life; but first the sorcerer told Wolf of recent events in Middenheim and Altdorf.

'You've been busy, Konrad,' said Wolf. 'I always thought I'd encounter Gaxar again and settle my score with him, but it appears you've saved me the trouble.' He looked at Litzenreich, then continued, 'But with Gaxar dead, what about the impostor he created? Wouldn't that also have died?'

'Not necessarily,' answered Litzenreich. 'Gaxar must have reanimated a corpse, transforming it into a likeness of the Emperor. The doppelganger was already one of the undead, and so how could it die?'

'But without the skaven's wizardry to keep it whole, it would have rotted away.'

'The replica still exists, I am sure. Although its creation was the most difficult part, it can still fulfil its function. There are many other grey seers who can see to that. Even without Gaxar, the skaven can carry out their plan to replace the Emperor.'

This was what Konrad had previously surmised, but he knew that Litzenreich did not care about the Emperor. As the wizard had already admitted, it was warpstone that he wanted. There were skaven in Altdorf, and that meant there was warpstone there. But he had to convince Wolf that the skaven were still a danger to Karl-Franz, and that only he could counter the threat.

Perhaps it was even true, or some of it.

Litzenreich had been a skaven prisoner beneath Altdorf, and he had no wish to be captured again. He must have believed that his return to the capital would be less dangerous if he were aided by Wolf and Konrad, and if he aided them.

'Our interests are the same?' said Wolf, repeating Litzenreich's earlier words.

'Yes.'

Wolf shrugged. 'Maybe.'

'Yes,' Litzenreich insisted.

'Then we'll head for Altdorf together.'

For a moment, Konrad wondered if Litzenreich had persuaded Wolf by using his powers of mesmerism. The two were sitting opposite, and the wizard had been staring directly at Wolf while they conversed. But then Wolf glanced at Konrad, and from his expression Konrad knew that he would still like to slit Litzenreich's throat.

'Good,' said Litzenreich, raising his wine glass in a toast.

Wolf and Konrad lifted their tankards. Ustnar gazed out of the window to the darkened city, and he belched.

'When do we leave?' asked the sorcerer.

'As soon as our army is ready.'

'Our army?'

'Ustnar can be handy with his axe,' said Wolf, 'and you have a few tricks up your sleeve, but it will take more than that to get us into the capital. We're going to invade Altdorf with an army of mercenaries.'

'Do you think that is wise?'

'I don't know, but it's the best chance we've got.'

'If you march an army on Altdorf, they will know that we are coming.'

'They'll know as soon as I start recruiting. And we'll be going by river, not marching.'

'I see,' said Litzenreich, nodding his head. He took a sip of wine, then wiped his mouth with the back of his left hand. There was a vivid scar in the centre of his palm, where it had been nailed to the ground. 'A diversion? I also considered it would be best if we four went alone. That is what we do, while your army engages the city troops?'

'Yes.'

'Will it not take some considerable time to recruit these mercenaries?'

'Maybe.'

'I have a better idea.'

Wolf sighed. 'What?'

'Instead of hiring an army and then hiring boats to transport them, why not simply enlist a pirate ship or two? There are Imperial spies in Marienburg who will soon discover what has happened and report to the capital. But to make sure that they do hear about the proposed attack, I am sure the brigands could be persuaded to burn a few Reik villages on the voyage upstream.'

Wolf stared at Litzenreich. It was clear that he was impressed with the wizard's strategy, and it was equally apparent that he did not want to show how impressed.

'Maybe,' he said, and he nodded. 'We could leave the vessels long before Altdorf, because the authorities won't want the ships to get anywhere near the city. They'll probably blockade the river, so the pirates will never be able to attack, and send out troops to destroy them. That in itself should provide enough of a diversion for us to get into the capital.'

'Excellent,' said Litzenreich. 'We will save the Emperor from the skaven, and for my services I will claim whatever warpstone can be found.'

They would be up against far more than the skaven, thought Konrad, but that would probably make little difference to Litzenreich. The only thing that had ever interested him was warpstone, and the mutated rodents were the most likely source of the material. This was why he had planned to return to the Imperial capital even before he encountered Wolf and Konrad.

'Despite my talents,' added Litzenreich, as he glanced from Wolf to Konrad to Ustnar, 'I always like to have the backing of skilled fighters with ready blades.'

'You'll need a new sword, Konrad,' said Wolf.

'How about a bow and arrow?' said Konrad.

'Peasant weapon,' said Wolf, with a slight smile.

It was an arrow fired by Konrad which had saved Wolf from being sacrificed by a goblin shaman. The shaman had been the first to die when Konrad had entered the subterranean temple where Wolf was held a helpless hostage.

'You've never had a sword of your own, have you?' Wolf continued. 'It's time you did.' He touched the hilt of his black sword – and Ustnar reached for the handle of his axe.

'Magnin the steelsmith has a good reputation,' added Wolf, ignoring Ustnar. 'We could pay him a visit after we have concluded our business in Altdorf.'

'If you want a sword,' said Litzenreich, 'perhaps I can help.'

'You can make a *magic* sword?' sneered Wolf.

'Ustnar knows the best swordsmith in Marienburg,' said Litzenreich, referring to the dwarf for the first time. 'What's his name?'

'Barra,' grunted Ustnar.

'He made Ustnar's new axe. Would you recommend his craftsmanship?'

'Yes, boss.'

'If you want a sword, Barra is the one to make it.'

'Can I look at the axe?' asked Wolf, holding out his hand.

'You can look,' said Ustnar, as he demonstrated by glancing towards the double-bladed weapon. 'But the only way you can touch is with it buried in your skull.'

Wolf smiled. 'One of these days, Ustnar, we'll resume where we were interrupted today.' He turned to Konrad. 'You want a sword?'

Konrad shrugged. 'I haven't got a sword so I need one, but I don't know if I want my own. When it comes to combat, it's the man who matters, not the weapon.'

'It's the man *and* the weapon. While I find some pirates who would like to try their hand looting Altdorf, you can have a sword made. I'm sure Ustnar will be only too delighted to introduce you to Barra.'

Konrad and Ustnar looked at each other.

'Delighted,' muttered Ustnar.

'LITZENREICH CAN BE useful,' said Wolf, once the wizard and the dwarf had gone.

'He thinks that about us,' said Konrad.

'As long as he believes that about us, and we believe the same about him, then everything should work out. I'd rather have Litzenreich with us, because that way I know exactly where the bastard is.'

'Are we going to do what you said? Find a gang of pirates to attack Altdorf?'

'Yes.'

'How are you going to persuade them?'

'With promises of untold wealth – because Altdorf is the richest city in the Empire, in the Old World – and with lies. I'll convince them that the capital is a succulent fruit, ripe for the picking, and that I have the keys to the orchard.' He grinned. 'I read that in a book once, although I think it was about some harem in Araby.'

'Will they believe you?'

'I don't know, but that's my problem. You think about what type of sword you want. Once you have your own blade, hand-crafted to your own specifications, you will never want to use another sword.'

That was what concerned Konrad, and what he began thinking of when he went into his own room. Over the years he had lost so many blades; the one snatched from his grasp today was simply the latest in a long line. They had been broken in combat, or they had decayed through contact with venomous enemy blood.

A sword was a sword, a killing implement. Some were better than others, but he had learned how to handle all types. He had been taught by experts, frontier mercenaries whom Wolf had appointed as his tutors, and he had taught himself.

Although he felt exhausted, sleep refused to come. He was too busy considering the events of the last hours, and what was to happen between now and their arrival in Altdorf – and after.

They had been attacked by a swarm of skaven, which meant that their enemies already knew they were in Marienburg. Cities always made Konrad nervous, and he felt vulnerable. The tiny room in the Eight Bells was like a trap. In spite of the draught, he lay near the open window in the hope that he could leap down into the river below if the tavern were assaulted, and he kept his dagger in his hand.

Konrad thought about the scheme to attack Altdorf. It was meant as a diversion, so that the four of them could enter the city more easily. But what if the pirates succeeded in smashing through the city's defences? What if the corrupted Imperial guard and all the other armies of the damned that secretly dwelled in Altdorf joined the invaders to burn and loot and destroy the capital? Was that not exactly what the legions of Chaos wanted to happen?

All that was left of the Imperial capital would be decay and ruins, the ideal environment for the skaven. No longer would the ratbeasts inhabit labyrinthine lairs beneath the city, because the whole of Altdorf would have become theirs.

CHAPTER TWELVE

'Ustnar! How's the axe?'

'Fine.'

From Ustnar, that was a real compliment, probably the closest that he would ever come to a show of enthusiasm. His expression, however, remained as impassive as ever.

Barra was another dwarf, but his thick hair and bushy beard were almost white. He looked almost as wide as he was tall, his torso and limbs rippling with muscle. Despite the season, he was stripped to the waist, wearing only a kilt and sandals. He was covered in sweat and must have stepped outside to cool down.

Beyond the door against which Barra stood, Konrad glimpsed an incandescent glow and could feel searing waves of heat blasting from the furnace.

It was the day after Wolf and Litzenreich had agreed to join forces. Ustnar led Konrad through the city streets, across many of the bridges of Marienburg, and he did not say a word. Konrad had saved him from the skaven below Altdorf, but that seemed to count for nothing, certainly not for an acknowledgement. The dwarf must have believed that they were now even. He had liberated Konrad from a similar situation beneath Middenheim, although he had gone there to rescue his brother from the skaven. But Varsung was already dead, and so Ustnar and the two dwarfs with him had saved Konrad. The other dwarfs, Hjornur and Joukelm, were now also dead.

The armoury stood almost alone in a run-down area of the city, and all the nearby buildings were either boarded up or burned out. The forge itself must once have been derelict, but much of it had been mended with new planks of wood. Repairs were still in progress, and another dwarf was on the roof, replacing some broken slates. He looked young, but was probably twice Konrad's age. There was a raven sitting on his shoulder, as if supervising the work.

'Konrad wants a sword,' said Ustnar, nodding to Konrad.

Barra said something in the dwarf tongue, speaking very rapidly. Ustnar replied with equal speed, gesturing at Konrad. Although he understood some of the language, Konrad could make nothing of their exchange, although it was evident that Barra was angry.

Barra studied Konrad for a while, then slowly nodded. 'Can you pay?' he asked, in Old Worlder.

Konrad patted his pocket, and the gold crowns that Wolf had given him jingled together.

'Barra's favourite sound.'

'A special sword,' said Ustnar.

'A good sword,' said Konrad.

'Barra only makes good swords. Everything Barra makes is the best.' He gestured to the curved bars of metal lined along a pole by the door; they were what he must have been producing that morning. 'Even horseshoes.'

Having completed his task, Ustnar turned and walked away. Konrad and Barra watched him leave the courtyard.

'Barra would rather make a weapon than anything else.' He ran his hand over the row of horseshoes, clanging them against one another. 'But Barra has to make a living.'

'I want–'

Barra held up his hand and Konrad became silent.

'Barra knows what you want. Barra knows better than you what you want. Barra will make what Barra wants, which is what you want.'

'But–'

Another silencing gesture, and Konrad obliged.

'What do you know about swords?'

'I know how to use them.'

'You pull your sword from its scabbard, you fight, you kill, you put your sword back in its scabbard. What else do you know?'

Konrad was silent voluntarily, and he shrugged.

'Barra knows *everything* about swords. Barra knows what nobody else knows. And what Barra doesn't know, nobody else knows.'

'I know how a good sword feels,' said Konrad, holding out his right hand, imagining that he was gripping a sword hilt. It was the same with a horse, he supposed. He could handle any kind of mount, and he could soon tell which was the best sort of animal to ride, but he could not explain how he knew. There was a bond between rider and horse, just as there was a union between a swordsman and his blade.

'But Barra knows how to make a good sword, a great sword. And Barra will make one for you, aye?'

'Yes,' agreed Konrad.

Then Barra added: 'If Barra thinks you're good enough for one of Barra's swords–'

'What?'

'Lodnar!' Barra shouted up to the dwarf on the roof. 'Two swords!'

'What?' Konrad repeated. 'I'm going to have to prove myself before you'll make me a sword?'

'Aye. Ustnar brought you here, which counts for something. But you have to show you are worthy of Barra's art.'

'And the horses who will have those nailed to their hooves,' said Konrad, gesturing to the horseshoes, 'are they all worthy of your art?'

'That is Barra's craft,' said Barra. 'Blades are Barra's art.'

Although he felt annoyed with Barra, Konrad was also amused by the idea of having to prove himself. He watched as the young dwarf climbed down the ladder. When he reached the ground, the raven flew from his shoulder and returned to the roof directly above the door. Lodnar was slimmer than Barra, his beard dark red. He went inside the armoury. Half a minute later he returned holding two blades which he gave to Barra, who then presented one to Konrad.

It was an excellent sword, well balanced, properly weighted, with good keen edges which were parallel almost to the tip, which was as sharp at the cutting edges. Its handle was bound with soft leather, and Konrad went through a few swift manoeuvres with the blade – more for Barra's benefit than to test the sword. The weapon was one he would have been happy to own and use in combat. He was tempted to ask for a price. There seemed no need to have a sword specially forged when this one was more than suitable.

'Very fancy,' commented Barra, once Konrad had completed his imaginary duel. 'You move like a warrior, and from your scars you must have been in a few battles. But how well can you fight? Try a few passes.' He raised the sword in his right hand.

'You aren't worried that I might kill you?'

'You kill Barra, and Barra can't make you a sword.'

'But if I do kill you, does that mean I would have been a good enough swordsman for you to make me a blade if you were still alive?'

Barra laughed and suddenly thrust his sword at Konrad's belly. If Konrad had not blocked the blade and turned it aside, he would have had six inches of steel in his guts. Barra could have pulled back before striking – but would he have done?

They fought, and Konrad hardly held back at all. It was more difficult fighting an opponent whose blade came at a different angle than one who was the same height. Barra was an expert swordsman, which was rare for a dwarf; axes were their chosen weapon. His technique was not very stylish, and he tended to swing the blade as if it were indeed an axe, but his anticipation and reflexes were very fast. It seemed that he was doing his best to injure Konrad, and that he did not care too much whether it was a fatal wound.

To unnerve the dwarf, Konrad suddenly switched his blade to his left hand and continued fighting. He maintained his guard and did not go on the offensive, and after half a minute resumed fighting with his right hand. He feinted to the left, drew back swiftly as Barra's sword came chopping down at his arm, and made as if to pass his sword back to his left hand. Barra quickly moved to counter the next stroke, but then Konrad sprang forward, his blade outstretched and still in his right hand. He leaned back a moment later, and there was a red cross upon Barra's chest, two intersecting lines of blood marking where his heart lay.

Barra stepped away, and he gazed down at the blood which mingled with his sweating flesh. He lowered his sword.

'I'm not surprised you have to make your living with horseshoes,' said Konrad. 'How many customers do you kill?'

'Not many,' said Barra, and he smiled.

'But if you made Ustnar prove himself, I'm amazed that you're still alive.'

'Sometimes Barra is surprised Barra is alive.' His smile became a grin, and he handed his blade to Lodnar. 'Barra will make your sword, Konrad. But you tell no one, ever, who made your blade. Understand?' His expression had become serious once more.

Konrad nodded, realizing this must have been why Barra and Ustnar had argued: because Konrad knew who had made the dwarf's axe. Barra was not for hire; he chose those for whom he would make his weapons.

'Give Lodnar some money.' Barra turned and walked into the armoury.

Reluctantly, Konrad returned the sword, and he stuck his hand into his pocket.

'How much?'

Wolf had given him a handful of crowns, finally admitting where they had come from. It seemed that the ancient dwarf temple had not been entirely devoid of treasure. The huge lens through which light had been directed from the mountain into the depths below had been made from semi-precious stone. Although split and fragmented by Anvila's gunpowder, it had been worth a considerable amount.

'Ten crowns,' Lodnar replied. 'That's to make sure you're serious. Bring some more tomorrow.'

Konrad counted ten gold coins into the dwarf's palm. Lodnar pocketed the money and then began to ascend the ladder. The raven flew down onto his shoulder as he climbed.

'Will it be ready tomorrow?' asked Konrad.

Lodnar glanced down at him. 'Barra was right. You don't know much about swords.'

WHEN KONRAD RETURNED early the following morning, he found Ustnar standing in the courtyard with Lodnar. Lodnar was doing all the talking. The raven was up on the roof above the door, gazing down like a living emblem. And Litzenreich was in the forge with Barra. Konrad began to sweat as soon as he stepped into the heat, but the wizard seemed as comfortable as the dwarf.

'We were discussing your sword,' said Litzenreich.

'What's it got to do with you?' Konrad asked. If he was not allowed to tell Barra the kind of weapon he wanted, why should the sorcerer have any influence on the blade?

'If you are to be with me,' said Litzenreich, 'you must have the best sword there is. We are going into Altdorf, and you cannot even begin to guess the powers possessed by those we will be up against. You will need all the help you can get. You need a special sword.'

That was what Ustnar had told Barra the previous day, and now Konrad realized exactly what 'special' meant.

Warpstone...

'I'm having nothing to do with that stuff!'

'It is a little late for you to worry about that now,' Litzenreich said, 'do you not think?' Not wanting Barra to overhear him, he walked out of the smithy, gesturing for Konrad to follow.

'I don't want any more of it corrupting me,' said Konrad. 'And if Wolf knew what you were doing–'

'Do not tell him.'

As far as Wolf was concerned warpstone was 'evil', and he had closed his mind to all other possibilities. Galea must have explained the origin of warpstone to him, just as she had revealed its source to Konrad. Or did she tell different stories to everyone who visited her mysterious island? Konrad had not spoken to Wolf about Galea and her revelations. It was almost as if he had absorbed her wisdom but was unable to discuss what he had learned.

'If that sword has warpstone in it,' he said, 'I won't touch it.'

'You think I want to lose what little warpstone I have?' said Litzenreich. 'I have a small amount which came from those skaven on the bridge, and I am putting it to its best use. I need you, Konrad. You need a sword. Your sword needs warpstone. You must fight Chaos with Chaos, there is no other way.'

'But I am Chaos! I'm part of it. I'm so tainted by warpstone that the skaven can smell me!'

'We are all part of Chaos, and Chaos is part of us all. Warpdust in the sword will help balance your unwanted Chaotic tendencies. If you believe you are already damned, what have you to lose? But this could be your salvation.'

Konrad stared at Litzenreich, knowing that he could not be trusted, but realizing that it was a risk he must take.

'And with the warpstone,' added Litzenreich, 'you will have much more chance of succeeding with your mission in Altdorf – whatever it really is.'

The wizard evidently suspected that Konrad had other reasons for venturing up the Reik than to save Emperor Karl-Franz, and Konrad wondered if Litzenreich had his own secret mission to the Imperial capital.

Was he really returning there in order to find more warpstone? He was obsessed with the substance, and Konrad well knew that the wizard would do anything to obtain more supplies. He had already been arrested in the capital, charged with treason for his work with warpstone. If discovered in the city, he would face a death sentence. No one else would willingly return under such circumstances, but warpstone fever seemed to blind Litzenreich to any danger.

Finally, Konrad nodded his agreement.

'Tell him to proceed,' said Litzenreich, and Lodnar went into the forge.

Litzenreich and Ustnar stood outside, but Konrad moved towards the door, watching as Barra and Lodnar set to work.

Barra selected a number of strips of metal from various piles within the armoury: one of bright steel, one of dark iron, one which seemed to be silver, one that could have been bronze, another with a bluish tint that Konrad did not recognize. All were approximately the same dimension.

Meanwhile, Lodnar was heating up a small metal container in the furnace. It looked like a cast into which molten gold was poured to make into ingots. Removing it from the flames, he waited until it had cooled down before adding various oils and powders, mixing them up into a paste.

Barra examined the mixture, stirring it and adding a few more drops of thick liquid. He said something to Lodnar, and Lodnar went to fetch Litzenreich.

The sorcerer followed the dwarf inside, reaching behind his beard to produce an amulet which was on a chain around his neck. It was black, in the shape of an inverted pyramid – and must have held the warpdust which Ustnar had collected from the dead skaven on High Bridge.

Litzenreich removed the chain, opened the pyramid, and sprinkled grey powder into the paste. He shook the amulet with his one hand, making sure that none of the refined warpdust remained, then thoroughly stirred the mixture. He and Barra spoke in low voices, and the dwarf picked up the first piece of metal he had selected. With a small brush, Litzenreich daubed the warpdust mixture over the surface of the steel. He did this four times, and each time another bar of metal was placed on top, so that the potion formed a layer between the five different metals. Bound together with wire, it made a bundle approximately the size of a broadsword.

Replacing his amulet, Litzenreich left the forge. He stepped past Konrad, but then stopped and glanced down.

'What is that?' he asked.

Konrad looked down at the pattern he had idly been marking in the dirt with a stick. He had drawn the coat of arms on the bow and arrows Elyssa had given him, but the mailed fist had been too difficult and he had wiped that part away with his boot.

'Two crossed arrows,' he said. 'Why?'

'Two?' said Litzenreich. 'Or four?'

He bent down. Where Konrad had sketched the arrow flights, Litzenreich rubbed them away and added arrow points. The two arrows now had heads at either end.

'That's still only two,' said Konrad, puzzled.

Litzenreich used his one index finger to draw two lines across the point where the arrows intersected, one vertical, one horizontal. He added an arrowhead at each end. The pattern was like the spokes of a wheel.

'The eight arrows of Chaos,' said the sorcerer. He stood up and showed Konrad the black amulet around his neck.

And on each inverted triangular surface a tiny pattern had been etched in gold: the same pattern which Litzenreich had drawn in the dirt.

'It is a symbol avoided by all but Dark Wizards,' said Litzenreich, then he turned and walked away. Ustnar followed.

When Konrad glanced down, Litzenreich's amendments to the pattern had vanished. All that remained was what Konrad had sketched. He scuffed the design with his boot, trying not to consider whether the elven crest really included a symbol of Chaos, and glanced in through the door of the smithy.

Barra had placed the stack of metal sideways upon the glowing coals of the furnace. While Lodnar pumped a pair of bellows, fanning the heat, he studied the end of the bundle in the hottest part of the fire. This began to change colour as its temperature increased, and the substance between the different strips started to bubble and hiss.

Konrad moved closer, watching what the dwarfs were doing. They took no notice of him. Although he was several yards from the forge, the heat was extremely intense, and after a few minutes he stripped off his outer garments.

After a few minutes more, Barra used a pair of tongs to lift the metal from the forge onto the anvil, and began pounding a heavy hammer against the glowing end of the bar with regular strokes. He kept stopping, examining his handiwork, turning the five strips, then hammering again until he was satisfied. The metal had grown darker as it cooled, and he used pincers to untwist the loop of wire lower down the bar, then lifted the bundle back into the fire. This time it was the area from which he had removed the wire that was positioned in the hottest part of the furnace. When he deemed that the metal had reached the correct temperature, he again swung it across to the anvil and began hammering once more. He repeated the process until the whole bar had received the same treatment. It was longer than it had been, and wider, and the five different strips were now welded into one solid bar.

Then Barra and Lodnar went outside to cool down, each swallowing several cups of water. Konrad followed them and wished that it was a Kislev winter.

'You don't mind working with warpstone?' he said to Barra.

Barra roared with laughter. 'Albion, where I come from, is far to the north, where the children build castles out of warpmud. There's so much warpstone there, it's in Barra's blood.' His fat fingers touched the cross which Konrad had made above his heart.

'And you?' Konrad asked Lodnar.

'It's just another job to me.'

'What about Ustnar's axe, does that have warpstone in it?'

'That's confidential,' said Barra. 'Between Ustnar and Barra. You could try asking him.'

Konrad knew he could try, but he also knew it would be a waste of time. 'To work,' said Barra. 'You coming back inside?'

Wolf had made it clear that he was conducting very delicate negotiations and that it was best if he ventured amongst the pirate lords alone. Neither Ustnar nor Litzenreich were Konrad's ideal companions, and he knew no one else in Marienburg. He could have gone for a drink in one of the city's many taverns, and after the intensity of the heat that would probably have been the best course of action. But he had become oddly interested in what Barra and Lodnar were doing, and so he said, 'Yes.'

They went back within the armoury, where Lodnar placed the tip of a strong chisel a third of the way from one end of the metal bar, and hammered most of the way through. He did the same halfway along the remaining length, then beat both of the ends over and down, so making the bar a third as long but three times as thick. More of the oily warpdust paste was daubed between the different sections, and one end was placed deep into the red-hot coals. The process of heating and hammering, hammering and heating, resumed until the bar of metal had become one solid piece fifteen layers thick.

So it continued all day, and the next, and Konrad handed over ten crowns, then ten more.

Each evening Ustnar arrived at the forge, to take the warp paste and the metal in which the raw essence of Chaos had been captured to Litzenreich for safekeeping during the hours of darkness. Litzenreich and Ustnar stayed at a different tavern each night, and Konrad wondered if the wizard hoped that the odour of warpdust would attract the skaven, and he would thus be able to obtain more of the enigmatic substance.

BY THE END of the third day there were three hundred and sixty thin layers of metal welded together. Konrad had kept count, and each had warpdust between itself and the next layer. Every patina was very thin, but because of the different colours they were all perfectly visible. Barra referred to the metal bar as a 'billet,' and it was approximately the same dimensions as when it had started out as five separate strips; the size of a sword.

'Tomorrow,' said Barra, 'the real work begins. Assuming that the skaven don't steal the billet away during the night. Once you carry it, they'll be drawn to that sword like mice to cheese!'

Barra laughed, but Konrad did not. Then he realized that it would make no difference. The ratbeasts could already smell the warpstone which flowed through his veins. His sword would attract no more attention than his tainted flesh.

'It won't only be skaven, of course,' Barra continued. 'You will have such a wonderful sword, everyone will want it! You'll have to kill more people, more non-people, just because of your blade. But because of the blade, it will be easier for you to defeat them. You need a good sword because you have a good sword; and because you have a good sword, you need a good sword.' He laughed again.

Although he was not sure how serious Barra was, Konrad knew what the dwarf meant. Robbers were more likely to choose their victims from amongst the wealthy, or those who appeared wealthy. If Konrad carried a blade which seemed to be valuable, he would attract more attention to himself. From the preliminary work Barra had put into the blade, Konrad already knew that it would be an exceptionally fine piece of workmanship.

'In that case,' he said, 'make it look like any other sword – until it is drawn. I don't want fancy quillons or an elaborate pommel, and the scabbard will be no more than functional.'

Barra had said he would make the sword the way he wanted to, but now he nodded in agreement. It would be several more days, however, before the sword was ready for its quillons and pommel.

The days passed, and Konrad was there for every minute, every hour, watching as Barra continued with his craft, his art, whilst Lodnar assisted him as he meticulously transformed the raw metal into a perfect battle blade.

The shape of the sword slowly appeared: the bevelled edges, the gradual tapering, the angle of the point, the groove down the centre of each surface. Twice the entire blade was heated in the furnace and suddenly plunged into a deep trough of water, which hissed furiously, giving off clouds of steam. This was the tempering process, by which the metal was hardened. All the time there was more hammering, filing and grinding, with a vast array of different hammers and instruments and tools used at the various stages; and in between there was always polishing and oiling, oiling and polishing. Barra never once took a single measurement. Everything was done by eye, by touch, by years of experience, by skill, by art.

The quillons were welded in place, solid steel, dark and functional, slightly upswept. The handle was wrapped in brown suede. It gave a good grip, being absorbent enough to soak up blood and sweat, and it could easily be replaced when it became saturated. The pommel was screwed into place on the end of the tang, a simple brass ball. Quillons, handle, pommel, they were as ordinary as could be. But the blade, the blade itself...

'Unless it's a two-hander,' explained Barra, 'a sword should be balanced about three inches from the quillons. The way a blade is made affects its balance, of course, the size and cross-section, but so does the weight of the pommel. Barra believes it is always best to have a small pommel, and this should be exactly right for the sword – and for you.'

Konrad was itching to hold the weapon, but Barra kept a firm grip upon it, explaining various points of its construction.

'By hollowing out these grooves on either side, the blade becomes lighter, yet without losing any strength. All the different layers of metal make the sword far more flexible and stronger. There is warpdust in there, as you know. There is also silver.' Barra sucked in his lower lip, baring his upper teeth. 'Good for vampires!' he laughed.

'Yes,' agreed Konrad, reaching out towards the polished weapon.

'And because of all the layers,' said Barra, drawing the blade away, 'the edge itself is far tougher and lasts longer. Resharpening is not too difficult, you'll find. Make sure that it's done evenly on both sides, slowly, a few inches at a time.'

'Yes, yes.'

'Barra will give you a whetstone, at no extra charge.'

Barra gripped the sword in his right hand, holding it up, turning it, inspecting it for flaws. It glinted in the red glow from the furnace. He walked outside, and Konrad followed. There was a wagon in the courtyard, and Lodnar was holding the blinkered horse which stood between the shafts. The animal seemed very nervous. Whatever was on the back of the wagon was hidden by a huge piece of canvas. Lodnar handed Barra a key.

'You must have heard stories of swordsmiths plunging new blades into living flesh to temper the metal,' said Barra, as he went towards the rear of the wagon.

Konrad nodded, and by now he knew what was under the canvas. He could smell it.

'It doesn't work. Barra has tried it. Heat softens a blade, and although a body might seem soft it's full of bones which can damage the hot metal. And after all that work, who wants that? A quenching tank filled with blood, however, can be quite effective.'

He pulled the canvas from the back of the wagon to reveal a cage – and inside the cage was a beastman.

The ugly creature roared at the sudden light, and rattled the solid bars with the claws of one arm; the lower joint of its other front limb had mutated into a curved blade. Over six feet tall, with a snake-like tail, it was covered in greenish scales. There was a crest of yellow spines on its head and its face was like that of a bird, with a sharp beak and tiny black eyes. Venom dripped from its fangs, and the claws and the talons on its feet were all razor sharp.

'This thing was captured last week,' said Barra. 'It got into the city through the sewers and killed three children who were playing by one of the canals. Or at least Barra hopes it killed them before it ripped them open and ate their guts.'

'Why wasn't it destroyed when it was caught?'

'Because it's valuable. They're used in sporting contests, battles against others of their kind, or against a pack of dogs, perhaps even against humans. Beast baiting. Sometimes fighting mutants are bred in captivity. It's illegal, but there's a lot of money to be made from gambling.'

'What's it doing here?' asked Konrad, although he was beginning to suspect.

'I bought it,' said Barra, glazing up at his growling captive. 'It may be a myth about plunging a red hot blade into living flesh, but it's a nice idea. Barra is a traditionalist, as you'll have noticed, which is why it takes so long to make a sword – and why Barra's swords are the best. And, although Barra says so, your blade is one of the very best. Barra makes the swords, then they are gone. That does not seem right. Barra ought to use this blade before you do, because it was Barra's blade before yours. Barra claims the right of first blood, to sacrifice it as an offering to Barra's own gods – the gods of Barra's ancestors, the gods of fire, of steel, of weapons.'

He reached up to the cage and slipped the key into the lock, turned it, then quickly sprang back as the barred door burst open and the reptilian mutant leapt free. Its ravenous jaws parted and its forked tongue rippled, loudly voicing its inhuman challenge.

Before its legs even touched the ground Barra darted forward again, the gleaming blade slicing through the scales of its deformed torso. A geyser of bestial blood erupted from the wound, and only then did the monster scream. The blade was so sharp it had not felt it slide through its repulsive body.

Spurting blood and spitting venom, howling out its anger and its agony, the brute towered above Barra. With a single slice of its mutated forelimb it could have split the dwarf in twain; a blow from its lashing tail could have crushed his skull.

The sword-limb slashed, but Barra dodged aside with agility, fending off the chitinous blade with the new weapon. The beastman's jaws snapped, its claws grabbed, its tail whipped, and Barra answered every assault with a thrust or a slice from the warpblade. He seemed to have grown in skill as a swordsman, his expertise increasing to match the magnificence of the blade which he wielded.

The mutant bellowed more loudly each time that Barra spilled more of its poisonous blood, and it grew more reckless in its assaults. But every advance was in vain, and the brute was unable to defend itself; attack was all it knew, what every primeval instinct commanded.

Roars of defiance were transformed into cries of desperation as it suffered more remorseless punishment. The beast's movements became slower and more clumsy as it was gradually cut to pieces, screaming out its alien agony as it slowly bled to death.

The dwarf did not hack at the thing, dismembering it by sheer force, but instead he carefully dissected its living body as a butcher would divide a carcass: flaying the outer layers, eviscerating the offal, carving the flesh, stripping the bones.

And the creature would not die. It was still screeching, still twitching, even though its body was a gory mass of flesh and blood and bones, when Barra ceased his vivisection and stepped back to examine the sword. Then he advanced once again, raised the blade and brought it down fast, severing scale and sinew, breaking bones and blood vessels in the final execution. The beastman's head rolled away, still screeching, while the body kept twitching in an ugly parody of life.

Barra leaned the sword against the wagon wheel, and the blade was greasy with fresh blood. He moved back, gazing at the weapon, then gestured towards it.

'It's yours,' he said, and he walked away towards the armoury.

'Here,' said Lodnar, and he handed Konrad a rag in exchange for the last payment of gold crowns.

Konrad walked across the cobbles, which were sticky with gore, and he took hold of the sword hilt in his right hand. Without lifting the weapon from the ground, he knelt down and slowly wiped it clean with a single downward sweep of the rag. As he did so, he saw the blade in close detail for the first time.

It was truly magnificent.

The surface was like quicksilver, seeming to shimmer if viewed from a slightly different angle. There were ripples upon the blade, like jewels with infinitely different facets, some of them whirlpools of iridescence which became more intense as they spiralled inwards, others coruscating prisms which radiated across the whole length of the metal.

The hollow down the centre was like a valley worn away over the aeons, revealing different strata of ancient rock: a whole rainbow of colours which had been formed from the original five layers of metal.

And the tip of the blade, so sharp, and the edges, so keen, they were a colour beyond the spectrum. Far more than the sum of their original hues, they had been multiplied by the addition of fire and air, by the water to quench and the coals to burn; the elements of the world. Every constituent layer of metal could still be distinguished where the blade narrowed at its killing edges: all three hundred and sixty levels, the five component metals tripled and doubled and doubled, then tripled and doubled once again.

Finally Konrad lifted the sword, feeling its weight, sensing its balance, holding the weapon firmly in his grip.

He raised the new sword high above his head, as though triumphant victory were already his.

It was as if the warblade had always been a part of him.

CHAPTER THIRTEEN

UNTIL THE PREVIOUS week, Konrad had paid little attention to whatever sword he carried. It was simply a weapon, and it was of no consequence how it had been made or where it came from. He had possessed many blades, but the only thing that mattered was whether they served their required function.

After what he had seen recently, he would view even the lowliest of daggers with respect. It, too, had once been a piece of shapeless metal, given form by the skills of a village blacksmith. And long before that, the metal had been a lump of ore, dug out of the ground and refined and made into ingots. Konrad had some knowledge of that kind of process, having seen the way that gold was produced at the mine in Kislev.

He thought about the five metals which had gone to make up his new sword, and he wondered where they had been originally mined. Had each come from a different region of the world, brought from distant continents and across vast oceans so they could be welded into one blade?

On the frontier, metals from broken weapons were often melted down and used again. But the blades of defeated Chaos renegades were never used, because they would corrupt any untainted metal, causing it to corrode and rust very swiftly. All kinds of metal were precious, and it seemed likely that some of the materials which Barra had fabricated into the new sword had once formed part of other weapons, weapons used by warriors in far-off lands who had fought in ancient battles. The men who had carried such blades were long gone, nothing but dust, and yet their weapons had been reincarnated in Konrad's exquisite sword.

And some day, long after Konrad was dead and forgotten, his own blade would have become part of a whole armoury of weapons carried by a legion of tomorrow's fighting men: spears and axes, lances and swords, knives and arrowheads.

All Konrad could hope was that such a time was very distant, and that his new blade would postpone the final day when he must inevitably fall in battle.

As he gazed up the River Reik, however, he realized that the voyage was bringing that day closer and closer. He was convinced that Skullface and Elyssa were still in Altdorf. As if he still had the gift of premonition, he *knew* that he would meet up with them both once he reached the Imperial capital. He also knew that he would not survive his confrontation with Skullface. But this encounter was what his whole life had been leading up to, and he could no more prevent himself from completing the voyage than he could have made himself stop breathing.

Konrad spent as much time as possible on deck, because he felt too confined if he remained below. His hand was on the pommel of his blade as he glanced up at the sails of the pirate vessel.

Just as he had never given any thought to how a sword was made, neither until now had he considered how a ship could sail upriver, against the flow of the water and also against the wind.

His first boat ride had been along the River Lynsk, upstream from Erengrad to Praag, and Konrad had paid very little attention to the ship and how it operated. He was too interested in watching the new land through which he was passing. Now, however, he was studying the vessel all the time, because that was preferable to considering what lay ahead once he reached Altdorf.

Wolf had arranged for two corsairs to sail towards the Imperial capital, persuading them that the city was vulnerable to assault because the army had been so depleted by the number of troops who had been sent to defend the Kislev frontier. He had also convinced the pirate chiefs that he was the only person who could unlock the secret of the city's untold wealth. Each ship was an ordinary merchant vessel, but its cargo was far from ordinary. The lower decks were packed with ruthless desperadoes, men whose whole life was devoted to death and destruction, to attacking helpless ships and looting their cargoes. They normally had two enemies, the craft they attacked and also the ocean. The sea could be a more implacable and dangerous opponent than the pirates themselves, but upon the Reik they had no such enemy with which to contend.

Instead, they were hidden beneath the hatches, kept quiet by uncounted barrels of ale, and whatever amusements they themselves had brought on board. They were not very quiet, however. Only at night were they allowed on deck, when the two vessels had tied up during the hours of darkness.

The ships stayed far apart, as if they were unconnected. Wolf's plan was that the first vessel should enter Altdorf and tie up at one of the port's many berths. The second would then show its true colours, reveal the guns which had been disguised as deck cargo, and begin firing upon the capital. The cannon had been transferred on board from the fast ocean-going ships in which the pirates usually set sail; they were huge, cast from solid metal and decorated with dragons and strange hieroglyphics. They had been built in Cathay, and the gunners were also from that fabled continent. Both ships were crewed by men from all over the world.

The cannon attack would be a diversion, during which the pirates on board the first vessel would begin their assault from within the city walls. Or that was what Wolf had told the pirates...

He and Konrad, Litzenreich and Ustnar, were on board the first of the two ships. Marienburg was very lax in its regulations, and the vessel had weighed anchor and sailed upstream without being inspected. There were a number of places on the Reik where it halted under the shadow of a fortress and was made to pay river dues. The fees payable depended upon the cargo being carried, but the majority of customs officials preferred to negotiate without having to board the vessels they should have examined. They were used to dealing with smugglers, and as long as their own personal charges were met they were happy to impose arbitrary official rates.

The Reik was the most important river in the Empire, in all of the Old World. Its headwaters lay far to the southeast, within the World's Edge Mountains. One of its sources was a spring in Black Fire Pass, which according to legend had originally bubbled to the surface when Sigmar first set down Ghal-maraz after his triumphant victory over the goblins.

This made the Reik the longest of all rivers, and it also carried the greatest number of vessels, craft of every type and dimension. So wide and so deep were its waters that ocean-going ships could navigate as far as the capital. Even the tallest of masts did not need to be lowered to pass beneath bridges, because every bridge on the river had a central section which could either be raised or swung aside to permit passage.

The pirate ship made its way slowly upstream, past the villages and towns which had grown up on the banks of the great river. All of them must have been tempting targets for the raiders, despite the brooding castles which stood high on the outcropping rocks above each centre of habitation.

They passed isolated farmsteads, lonely windmills, terraced fields where vines grew, and mile after mile of impenetrable forest. The river was seldom straight for very long, was always twisting between high valleys or meandering across fertile pasture, and all the time it carried the vessel closer to Altdorf.

The days passed, and the nights, and Konrad was glad that his sword seemed so ordinary. Any one of the pirates would have slain him for his blade, even though they were meant to be allies. They must all have killed for far less, and the same was true of their officers. Konrad seldom saw the captain of the ship; it was the first officer who handled all the daily routine.

He came from the Estalian Kingdoms, and he gave his name as Guido. He said he could not reveal his family name, because he was of royal blood and preferred to hide his identity. The best way to have hidden it, thought Konrad, was not to admit that one was trying to do so.

'I ran away to sea,' said Guido, 'and now I'm surrounded by land. It makes me ill looking at it, the way it keeps still all the time.'

Guido was about thirty years old, of medium height but slender build, and he was far removed from Konrad's idea of a pirate. He was cultured and educated, and perhaps really was of high birth. Always dressed in the finest of clothes, which he changed every day, the others on board the ship obeyed his every order with utmost alacrity. His authority came from his position, not his physical strength. The only time there had been any trouble on board was when a topsail was not rigged to Guido's satisfaction. The two men responsible were immediately flogged, and Guido watched while the cabin boy gave him his regular morning shave. Even Captain de Tevoir treated his first officer with respect, almost as if it were Guido who were the ship's master.

'My ancestors were bandits and brigands,' said Guido. 'They carved out a slice of Estalia hundreds of years ago, and established themselves as rulers. But there was no place for me there. My eldest brother inherited the throne from my father before I was even born. It was lucky he let me survive. Lucky for me, but not for him. One day I'll return, depose Alphonso and seize my father's kingdom for myself.' He shrugged. 'If I can ever be bothered going back to that dump.'

He watched as a sailing barge passed slowly by, heading downstream. His gaze was predatory, and he must have wished that he could drop his vessel's masquerade and loot the passing vessel.

At first, Konrad tried to avoid Guido. He did not want to have too many dealings with a man he would have to betray, and perhaps even kill. But it was difficult to stay far away on the deck of such a small ship, and they began to spend more and more time in each other's company. Guido loaned him books, histories the like of which Konrad had never imagined.

It took a while for him to realize that he had been reading mere fables, invented tales whose resemblance to actual events was very remote. Once he discovered this, and knew that he did not have to study the books as diligently as all the others he had previously read, he enjoyed the improbable adventures considerably. And Guido's own tales were almost as wildly spectacular as those which Konrad had read.

In the years since he had left his native village, Konrad had travelled from one side of the Empire to the other, and even beyond. But Guido had travelled from one end of the world, completely circumnavigating the globe, before returning to where he had begun.

Konrad had no idea how much was true, or how much of what Guido related had actually happened to the pirate himself, but he was fascinated by the tales of all the different lands and the people and creatures who dwelled there.

'I've been everywhere,' Guido said, 'seen every kind of person – and killed every kind!' He drew his finger across his throat as he spoke, smiling grimly.

It was only on such occasions that Konrad recalled who he was dealing with: a cold-blooded killer, someone who would murder a helpless baby without hesitation. That was Guido's life – to kill and to plunder – and that was why he and his ship were heading towards Altdorf. He was after the richest prize in the Old World, the Imperial capital itself. It was of no consequence how many had to suffer or die so long as Guido and his comrades showed a profit from their marauding voyage.

They passed safely beyond Carroburg, where the River Bogen flowed into the Reik, and finally came to a halt some twenty miles upstream from the capital, between the villages of Rottefach and Walfen.

'It's time for us to go ashore,' Wolf told the captain. 'We must go ahead and reconnoitre.'

For almost the first time since leaving Marienburg, all three of Konrad's companions were on deck together. Many of the crew were aloft in the rigging, furling the sails; others were securing the vessel to the riverbank.

'But of course,' agreed de Tevoir. 'You'll get horses in the next village?'

'Yes.'

'You will only need two.'

'Two?' said Wolf, and a moment later his hand was on the hilt of his black sword.

Konrad reacted simultaneously, as he also realized what the captain meant, and he began to draw his new blade for the first time. But neither of them was fast enough, and in moments they were ensnared by the ropes which had been dropped down onto them by the sailors on the spars above. Litzenreich and Ustnar were also caught, although the dwarf was able to tear his way through the first coils which looped around him. Before he could swing his axe, however, he was clubbed senseless and fell to the deck.

'Two horses,' said Captain de Tevoir. 'One for you, one for him.' He gestured towards Litzenreich. 'Be back here by dawn, or else these two die.'

It was almost noon, and Konrad turned as he saw another vessel rounding the bend downstream. He recognized the second pirate ship. They were joining up for the first time since leaving port.

'That isn't enough time,' said Wolf.

'Dawn,' de Tevoir repeated. 'Both of you be back here by then, or–'

'We'll be back,' agreed Wolf, and he looked at Konrad.

'And by then you'll have fixed it so we can all sail peacefully into Altdorf together.'

'Naturally,' said Wolf, as though that had been his intention from the very start.

The captain gave a command, and the mercenary and the magician were released from the ropes which had trapped them.

'If you're not here,' added de Tevoir, 'we're still sailing upstream – only there won't be as many of us on board.' He used his cutlass to indicate his captives, in case Wolf was unsure who he meant.

Konrad struggled against his bonds, but to no avail. Instead he was seized and bound more tightly, tied upright against the mainmast. His belt was unbuckled, his new sword taken away. He had never had a chance to draw the blade, never fought in combat, never shed enemy blood.

Guido leaned on the bulwark, watching as Wolf and Litzenreich departed. He turned around as Ustnar was hauled to his feet and securely lashed to the same mast as Konrad. They stood back to back, and the first officer walked slowly across the deck to stand in front of Konrad. He held out his hand, and one of the pirates handed him Konrad's sword belt.

'If it was me,' he said, 'I wouldn't come back.'

'They aren't you,' said Konrad.

'No, but you think they'll come back?'

Konrad said nothing.

'Would you?' asked Guido.

'Yes.'

Guido nodded slowly. 'You probably would; Wolf probably would; the sorcerer wouldn't.'

That was what had been bothering Konrad. Litzenreich thought only of himself. He would not return, not even to help Ustnar. Even if he were not in danger, Litzenreich would do nothing that was not in his own interest. And returning to the pirate vessel could certainly be excluded from that category.

'But they both must return,' said Guido, turning his head towards the south-east, towards Altdorf. He glanced at the weapon he was carrying, took hold of the scabbard in his left hand and the hilt in his right, then began slowly drawing the blade from its oiled sheath.

'Nice,' he said. 'Very nice indeed.'

'IF IT WAS up to me,' said Guido, that afternoon, 'I'd untie you, Konrad. But I have to follow orders. And I suppose you wouldn't want to be unbound if the dwarf was kept tied. I could trust you, but not him. You see my dilemma – and yours?'

'Just shut up, will you?' said Konrad, angrily.

'It annoys you, does it, my talking? In that case, I'll keep on talking.'

Konrad felt very weary, and his limbs were stiff. He had been expertly tied; he could hardly move, yet the ropes did not cut excessively into his flesh or impede the circulation of his blood.

'We aren't stupid,' Guido continued, 'or at least some of us aren't. Did you really think we would let all of you leave? In our business, we often take hostages. Some people are too valuable to kill, and they can be held for ransom.

'How much are you worth, Konrad? Is there anyone who would pay for your freedom? No? It's the same with me. We are so alike, you and I. We both have only one name, although I doubt somehow that you are of noble blood. And speaking of blood, it seems that you will soon be losing a great deal of yours. As well as your life, of course.

Have you ever thought much about blood, Konrad? Why do we have it, I wonder? What is it for?'

Guido paused, as if considering the nature of blood, then said, 'Would you like me to read to you, Konrad? Would you like to hear a fabulous tale of distant Lustria?'

'No.'

'A story of what once happened to an unfortunate wastrel in Naggaroth?'

'No.'

'What about one of my own adventures in Araby?'

'No!'

'There's no pleasing some people.' Guido sighed, but he was becoming more amused at Konrad's irritation. 'One day, you realize, I will be telling of how I took part in the sack of Altdorf. It will go down in history. Such a pity you won't see the great event. You will be there, let me assure you, tied to one of the yardarms. Captain de Tevoir thinks that the bodies of his most recent victims bring the ship good luck. I wonder how he will have you killed?'

Konrad bit his lower lip, forcing himself not to respond.

'I think it should be with your own sword. Quite appropriate, and poetic, don't you think? I'd consider it an honour to execute you, Konrad. And, believe me, it would be done swiftly and as painlessly as possible.'

Konrad bit even harder, tasting blood. He clenched his fists and closed his eyes. Would he be the first human victim of the magnificent blade which had been made especially for him?

'But what about the dwarf? What should I do with him? Cut off his head with his axe?'

'Why don't you shove your own head up your arse?' grunted Ustnar, speaking for the first time since his capture. 'That's where your mouth already is.'

'We could do that with your ugly head,' said Guido. 'Would that be your dying wish?'

'Go mutate!' growled Ustnar.

'Perhaps we could hold a contest between the two of you,' Guido suggested. 'You fight each other. That would produce one of your deaths. The crew love to watch such duels, it saves them having to fight each other. Human against dwarf, sword against axe. You could use each other's weapon. Perhaps I should suggest that to de Tevoir.'

'You seem very certain that Wolf and Litzenreich won't return,' said Konrad – although he felt almost certain himself.

'I know they won't return,' said Guido. 'Ah well, I can't stand around talking all day. Unlike you two, I have work to do.'

The rest of the day passed by slowly. It seemed to Konrad that there were fewer boats on the river than usual, but he could have been imagining it. He kept imagining all kinds of things – that a war fleet from Altdorf was about to attack the pirate ships, while an army battalion did the same from the shore; that Wolf and Litzenreich would return to rescue him and Ustnar.

But nothing happened. The ships lay quietly against the side of the river, their timbers creaking as they rocked gently back and forth.

On board, the crew sharpened their swords and their knives, making ready for their impending assault on the greatest city of the Old World.

Night fell, and with the darkness came the cold. Mannslieb rose to the east, but never climbed far above the horizon, setting a few hours later.

Morrslieb made no appearance. Konrad would have welcomed the lesser moon, despite its spectral light. No lanterns had been lit on deck, the two ships blending in with the night. He gazed up at the stars, unable to sleep, not wishing to sleep, and wondered if he would live to see another dawn.

He woke to the sound of soft footsteps on the deck, at first angry that he had fallen asleep, then on edge because of what he had heard. The sky was still black, without any hint of impending sunrise. They could not be coming for him yet, he realized, and he had detected only one pair of footsteps.

There were two guards positioned nearby, and it was not they who were moving. The sound was so faint that it seemed neither of them had heard it. Perhaps they had also fallen asleep. Konrad listened as the first sailor was killed. It was done so expertly that the second crewman knew nothing about it. Then once again came the sound of a blade slicing through a throat, and another body crumpled onto the deck.

Konrad felt the ropes which held him being cut, and he turned, trying to see Wolf's face.

'Let's get out of here,' a familiar voice whispered to him and Ustnar.

It was familiar, but it was not Wolf – it was Guido.

This was not a time for questions, and he and the dwarf followed the dim shape of the first officer as he led them to one side of the ship, down a rope ladder and into the small boat waiting for them. Guido took the oars and began rowing upstream. They made their way slowly against the current, away from the two corsairs, and towards Altdorf. Guido rowed for an hour, by which time the sky had begun to redden above the hills in the east. He turned the boat towards the south bank of the river, running it onto the mud.

'Here,' he said, shipping the oars and then reaching behind him. He produced Konrad's sword and Ustnar's axe.

Konrad stood up and buckled on his sword belt; Ustnar gazed at Guido, then slung the axe across his back; and the three of them climbed from the boat and dragged it ashore, hiding the frail craft in the thick foliage a few yards from the river bank.

'What's going on?' asked Konrad.

'Wolf recruited me in Marienburg,' said Guido. 'He knew that de Tevoir would never allow you all to leave. It was my job to get anyone who was left off the ship.'

'What's in it for you?' asked Ustnar, eyeing him suspiciously.

'I think it may be healthier to be on land than on board ship today, and also far more profitable.'

It seemed Guido still believed that it was Wolf's intention to raid the Imperial treasury – and maybe, thought Konrad, it was...

'Wolf and Litzenreich are waiting for us in Altdorf,' said Guido, 'but the two ships will reach the city first. By the time we get there, it should be quite lively.'

CHAPTER FOURTEEN

GUIDO WAS WRONG in one respect: the two pirate ships did not reach Altdorf before they did. The one upon which Konrad and Ustnar had been held captive was sunk by the Imperial forces that had attempted to block the river. The other vessel succeeded, however, its guns blasting a fiery passage through the defensive flotilla. It sailed on up the Reik towards the capital.

The three of them had managed to pass upstream of the blockading ships before the battle commenced, and they watched the conflict from the riverbank. Units of the Altdorf city guard were patrolling each side of the river, to kill any survivors from the fir st corsair, and to ensure that no hostile battalions could reach the city by land. They probably believed the river boats were part of a combined assault.

It took quite a while for Konrad, Ustnar and Guido to evade all the patrols. After his hours of confinement, the dwarf was eager for action, to seek vengeance for what had happened to him, and it did not really matter who he killed. At one point they were hiding only a dozen yards from a foot patrol. Ustnar gripped his axe tightly, as if restraining the weapon, that without him it would launch itself at the soldiers. He recognized that he must subdue his bloodlust for a while. They were far too outnumbered and could not take on the military might of the city's army and hope to survive.

Once they reached Altdorf, Konrad realized, they would be up against far more than the army. Everyone was their enemy: the pirates who were attacking the city, as well as the forces who were defending it, and also all the creatures of damnation who dwelled beneath the capital. And what of the Imperial guard? Had every human who wore the uniform of the Emperor's bodyguard been subverted, become transformed into a slave of Chaos?

Long before they came in sight of the white walls of the city, they heard the sound of gunfire once again. Altdorf was under bombardment from the surviving pirate ship. They saw many fires within the capital, and clouds of thick black smoke rose from the various conflagrations. It seemed that Wolf had conjured up the diversion he had wanted.

'Where is Wolf?' Konrad asked.

'We meet him at sunset,' said Guido.

It would be almost then by the time they reached the city. Their journey had been long and slow, keeping away from all the woodland tracks in order to avoid the soldiers.

'And Litzenreich?' asked Ustnar.

'Who knows?' said Guido.

Konrad wondered if the wizard had been aware when he left the ship that Wolf had arranged for Guido to release de Tevoir's hostages – even though Konrad and Ustnar themselves did not know – or whether he even cared. But Litzenreich had made sure that Konrad's new weapon had included warpstone in its fabrication, and he knew the sorcerer never did anything without a reason.

Ustnar would do whatever Litzenreich required. Guido seemed to be after as much plunder as he could steal.

Having arranged the voyage to Altdorf and all the current mayhem, Wolf must also have had a course of action in mind.

As so often, it seemed that Konrad was simply carried by events. But there was far more to it than that, he had come to realize. The disparate parts of his life were at last falling into place, forming a pattern that he could almost recognize. He intended to thwart the plans of the armies of damnation, to prevent them from placing an impostor upon the Imperial crown. Skullface was at the centre of this nefarious scheme, Konrad was sure – which meant that he would inevitably be in conflict with the mysterious figure.

But Konrad wanted more than mere conflict, he wanted a confrontation with Skullface.

And, no matter what had happened to her, he also wanted to find Elyssa.

Last night he had been a prisoner on board de Tevoir's ship, and he had begun to believe he would never see another day. Instead it was the pirate chief who had died. Konrad had watched the captain being butchered when he waded ashore after his vessel had been destroyed.

Another night was falling, and this time Konrad more than believed he would not see the subsequent dawn. He *knew*...

From their vantage point, he was able to observe that the other pirate ship had not penetrated the city walls, where it could have bombarded Altdorf to more deadly effect. It was mid-river, firing at the fortifications and repelling all boarding attempts. It was difficult to distinguish precisely what was happening, however, because of the gloom and all the smoke from the guns and the fires.

As they came closer to the city, Konrad noticed that it was not simply drifting smoke which was obscuring their vision. A pale mist was forming on the river itself, rising eerily up to blend with the impending night, apparently causing the sun to set earlier than it should have done. It was not only the eyes which were affected by the thick mist, but the other senses. Some sounds became magnified, whilst others were severely muted.

The distant clash of weapons and the screams of the dying that echoed across the river seemed to be made by a whole legion of warriors fighting another army. There appeared to be far more damage within the city than could have been caused by one renegade vessel, no matter how many cutthroats were on board – and none of the pirates had yet invaded the capital.

Had the regiments of Chaos chosen this time to rise up against the Imperial forces? Was that the true purpose of Wolf's diversion? Konrad had discovered that his comrade, like himself, was touched by Chaos. But had Wolf's infection completely corrupted his whole body? How much had his body mutated beneath his black armour?

Guido had been leading the way, and they cut across from the Reik, heading diagonally towards the south-west corner of the city walls. The river battle was obscured from sight, but not from their hearing. Konrad kept watching the battlements. If one of the defenders happened to look down, the three of them would have been immediately visible and would soon fall victim to a volley of arrows. But the observation turrets seemed deserted. The mist from the river had begun drifting across the land and encircling the city, as if following the three of them. At first it was at ankle height, but slowly began to rise. The fog was cold, very cold, biting through Konrad's clothes like a winter Kislev wind. He shivered, chilled to the bone.

They reached a narrow door by the side of one of the main entrances to the capital. Both the heavy gate and the smaller entrance were firmly closed, which demonstrated the seriousness of the situation within the city. Altdorf prided itself on allowing access even during the middle of the night; it was no isolated village frightened of the dark, terrified of the creatures which inhabited the midnight hours.

Guido halted and leaned against the wall. He put his hand to his mouth, trying to mask a sudden cough as the mist rose up to his face. Konrad could hardly see him, and Ustnar had vanished beneath the rising mist.

'We wait,' whispered Guido, pulling his collar up to cover his mouth.

'You seem to know your way around,' said Konrad, gazing up towards the towers above the massive gate. They also appeared unoccupied.

'I've been everywhere,' Guido replied, as the fog enveloped him. He was only a yard away, but totally invisible.

Konrad drew his new sword. He had done this many times since Barra had made the blade for him, although never on board the corsair. Previously, his only purpose had been to admire the sword, to wish that he could wield it in combat. Now he held the blade because he felt safer with it in his hand, but this was also the first time he believed he might need to use the weapon.

The fog was as cold in Konrad's nostrils as it had been on his skin, and he attempted to breathe shallowly, taking as little of the unnatural air into his lungs as possible.

He heard the peal of a bell, a sound he knew must have come from a distance, although it appeared quite near. He had heard the same sound every evening during his stay in Altdorf. It was the sunset bell, although because of the mist this could have been any time of the day or night.

Then he heard another sound, and he spun around. The gateway where they stood was suddenly open, and two figures stood on the other side of the wall. Wolf was clad in his black armour, Litzenreich wore his dark robes. The three newcomers hurried through, and Wolf swung the gate closed behind them, cutting out the pale mist.

'You took your time,' he said.

Konrad jerked an inquisitorial thumb towards Guido.

'He's with us,' said Wolf. 'Did I forget to tell you?' He grinned, baring his sharpened teeth.

He carried his helmet under his arm. If his body had become transformed, it had not yet affected his tattooed face.

There was no sign of the fog within the walls, or of anything else. No one was in sight except the mercenary and the magician. It was as if the entire capital were deserted.

Wolf turned then suddenly halted, gazing into the city.

'Why is it dark?' he demanded, drawing his black sword and glancing at Litzenreich. 'And where is everyone?'

It must have been light a few seconds ago, the streets full of people.

Now everything was almost black. Outside it had been sunset, here it was the middle of the night. Only Morrslieb was visible in the sky, casting its greenish hue over the Imperial capital. The spectral moon seemed larger, nearer, than Konrad had ever seen it previously. It appeared to be directly above the Imperial Palace, almost touching the replica of Sigmar's warhammer mounted on top of the spire.

Everything was silent, as if there were no desperate battle taking place beyond the walls, as if there had been no uprising by the Chaos legions who lurked within.

Konrad saw a sudden movement at his feet, and he thrust out his sword. There was a screech. He raised the blade, upon which was impaled a rat. He flung its writhing body aside, noticing that there were thousands of the creatures scurrying through the streets. It was as if it were a rodent city, that nothing human dwelled within the walls of the capital.

Shrouded by the freezing mist, the entire city was in thrall to a potent magic spell.

He glanced at Litzenreich who was muttering under his breath and ritually pointing his staff, evidently conjuring up his own enchantments to protect himself and his comrades.

'Now what?' he asked Wolf.

'We save the Emperor, of course,' Wolf told him. 'What else?'

'Save the Emperor?' echoed Guido. 'Save him from what?'

Konrad turned his gaze back to Litzenreich. It seemed he had no objection to what Wolf had said. The wizard was watching the swarming rats, and he nodded with approval. The skaven must have been responsible for what was happening to the Imperial capital – and that meant they were using warpstone for their depraved sorcery.

'To the Imperial Palace,' said Wolf, and he lowered his helmet into position. The palace was where Karl-Franz resided when he was in Altdorf, and so he must have returned from his sojourn in Talabheim.

Wolf turned and hurried away. Litzenreich and Ustnar followed, as did Konrad.

'I don't know about saving the Emperor,' said Guido, who ran to catch up with Konrad, 'but I'm not staying here on my own.'

Altdorf was the largest city in the Old World, yet it seemed totally uninhabited – except by a plague of rats. There were lights in the houses, the taverns, but there was no sign of anyone within; no one else was on the streets except the five of them.

But then Konrad realized they were not alone, that there were numerous faint shapes in the square. Scores of immobile translucent figures only became visible when he was almost upon them. These were the citizens of Altdorf, and they had become like characters in a painting – although far less substantial.

Were they all dead, and these their spirits?

But a wagon could not have a ghost, and directly ahead was such a vehicle being pulled by two horses. Konrad reached out to touch the flank of one of the animals, and his left hand sank through its ethereal flesh as easily as if it were water. His fingers were instantly numb with freezing cold. He drew back his arm immediately, flexing his fingers and shaking his hand to restore heat and vitality, then hurried on past the frozen apparitions.

Civilians who had been fleeing the assault, troops who had been rushing into combat: they were all ghosts, more than dead but less than living.

And they would become truly dead once Chaos took its final fatal grip on the capital.

KONRAD RAN WITHOUT sound, his body casting no moon-shadow. When he noticed the other four, it seemed as though they were moving at half-speed. They ran like figures viewed in a dream landscape. He felt that he was running normally, but he was maintaining the same pace as the others, and so his own movements must have been similarly slowed.

Konrad was glad of the sword hilt in his hand, something he could feel and could trust. He wished for an enemy, even for a hundred enemies – and he knew he would not have long to wait.

They entered the palace by way of the main entrance. The gates were wide open, but the intruders went unchallenged because there were no sentries at their posts, not even spectral ones.

The Imperial guard were responsible for protecting the palace, but if they had all become servants of Slaanesh their absence could be explained. Whenever Morrslieb was full, it was a night when Chaos was on the ascendant.

And Konrad had never known a time when the portents were more menacingly auspicious. It was as if the legions of Chaos were massed directly outside Altdorf, and at any moment the city walls would burst asunder and the capital would forever become a part of the benighted Wastes.

Wolf had halted in the courtyard, deserted except for a wraith-like cavalry troop. The knights were Templars of Sigmar, riders and horses petrified into intangible equestrian statues. Litzenreich and Ustnar caught up with him, then Konrad and Guido joined the other three, and they all stared up at the immense building which lay before them.

'What's happening?' Konrad asked Litzenreich.

'Nothing,' answered Litzenreich. 'Nothing at all. The world has ceased to move. All of time is standing still.' He gazed around him. 'It is very impressive, is it not?'

Konrad and his comrades were unaffected, as were the rodent vermin which normally inhabited the sewers beneath the city. And time could not have been frozen for the ones who had cast the powerful temporal spell – the creatures of damnation who had claimed the Imperial Palace as their own.

Wolf held his black sword, Konrad his new blade, Guido his cutlass, Ustnar his axe, and Litzenreich his sorcerer's staff. Side by side, the five began to climb the curved flight of wide steps which led up towards the palace entrance. The stone steps were huge, as if built for giants, and everything within the main building had also been constructed on an exaggerated scale.

The first doorway was almost big enough for de Tevoir's corsair to have sailed through. The chamber beyond was vast, its high vaulted ceiling supported by flying buttresses upon which were carved all kinds of mythical beings and fabulous beasts. The walls on either side were lined with enormous statues of every previous Emperor, like a rank of troops all arrayed in their Imperial finery.

Flights of marble steps to either side led up to the higher levels of the palace, where the day to day business of administering the Empire was conducted, and to the Emperor's private quarters.

'That way,' said Litzenreich, his staff pointing directly ahead.

Wolf hesitated, but Konrad did not. He ran towards the arch. Beyond, he knew, each successive room was dedicated to a different Imperial ruler. Filled with trophies and the spoils of forgotten campaigns, the chambers were decorated with paintings and tapestries depicting the entire history of each reign.

And in the centre of each room was a stone plinth bearing the mortal remains of each Emperor. Sometimes there would be a stone coffin, sometimes a gold sarcophagus; sometimes there were gilded bones, and sometimes nothing. Altdorf had not always been the Imperial capital, and many Emperors had been interred elsewhere. But each of them had their own chamber within the palace, and by each plinth, whether empty or not, stood a member of the Imperial guard. Not only were they the guardians of the present Emperor, but of every previous one.

The other four followed as Konrad entered the first room, which was that of Luitpold, the father of Karl-Franz. His body lay encased within a bejewelled casket, upon which his effigy had been embossed. It was illuminated by the haunted light of Morrslieb, which filtered through the panels of the stained glass circle in the high ceiling. His bodyguard stood on duty by the coffin, resplendent in his shining uniform. Everything appeared as it should have done – except that the guard was not human...

Unlike everyone beyond the confines of the Imperial Palace, the sentry was more than an immaterial spirit. But, like those who had attacked the Grey Stoat tavern, he was a beastman with bovine features. His face was tusked, his head horned.

Konrad was about to attack when he noticed that the creature appeared to be as dead as Luitpold. The brute stood without breathing, without even blinking, as lifeless as one of the statues in the outer hallway – or as everyone else in Altdorf.

Day or night, each of the sacred halls was lit by a series of perfumed candles which rested in sconces along the walls. There was something strange about the candles, and Konrad paused to examine one of them. It was lit, but the flame did not flicker. There was no smell from the scented tallow, no heat from the flame, and the light cast no shadow. He hesitated for a moment, then ran his hand through the flame, and it felt cold, almost as if the fire were frozen. He shivered and tried to blow out the flame, then to extinguish the tiny ersatz blaze between his thumb and forefinger, but all to no avail.

The five went on, and the next chamber was similar to the first: a coffin reverently protected by a beastman in the uniform of an Imperial guard, surrounded by relics of the Emperor and decorated by scenes of his triumphs, all illuminated by numinous moonlight and the ghostly candles.

Each successive room was more ancient than the one before, having been constructed upon the death of that Emperor. The halls had been added wherever there was space, sometimes at right angles, sometimes on a different level. Racing through the chambers, travelling back over the aeons, was like going through a maze.

Wolf was a few paces behind Konrad when he suddenly yelled, 'This time you die!'

Konrad instinctively leapt aside, turning and raising his new sword – but Wolf's challenge had been issued to someone else, some invisible entity.

He swung his black sword, slicing the blade through the empty air. He lunged forward, swiftly bringing up his shield to protect himself.

Konrad watched in disbelief as Wolf was thrown back by the weight of a disembodied foe, which sent him crashing against an antique lacquered cabinet containing a priceless collection of porcelain, every piece of which crumbled into powder. Then Wolf sprang back into the attack, launching himself against an opponent only visible to him. His sword thrust forward, striking at nothingness.

While the other three went on, Konrad held back, hoping to help Wolf in his battle – but he could see no enemy.

Wolf was fighting against an unknown adversary from his past. It was his own personal battle, and there was nothing that Konrad could do. He had to go on, he must go on.

He turned and followed the wizard and the dwarf and the pirate as they proceeded through the next chambers, their footsteps silent upon the marble floors.

A minute later it was the turn of Ustnar to fall prey to the spectral adversaries who haunted his past.

He was advancing past an ancient sarcophagus when suddenly he yelled out a dwarf warcurse. His axe swung, and he screamed out his battlecry, his eyes focused on something which no one else could see. The weapon which Barra had made for him caused mayhem within the hallowed hall. The bestial guard was not his foe, but a wild swing of the battleaxe sliced through the sentry's armour – and the sentry within, splitting him in twain. The two halves of the beastman fell slowly to the floor. Like a statue, the corpse did not bleed.

Ustnar's axe repeatedly hacked through the air and whatever else was in range, seeking out the insubstantial enemy which seemed to be taking refuge behind the material objects in the chamber. Tapestries were shredded, paintings slashed, ancient armour wrecked, the fragile stone coffin itself dislodged from the plinth where it had lain undisturbed for centuries, cracking open and spilling the ancient emperor's fragile bones onto the floor. Ustnar kicked the skull away, yelling another fearsome oath as he launched himself once more at his unknown foe, destroying everything else that lay in his path.

Again, Konrad could do nothing. There must be no diversions, and he ventured deeper into the palace, amongst the tombs and memorials of the emperors who had lived and died a millennium and a half ago. The sound of Ustnar's battle was soon lost, as if it were taking place far away – or long ago.

He felt cold, colder than when the mist had enshrouded his body, but his skin prickled with sweat. He and Litzenreich glanced at one another for a moment, and the wizard must also have been wondering who would be the next to succumb to the palace's secret defences. They advanced together, separating only to pass on either side of each plinth and the mutated sentry who guarded it, while Guido followed.

'Please!' begged Litzenreich, falling to his knees and gazing up at nothing – nothing and everything.

But even as he pleaded, he was pointing with his staff and conjuring up a spell: aiming at the unseen threat, about to use his magical powers to strike out in defiance.

The chamber was suddenly ablaze with streaks of multicoloured lightning, appearing from the empty air, all of which were aimed Litzenreich. He used his staff to fend them off, as a swordsman would parry blows with his blade. Then he was back on his feet, retaliating in kind, and bolts of energy cascaded from his wand.

It was even more dangerous to be near Litzenreich than Ustnar, and Konrad left him to fight his own battle. He and Guido hurried on into the next hall of the dead, and then the next. Every chamber through which they passed was a step back in time, as if they were walking across the centuries.

Until at last they reached the final sacred hall, the one which was dedicated to Sigmar himself.

CHAPTER FIFTEEN

THERE WERE MORE legends told of Sigmar Heldenhammer than of any other Emperor, and yet this chamber was the most barren. Sigmar had founded the Empire, and the walls were covered with numerous friezes in his honour; but all of the paintings and sculptures had been made long after Sigmar's reign. The first emperor had lived two and a half thousand years ago, and he had not been seen since he had made his final journey back to Black Fire Pass to return Ghal-maraz to the dwarf race – not seen by anyone human. Upon the plinth where his mortal remains should have lain was a black velvet cushion which bore the only known relic of his reign. It was the handle of the dagger which Sigmar had carried at the battle of Black Fire Pass.

Konrad halted. There could be no going on, because this was the last chamber and there was but one doorway. He stared around, knowing that whatever was waiting for him must have been here. He gazed up, seeing the deformed shape of Morrslieb through the stained glass. The moon had been in exactly the same position in each chamber of the necropolis. Normally it passed across the night sky far more swiftly. But tonight it had become still. Time had indeed ceased to exist. There was no time – and there was every time.

He looked at Guido, who returned his gaze. The pirate frowned and raised his hand towards his lips. He opened his mouth as if to speak, and Konrad saw his tongue move – then realized it could not be a tongue. It was brown, it was covered in fur...

The head of a rat appeared from Guido's mouth!

One of the pirate's cheeks bulged and split, and the bloody snout of another rat ripped through the flesh. His left eye disappeared, and a third rat burst through the cavity – its sharp teeth chewing upon the eyeball.

Guido's entire body shook and trembled, then was suddenly torn apart from within as a fetid horde of blood-drenched rats spewed out from his innards, from his chest and his guts, his arms and his legs. He had been devoured from within, his human shape supported by a skeleton of rodents.

Konrad gazed in horror as Guido's clothes and shed skin and cutlass fell to the ground. The squealing pack of rats dispersed throughout the chamber, vanishing into the holes along the edges of the walls.

This was truly skaven sorcery. The Imperial guard may have become devotees of Slaanesh, but it was the servants of the Horned God who had drawn Konrad into the heart of the Imperial Palace.

Clutching his new sword, Konrad remembered that the warpstone within the blade had come from the ratbeasts who had attacked on High Bridge. Had those skaven been a deliberate sacrifice, to beckon him along the Reik? And when he had voyaged towards Altdorf it was Guido, a skaven construct, who had made sure that he escaped from the pirate ship.

And now Konrad was alone once more, as he had been so often in his life. His mouth was dry, his heart thudding in his chest, his palms damp.

He had been drawn into a trap. The only escape was to retreat the way he had come. He turned – and saw a deformed creature rushing towards him. It had appeared from nowhere, and all his reasoning told him that it could not possibly exist.

Its body was translucent, and it was one of the most primitive mutants he had ever encountered: shambling and ungainly, with matted grey fur, the face of a dog, fanged and taloned, carrying a rusty sword.

The beast seemed somehow familiar, but Konrad did not know why. He raised his own sword, bringing it swiftly down across the thing's neck, trying to decapitate the brute. His sword passed straight through, without any resistance. The apparition began to dissolve, however, but was immediately replaced by another beastman.

This one was huge, its face upside down, clad in pieces of tarnished armour, wearing a weapons belt around its fat belly and with an axe growing out of the end of its right arm. And this one Konrad did recognize: it was the first beast he had slain the day that his village had been annihilated. It was the one he had skinned, whose hide he had used to camouflage himself. He tried to kill the creature again, plunging his blade into its chest, but the mutant was already disintegrating, its place immediately claimed by yet another creature of the damned – this time a skaven.

Then he remembered the first monstrosity, where he had seen it before. It was the beastman he had stabbed to death when it attacked Elyssa. They had met the first time that day because he had saved the girl's life.

He swung at the skaven, and that also melted away, to be replaced by a creature which seemed to be half-insect, half-human. It had the legs of a man, the upper body of what might have been an ant, with four thin limbs growing from its black carapace. And like all the others, it was already dead. He had slain the beast with his bow and arrow when his village was assaulted. It was a ghost, they were all ghosts. It seemed that he was being assailed by the spirits of all the beastmen he had ever slain – and each time he swung at them, each time one vanished and was supplanted by the next, Konrad felt weakened.

When yet another creature materialized, this time above him, he tried to lift his sword but it felt almost too heavy. It was one of the flying beasts which had swooped upon Konrad when he had returned with Wolf to the site of his destroyed village. The creature had more substance than the previous mutants, and yet Konrad's sword could make no impact upon his assailant. As with all the other brutes, the blade passed harmlessly into its scaly hide and through its incorporeal body.

Then Konrad saw that his weapon was becoming transparent – and so was his own arm! His sleeve seemed to have vanished, his skin to have evaporated. He saw the veins which carried his blood, the tendons and sinews beneath the missing flesh. Then they too faded away, leaving nothing but whitened bone, which also disappeared as if disintegrating over the aeons.

His energy was being drained through the sword, sucked into those he was trying to destroy. Instead it was they who were destroying him, making themselves stronger and more substantial while his vitality ebbed away. His whole essence seemed to be vanishing, his entire body growing invisible.

He backed away, not wanting to use his blade, because that was how he was being depleted. The warpdust had come from the skaven, and it was the warpdust which was leeching his lifeforce.

But without Konrad trying to defend himself, the flying beastman pressed forward, its own sword sweeping at him. The weapon passed through Konrad's body, leaving no physical mark, yet stealing more of his substance.

More and more hideous shapes materialized all around him, the shadows of his bestial victims. They had long ago perished, but they seemed far more alive than Konrad. It was he who belonged to the ghostly realm.

He was fading, fading faster, while his enemies screamed in silent triumph, growing more tangible with every moment. And with every moment, Konrad dissolved a fraction more.

He found himself pressed up against the plinth upon which lay Sigmar's one holy relic – against it and into it...

He reached out with his left hand, trying to hold himself back, and saw his fingers melting deeper into the stone. Raising his hand up through the plinth, through the velvet cushion, he touched what remained of the knife, and was able to feel the ancient ivory handle against his palm. He took a firm grip, and as he did so his fist regained its shape and colour.

Konrad saw his hand again properly – and he also saw the blade of the knife.

The metal of Sigmar's knife which had rusted away centuries ago was visible once more, sharp and gleaming as if newly forged. Where there had been a cold numbness in Konrad's fingers, there was now warmth. He sensed a glow rising up his arm, and his limb swiftly lost its transparency.

He was becoming whole once more, becoming more than whole. A surge of energy suffused his entire body, replenishing his lost strength. He felt totally invigorated, and he leapt forth against his legion of enemies. He had destroyed them once, and now he must obliterate them again.

Instead of draining his spirit, the warpblade now gave Konrad new vitality. The sword sliced through the air – and through ugly feral flesh, killing the undead. These were the Chaos breed that he had battled on the Kislev frontier, which had now been reborn in the heart of the Empire, and which he had to defeat once more. Their mutated bodies had long ago rotted, but this time he was conquering their souls, casting their foul spirits into eternal oblivion.

He also used Sigmar's knife to drive the unliving horde away, stabbing and gouging at the flesh which was not flesh, and which lost its substance at the same rate with which his own powers increased.

Yet it was as if the dagger were wielded by some external force, that Konrad had control of the right side of his body, whilst his left was under the influence of some greater entity.

He had felt this way before, during the battle with the cave-dwelling goblins. Then, he knew, he had been truly possessed, driven to supreme feats by the authority of the spiritual power which had manipulated his complete being.

'There is some part of Sigmar in everyone,' Galea had told him. 'There is more of Sigmar in you than in most.'

Again Konrad was Sigmar's chosen warrior, destroying the malevolent invaders who had dared to invade the god's most ancient sepulchre.

Awareness was immediate: it was not the skaven who had lured Konrad here, although that was what they believed; it was the spirit of Sigmar who had guided Konrad to this place, to this time.

Konrad opened his mind to the founder of the Empire, to the man who had become a god.

Together, yet as one, fighting within a single physical body, they slew the battalions of damnation, driving them back to the abyss of darkness whence they had been spawned.

Rivers of invisible blood gushed forth, dozens of insubstantial limbs were severed, scores of unseen bones were snapped, organs sliced, entrails spilled. All of Konrad's years of carnage were compressed into one titanic ordeal of death.

He slew them all again, all the festering Chaos vermin he had ever fought. The goblins in the dwarf temple and Kastring the pagan chief, the pale troglodytes beneath Altdorf and Zuntermein the Slaaneshi priest, Taungar the corrupted sergeant and the skaven pack who had attacked on the bridge in Marienburg.

They were all but faint incarnations of their previous selves, forever banished by the potency of Konrad's warpblade and the innate power of Sigmar's holy dagger.

And then the battle was over, every opponent defeated, and Konrad was alone within himself. The spirit of Sigmar had returned to the outer realms where he dwelled, and Konrad felt both exhausted and yet revitalized.

He glanced around, and nothing seemed to have changed. The Imperial guard stood in his place, still immobile, still a bull-creature. Morrslieb cast its haunted luminescence over the mausoleum, while the candle flames remained frozen.

Konrad looked down at the knife in his left hand, the hand which was once more his own, and he watched as the blade slowly faded into invisibility. Once more all that was left of Sigmar's dagger was the fragile bone handle. He put the ancient weapon back in its place upon the black velvet cushion. Then, except for Guido's remains upon the marble slabs, everything was truly as it had been before he entered the chamber.

Except for Silver Eye.

'KONRAD,' HISSED THE skaven, 'you going to try and kill me once more, yes?'

The ratbeast was standing in a corner of the chamber, as if he had materialized out of the shadows. He looked like Silver Eye, with the same tribal markings, the same scavenged armour, the same metal teeth, the same piece of warpstone in place of his left eye, the same jagged sword, and he carried the triangular shield which bore the golden crest of mailed fist and crossed arrows. But he did not sound like Silver Eye.

'Gaxar!' gasped Konrad.

'Who else?'

Konrad raised his sword and rushed towards the skaven.

'Stop! Stop!' commanded Gaxar, and he lifted his own sword. 'One step and the Emperor dies!'

Only then did Konrad notice that the transformed grey seer was not alone in the gloom. There was a human figure to his right, a figure that Konrad recognized from paintings and from the Imperial currency. It was Karl-Franz of the

House of the Second Wilhelm, the Emperor himself – or the doppelganger that Gaxar had created in his subterranean lair beneath Middenheim.

'That's not the Emperor,' Konrad said, but he halted.

'Perhaps not,' said Gaxar. 'But if that's not the Emperor, then this is!'

He gestured to his left, and there was another man with him in the dimness. Another Emperor Karl-Franz.

One of them was the true Emperor, but which? Or were they both impostors, created by Gaxar's necromantic talents?

'I knew you could give the dead a semblance of life,' said Konrad, 'but how did you revive yourself?'

'That was thanks to my loyal bodyguard. After you slew me, Fenbrod did me the honour of devouring my innards – my brain, my heart, my liver. He consumed the essence of my being so that I might be reincarnated within his body.'

'And Fenbrod?' Konrad had never known Silver Eye's true name until now, and neither had he cared.

'There was only room for one of us within his body. He sacrificed himself for me, as a loyal servant should do. I must admit it is pleasant to have two paws once again, although the lack of an eye is disconcerting.'

'So I did you a favour by killing you?'

'Ha!' Gaxar barked out his laughter. 'Now it's my turn to kill you, Konrad. But when you die, you die forever!'

'What about the shield?' said Konrad.

'What?' asked Gaxar. 'The shield?'

'Where does that shield come from?'

For a moment, Gaxar gazed down at the battered shield he held. 'How should I know?' he growled. 'Let us fight!'

'Why?'

'Why? Why! Because I want to kill you, Konrad, that's why, that's why! I now possess Fenbrod's brutal strength, and I still have my own magical skills. I intend to destroy you. No one kills me and gets away with it!' Gaxar barked out his rodent laughter once more.

Perhaps the bodyguard's memories had been obliterated when the grey seer had claimed his fur and bones, and so Gaxar knew nothing of the shield. But he must have known something of Elyssa, because she had been in the underground chamber with the skaven sorcerer, watching as Litzenreich and Ustnar were crucified – and Skullface had also been there.

Konrad shrugged and stepped backwards.

'You've got to fight! Don't you want to save your Emperor?'

'*My* Emperor? Why should I care what happens to him?'

'I'll kill him, I'll kill him!' yelled Gaxar, and he moved threateningly towards the figure to his right. Then he paused and spun around, his blade aimed at the second identical shape. 'So cunning, you humans, so very cunning.'

The twin figures were both wearing the clothes of a courtier, and both stood without moving. Although not as rigid as the members of the Imperial guard who were stationed throughout the palace, it was clear that Gaxar had them under his spell and that they were unable to act of their own free will. But only one of them could ever have had any volition; the other had always been a creation of the grey seer's, brought by him from Middenheim to the capital.

Captured by the skaven, the true Emperor was about to be replaced by his double, a puppet of the ratmen. The exchange must have been intended for tonight. If Karl-Franz were replaced by a servant of Chaos, the awesome consequences would be unimaginable.

'Kill him,' said Konrad, feigning unconcern. He shrugged again.

'No,' said Gaxar. 'You kill him! You choose, Konrad. Which one should live, which one should die? One is the true Karl-Franz. You must decide which one – and execute the other!'

'Why should I?'

'Because I am commanding you to!'

Gaxar's fierce gaze seemed to burn through Konrad's eyes and into his brain. He tried to look away, but it was already too late. Gaxar had mesmerized him, and he felt himself advancing reluctantly forward. He attempted to hold back, but to no avail, and his right arm began to raise his sword. It was not he who was deciding which Karl-Franz would die. Gaxar would ensure that the impostor lived, that the throne was claimed by his own creation.

Above Gaxar was a frieze which showed the coronation of the first Emperor. It caught Konrad's attention because instead of Sigmar being crowned, there was a skaven upon the throne – the Horned Rat himself...

And if Karl-Franz were murdered, it would be as if the last of Sigmar's heirs had died – assassinated by Konrad.

Konrad took another unwilling step forward, and the warpblade rose even higher.

Summoning all his inner reserves of energy, Konrad managed to utter two syllables.

'Sigmar,' he whispered.

There was a sound in the distance, a rumble like far away guns. Perhaps the pirate ship had broken through the boom across the Reik and was bombarding Altdorf itself. Konrad felt the ground move, and he glanced down in time to see the marble tiles beneath his feet splinter and crack. The entire world must have been in turmoil, shaking the foundations upon which the Imperial capital and the palace itself were built.

As he advanced, Konrad missed a step and almost slipped, perhaps because of the earthquake, perhaps because Gaxar's hypnotic control was beginning to fade. He fought even harder, trying to resist the skaven's malign influence, and he concentrated on his own mental resources, upon the hidden depths he had so recently discovered.

'Sigmar,' he prayed, once again, louder, and the word gave him enough strength to shout: 'Sigmar!'

There was a sudden flare of brilliant light far beyond, reflected through the circle of stained glass, and Konrad raised his head in time to see twin streaks of lightning flash across the sky, so bright that they totally eclipsed Morrslieb's macabre glow.

A thunderous roar came from high above the palace. The thunderbolts must have struck the pinnacle, which was built from granite blocks brought from Black Fire Pass, and the whole of the great building shook once more. This time, a jagged crack appeared down the side of the chamber, ripping apart the wall.

Gaxar gazed anxiously upwards, surrendering his preternatural hold over Konrad's will.

Then, without warning, the ceiling was torn asunder by the untold weight of a gigantic block of falling masonry.

Konrad leapt back, Gaxar sprang aside, and the massive chunk of rock landed between them, spraying shards of stone throughout the chamber.

The hall was filled with clouds of dust, but everything was abruptly silent. There was no sign of the Emperor, or of the impostor, whichever was which. And, as the dirt and debris settled, Konrad observed what it was that had crashed down into Sigmar's mausoleum: it was the replica of Ghal-maraz which had topped the palace spire. Thrice the size of a man, the stone warhammer had been dislodged by the lightning and plummeted straight down into the central chamber of this wing of the palace. There was a vast hole in the ceiling, but only the sky and the stars were visible. Morrslieb had been banished from the heavens. All the candles were properly alight now, flickering in the wind which blew through the cavity in the roof.

On the ancient frieze, Sigmar had been restored to his rightful place on the Imperial throne as the first Emperor.

Hearing another sound, Konrad looked around. The force of the titanic impact had knocked over the Imperial guardsman who had been on duty in the chamber, and now he was rising to his feet – and he hurtled towards Konrad, his sword raised to attack.

Time had been restored, the guard's heart had begun to beat once more, but it was a mutant heart. He was still a slave of damnation, a depraved worshipper of the lord of hedonism.

Konrad's warpblade sliced through the creature's throat, half-severing his head. Blood spurted, the beast screamed – and died.

Turning, Konrad noticed that one of the two figures Gaxar had magically ensnared was still standing upright, gazing around in bewilderment. The other had been squashed beneath the huge granite carving, and all that remained was a mess of festering and decayed flesh. Sigmar's legendary warhammer had claimed yet another victim. The impostor was a corpse once more.

Gaxar had been rendered immobile for several seconds, as though stunned by what had happened. Konrad ran to put himself between Karl-Franz and the skaven.

'I am,' said the Emperor hesitantly. 'I am...' He shook his head, then staggered slightly.

There came the sound of many footsteps, all running towards the chamber. Several more members of the Imperial guard rushed into the hall. Once the Emperor's most loyal servants, now they were devoid of all trace of humanity. Their bull-heads roared out their challenge.

Konrad glanced at Gaxar, but there was no time to slay the grey skaven – to slay him again – before the guards were on him. He stepped in front of the Emperor. He had to defend Karl-Franz at all costs. That was his mission, why Sigmar had brought him here. His whole life had been a prelude to this moment.

He fought, his new blade thrusting out to claim another victim, then slashing up and across to kill yet one more. The chamber echoed to the sound of clashing steel, to the screams of the dying mutants. Konrad lost himself in combat, yelling his own defiant warcries as loudly as his enemies vented their insane bloodlust – and howled their death screams as their inhuman blood was mercilessly shed.

The hall filled with more figures, but that did not matter. Konrad was already outnumbered. He could only die but once, whether attacked by a dozen feral foes or a hundred.

Then he saw a black blade slice through the air, and he knew he was not alone. Wolf was with him. The odds had been halved, and Konrad fought with renewed vigour. A thunderbolt flashed, a burst of bright flames illuminated the hall, and Litzenreich had joined in the battle.

The thunderous sound of racing hooves echoed through the palace, and Konrad looked towards the next chamber, wondering whether a whole legion of the damned had arrived as reinforcements. But then a rider charged into the hall – a Templar of Sigmar, his red lance impaling one of the mutated Imperial guard.

More of the mounted troops arrived in Sigmar's sepulchre and entered the fray. These were the cavalry who had been ensnared by frozen time in the palace courtyard. Their helmets were crested by twin horns – but the horns of their victims grew from their deformed skulls, and they were slaughtered like the beasts they truly were.

Gaxar had been lurking in the corner, hoping to seize the moment when he could pounce upon Karl-Franz. But now he recognized that the odds were too great, and he spun around.

A hole appeared in the floor near his feet, a tunnel which had opened up at his sorcerous command, and he stepped towards it, about to escape.

'Gaxar!' Konrad commanded, and the skaven hesitated.

The grey seer turned, or perhaps it was the warrior part of him which could not be denied. Silver Eye's body must still have retained his fighting instincts. A challenge could not be refused.

The skaven grinned, baring his metal teeth, and he licked at his jowls. Konrad remembered the rasping feel of Silver Eye's tongue when it had licked at his blood, tasting the warpstone which coursed through his veins. Gaxar – if it were Gaxar who was in control of the rat shape – raised his jagged sword, lifted the enigmatic shield, and launched himself at Konrad.

They fought, trading blow for blow. Gaxar had the advantage, because he was protected by the triangular shield. But it was the skaven who was on the defensive, realizing that he was trapped. Even if he managed to defeat Konrad, there were plenty more warriors within the ruined chamber that he would have to destroy, and they would not attack him singly. Many of the knights had dismounted to form a protective phalanx around the Emperor, and from the corner of his eye Konrad could see both Wolf and Litzenreich watching the deadly duel. Neither of them would allow the grey seer to escape alive – although Litzenreich would probably be willing to consider some kind of deal if it meant he could get his hands on a cache of warpstone.

Konrad's new blade clashed against Gaxar's hooked sword. The warpblade was part skaven, and it was time it claimed skaven blood. The sword slashed through brown fur, and blood dripped onto the dust which covered the marble floor of the palace. Gaxar screeched in pain, and Konrad thrust forward again. He stabbed the point of his weapon into Gaxar's chest, then sliced the edge of the blade across the skaven's sword arm. There was more blood, more screams. Gaxar fought more wildly, throwing himself forward, leaving himself wide open to counter-attack. There was even more blood, more screams.

Gaxar was becoming more desperate, and suddenly he flung his shield at Konrad, spun around, and sprinted for the exit he had created. No skaven could ever outrun a man, and Konrad caught up with the grey seer before he could make his escape. He grabbed hold of the creature's tail, yanking him backwards.

Gaxar howled, more in anger than in pain. He twisted around, hacked through his own tail to release himself, then ran on. Konrad fell back for a moment, and Gaxar had almost reached the hole in the ground when Konrad drove his sword between two plates of armour and into the rat-thing's back. The skaven froze for an instant, and Konrad withdrew his sword. Then Gaxar slowly turned, and blood was pouring from his chest as well as his back.

He raised his sword, as if to strike, but the weapon dropped from his paw. He opened his mouth as if to speak, but no sound came. He fell, and he was dead before he hit the ground. The dark opening which his magic had caused to appear vanished simultaneously.

Konrad looked down at his warpblade's victim. He raised his sword, examining the blood. The weapon gleamed in the candlelight, the skaven gore emphasizing all the different layers of metal, glinting from all the different hues.

'Gaxar,' Konrad told Wolf and Litzenreich, nodding to the skaven's corpse. He looked past them. 'Ustnar?' he asked.

'Dead,' said Wolf. His helmet was gone, and there were fresh cuts across his face; his armour was dented and scored, gouged open in several places.

Litzenreich had fared no better. His clothes were ripped, some of his hair and beard appeared to have been burned, and his face was scorched and blistered. His staff had been blackened by fire, the lower end turned to charcoal by some intense heat.

'Who are you?'

The three of them looked towards the Emperor, who had pushed himself between two of the knights.

'This is Konrad,' said Wolf. 'This is Litzenreich. My name is... Wolf.' He hesitated, but did not give his full identity.

'I have few memories of what happened to me,' said Karl-Franz. 'But I realize that I owe you all my life.' He glanced over to where the rotting corpse of his doppelganger lay crushed beneath the replica of Skull-splitter. 'To you in particular, I believe,' he added, addressing Konrad. He was speaking slowly, as if in a foreign language. 'I must rest. But you will be rewarded, all of you. I will not forget.' He turned and was helped away by two of the templars.

'He'll forget,' said Wolf, watching the Emperor leave the ruined chamber. The rest of the cavalry departed, leading their horses – and leaving the dead and the damned beastmen behind.

The only thing which remained intact was the stone plinth in the exact centre of the vast room, and upon it was the velvet cushion and the ivory handle of Sigmar's knife.

'We've saved the Emperor,' said Konrad, wearily. 'We've saved the Empire. Wasn't that what we were supposed to do?'

'Was it? I knew we came here for something.' Wolf grinned and wiped his face with the back of his hand, smearing sweat and blood across his tattooed features. His sword was in his hand, dripping with blood and gore.

Konrad knelt down to study the triangular shield, examining it as closely as possible without touching it. It was old and dented, streaked with rust where the black paint had flaked away. The golden emblem was almost intact, however, and was identical to the crest which had been on the arrows, the bow, the quiver which Elyssa had given him so long ago.

'An elf?' asked Konrad. 'Was this the elf's shield?'

Wolf shrugged, making it clear that he did not wish to discuss the time an elf had defeated him, then spared his life.

Had all the weapons belonged to Elyssa's true father, who was an elf? And where had Silver Eye scavenged the shield?

Litzenreich had been gazing at Gaxar's body, walking all around him, tapping the floor with his charred staff. He said something, which was too low for Konrad to hear, and he kept muttering to himself. Then when the floor opened up, Konrad realized that he had been casting a spell.

There was a dark hole in the ground, in exactly the same position as the one which Gaxar had created. Litzenreich peered down, and Wolf walked across and did likewise.

It was almost dawn, Konrad realized. The whole of the night had been stolen by Chaos.

In the growing light, Konrad could see that there were steps leading down from the entrance which Litzenreich had conjured. It must have been some secret passage beneath the palace.

'Shall we go?' said Litzenreich, staring into the depths of the darkness.

He must have believed there were more skaven down there, and where the ratbeasts dwelled there would be warpstone – and warpstone was the source of magic.

Wolf nodded, and Konrad wondered why he should want to descend into the maze of passages beneath the city. Perhaps because that was where there was Chaos infection, which meant Wolf would have more enemies to fight.

The two of them looked at Konrad. The last thing he wished to do was return to the treacherous labyrinths which lay under Altdorf; but he knew that he must venture into the subterranean world once again.

Elyssa was there.

And so was Skullface.

Konrad picked up the black shield, slipping his left arm through the handle and holding the grip in his fist. Like his new sword, it was as if the shield had been made for him.

Wolf seized one of the large candles and led the way down; Litzenreich took another and joined him. Konrad also drew one of the scented candles from its sconce, then gazed upwards, seeing the first trace of blue as night was banished from the sky.

Aware that he would never see daylight again, or ever return from the land beneath the world, Konrad took his final breath of surface air then followed the other two down into what he knew must become his grave.

CHAPTER SIXTEEN

THE TUNNELS WERE like those beneath Middenheim, hewn from solid rock. Like those under the City of the White Wolf, they must have been constructed by dwarf engineers. Long before the rise of humanity, the Old World had been inhabited by the dwarfs – and before that by the elves. The dwarfs had built tunnels across what was now the Empire, linking many of their towns and cities. Their abandoned centres of habitation had been taken over by the younger human race, and the network of passages still existed.

The humans had taken over the cities, but the tunnels now belonged to the skaven...

And that was what was so familiar to Konrad: the stench of the mutated rodents seemed to have saturated the narrow tunnel through which the three humans ventured. The ratbeasts could smell the warpstone which had become a part of Konrad, but he could also smell them.

More than any other creature of Chaos, Konrad hated the skaven. His hatred went back further than the time of his imprisonment by Gaxar. Maybe it was connected with the way that the skaven were so like humans, yet so radically different. They were intelligent, well organized, but they appeared almost like a parody of humanity.

Wolf hated every manifestation of Chaos with equal ferocity. To him, the skaven were no worse than any other of the hellspawned legions. They were vermin to be eradicated like all other mutants. As for Litzenreich, his relationship with them was almost symbiotic. He needed the skaven, because it was they who refined warpstone – and Litzenreich needed warpstone to pursue what he called his 'researches.'

Konrad felt very nervous knowing that there were skaven about. He was behind the other two and could see nothing ahead as they pressed on through the maze of dark damp passages. Wolf was leading the way, and they were going further and further down with every step, but where was Wolf leading them?

It was not only skaven who dwelled deep below Altdorf and who used these tunnels, because every so often they came across a glowing lantern. The skaven needed no such illumination, so what other creatures inhabited these depths? Whatever they were, Konrad was far less concerned about them than the treacherous ratmen.

Time passed, they went deeper, and he was beginning to feel less uneasy. Why had Gaxar been alone? Could it be that there were no other skaven beneath Altdorf, that they had all departed the city? Some other beings had taken over their nesting sites, and that was why the rat-things had not attacked.

But at that very moment they did attack...

Suddenly from ahead there came the repulsive sound of skaven screeches, of metal upon metal as Wolf's sword repelled his abominable assailants. Konrad tried to push forward, but Litzenreich was in the way, and the wizard was reluctant to advance into danger. Konrad forced himself past and into the wide cavern which abruptly opened up in front of him. The cave was low but wide, and lit by a few lanterns hanging from the walls. Konrad almost wished that there was no light, because then he would not have seen what confronted him: the packed ranks of scores and scores of skaven, all of whom must have been waiting patiently for the unwary humans to emerge from the darkness.

Konrad joined Wolf, and together they fought against the flowing tide of mutated rats, their blades scything through the enemy, chopping them down, hacking them apart. They were both soon splattered with skaven gore; but for every creature that they slew, another took its place. All of the enemy were warrior rats, the size of men, and armed with their usual jagged swords and hooked lances. But when their weapons were lost, they also fought with teeth and claws. Despite his shield, Konrad was soon bleeding from a number of wounds.

Instead of standing his ground in the tunnel from which they had emerged, Wolf began advancing through the ranks of skaven, hacking a route through the multitude of malevolent creatures. There was another passage ahead, on the far side of the cavern, and that was where he seemed to be heading. Konrad followed, back to back with Wolf, each defending one another, blades slicing and slashing.

Litzenreich had been searching the skaven corpses, hunting for any which carried warpstone. But none of the living creatures attacked him. They concentrated all their attention on Konrad and Wolf. Konrad guessed that the wizard was protecting himself with some kind of spell. Now that he had found a source of warpstone, he no longer needed his allies.

But then Litzenreich stood up, pointed with his staff, and a bright streak of light flashed across the cavern. One of the skaven which had been about to hack at Konrad suddenly burst into flames, screaming hideously as it burned alive. The wizard began to make his way through the cave, immolating every skaven who dared to get in his way.

Wolf carved a gory path through the ratmen, his sword never still. He was shouting out some atavistic warcry as he fought, and finally he and Konrad made it to the other side of the cave. Litzenreich joined them a few seconds later. Dozens and dozens of the skaven lay dead or dying, burned or burning, but there were far more within the chamber. Reinforcements poured from the tunnel by which the three humans had entered the grotto.

The skaven horde attacked with renewed vigour. Wolf pushed the other two past him into the tunnel and then took up position at the end, blocking the entrance with his body and his sword.

'Go!' he shouted to Konrad, and Konrad hardly understood because his voice sounded so strange.

Then he noticed Wolf's face.

It had begun to change, for the brow to deepen and the jaw to lengthen, for the white hair of his scalp and beard to spread over all his features, while his sharpened teeth became longer, like fangs. He had appeared this way when the goblins had taken him prisoner, although at the time Konrad had thought his eyes must have deceived him.

This was how Wolf had been tainted by Chaos.

He was taking on the likeness of the animal for which he was named. He was becoming *were*...

His whole shape was altering, not only his face. He bent lower, becoming more stretched, and the armour split as his wolfish body burst through the black metal.

'Go!'

And now the word was indecipherable. It was an animal roar, but Konrad knew what it must mean.

No longer human, the mercenary had been transformed into a huge white wolf. The armour was gone, and all that remained was the chain around his neck – the chain which had once held Wolf a prisoner, and which he wore to remind himself that he would never be captured again. The black sword lay on the ground. Wolves did not need weapons. They had powerful jaws which could snap through the throat of a skaven in a moment, claws which could rip out foul rat entrails in an instant.

'This way,' Litzenreich ordered.

He had already started down the second passage. Konrad hesitated, but then obeyed and followed the dark wizard. As in the hall above, when Wolf had been called to battle by an unseen adversary, there was nothing that Konrad could do. The creature who had once been Wolf needed no human help to destroy every skaven which attempted to get past. The tunnel was filled with the noise of lupine roars, of rodent screams.

There were several intersections which they passed, and at first Litzenreich had no hesitation in his choice of direction, but after a while he advanced more slowly.

The sounds of feral combat echoed through the maze of tunnels, and now it was not only the skaven which yelled in agony. Wolf's challenging growls were punctuated with howls of torment.

He was totally outnumbered, and he must inevitably be overwhelmed. He had chosen his position as rearguard in order that Konrad could go on, and so Konrad must not betray his comrade by faltering now.

Instead it was Litzenreich who halted.

'Keep on in this direction,' he said, and his voice was faint.

'What will I find?'

The sorcerer shook his head. 'I must go back,' he said, almost whispering.

In the dim light Konrad noticed his face. It had suddenly become old, very old. Litzenreich had appeared middle-aged, but now his true age was revealed. Above his white beard, his face was deeply creased; his left hand was withered and gnarled; and his back was bent, his whole body hunched. He had become the oldest human that Konrad had ever seen.

'I deserted Wolf once,' Litzenreich continued, his breath coming in short bursts. 'I left him to die. Perhaps I can make amends if we die together. And together maybe we can hold back the skaven a little longer – so that you can go on.'

'But why?' Konrad demanded. 'Go on where?'

The ancient wizard seemed not to hear. He made his way back along the passage, returning towards the sounds of wild animals locked in deadly combat, his crooked shape vanishing into the shadows.

Litzenreich was an old man, Wolf was a canine beast. And they were both about to die in order that Konrad could continue down through the black tunnel which lay ahead.

Konrad stood without moving for a while, unwilling to advance into the unknown darkness. His doomed companions both seemed to know far more than he did about why he was here and what lay ahead.

He made up his mind – and turned and ran back. He and Wolf had been comrades for so long that he could not abandon him, and Litzenreich had become an ally. They would all survive together, or not at all.

He sprinted through the tunnels, led by the sounds of desperate combat, finally seeing a faint glow of light in the tunnel ahead. The air reeked of the pungent odour of skaven blood.

When he reached the cavern, he halted as he gazed at the scene of carnage. Swarms of skaven had been massacred, but there were still as many of them armed and fighting. Wolf was in their midst, more dead than alive. Instead of a white wolf, he was now red, every inch of his fur matted with blood – and much of it must have been his own. He was bleeding from a hundred wounds, but still he fought, his jaws snapping, his claws slashing. At any moment he would be defeated, drowned by the pestilential tide of skaven which flowed towards him, screeching and hacking.

Litzenreich was also there, standing near the end of the tunnel, again ignored as if he were no threat.

This would be the final battle, Konrad knew. There could be no escape from the subterranean chamber. But what better way was there to die than with a sword in one's hand, fighting with one's comrades against the most hated adversary of all?

He started to advance, but then suddenly halted when Litzenreich spun around, gazing at him.

The wizard thrust his staff at Konrad, gesturing for him to go back, and then he drove the end of his staff upwards, and a single bolt of white lighting flashed. A moment later came a tremendous crack, the sound of massive rocks being split asunder. Then the whole roof of the cave collapsed. Countless tons of rock crashed down, crushing all of those beneath – both skaven, human and once human.

There was no way that Litzenreich or Wolf could have survived.

They had died so that Konrad could continue, and so all he could do was turn and go on.

He headed deeper into the darkness and towards his nemesis.

HAVING PASSED BEYOND the point where Litzenreich had turned back, Konrad instinctively took the left fork when the tunnel branched into two. At the next dark junction he went right, again aware that this was the direction which he must take, although still unsure of what his destination would be. It was almost like *seeing*, as if his lost talent of foresight had returned to guide his direction.

With the mysterious shield in one hand, his new blade in the other, Konrad advanced deeper into the gloom, his route illuminated by the flickering lanterns, their reflections beckoning him onwards.

All was totally silent. There could be no clash of weapons far behind, no agonized screams of death. The exit from the cavern had been totally blocked by fallen rocks, and no ravening rodent horde would pursue him – for a while, at least.

But this underworld was the skaven domain, and they would know every labyrinthine route beneath the Imperial capital. Konrad would not be alone for very long, and he listened for the distant echo of his verminous foes.

The only sounds were of his own boots treading the cold stone floor, of the shield occasionally brushing against the narrow sides of the damp passage. Konrad's pulse had slowed since the ferocious battle across the cave, but he could still feel the blood race through his veins; he imagined that he could hear his own heart pounding, that the sound was like an alarm to the enemies who lurked ahead.

Perhaps the ratbeasts had been joined by swarms of their hideous allies. Every step which he took brought him closer to another ambush, and he expected to be attacked every second; but every step led to another, and then another, and there was still no sign of any skaven. And each step took Konrad deeper beneath the city, further away from the surface.

It was almost as if he were no longer in command of his own body, that even had he wished to halt and turn back he could not have done so. This was where he was destined to be, what he was fated to do, and he must live out the role which had been assigned to him – and for which Wolf and Litzenreich had laid down their own lives.

He reached another junction, and he immediately went to the left, and he saw a distant light ahead; but this was not one of the oil lamps which he had kept passing. It was a single line of natural light, its intensity unwavering; and it was at ground level, like the light which spilled out from beneath a doorway.

He moved forward cautiously. There was indeed a door directly ahead, he realized. It seemed as if it led out of the maze of tunnels, because daylight was visible beneath. But that was impossible; he was far too deep underground.

Konrad halted at the end of the passage, a sword's length from the wooden door. The door seemed familiar, as if he should recognize it. His heartbeat began to increase once more, cold sweat to break out again on his hot flesh. He looked around, staring over his shoulder into the darkness. The narrow tunnel was still absolutely silent, and yet he knew that he was no longer alone. There was something ahead, something waiting for him beyond the door.

Something or someone.

It would have been so simple to open the door, but he was terrified of what he might discover within.

He wiped the sweat from his forehead with the back of his arm. His face was sticky with the blood from his own wounds and the streaks of gore from the skaven he had slain.

Konrad had no idea how long he stood in the silent darkness, his sword poised to strike whatever might appear in front of him when the door opened. But the door would not open, not unless he were the one to do it.

He touched the tip of his warpblade against one of the wooden planks, stretched out his arm and pushed the door open, then leapt through, poised to defend himself from whatever was waiting to attack.

As he had suspected, he did not find himself outside.

He was inside – inside Adolf Brandenheimer's tavern!

The door slammed shut behind Konrad, trapping him in the past, capturing him within the tavern where he had slaved for most of his life.

This was all an illusion, a vision of the past designed to ensnare him. The inn had burned down the day that the Chaos swarms had totally annihilated the village.

The place was devoid of people, but every detail of the building was accurate: the fire in the hearth, the straw upon the dirt floor, the roughly hewn tables and benches, the blackened thatch ceiling. Konrad could see that the rest of the village was visible through the windows. A boar was roasting over the fire, pewter tankards stood on the table in front of the barrels of ale. At any moment Brandenheimer would be yelling at Konrad to turn the spit or to fill the beer steins.

But the landlord was long dead. Konrad had watched as Brandenheimer's head had been used as the ball in a vicious game which the triumphant mutants had played after the slaughter.

None of this was real.

Then Konrad's attention was caught by something which did not belong in the tavern, and he moved for the first time, slowly walking towards the table upon which the misplaced object lay.

It was an oval mirror; the frame and back and handle were silver, studded with jewels.

It had been Elyssa's mirror.

It was the mirror in which Konrad had first seen his own image, first seen that his eyes were of different colours, and first seen so much more...

This must also have been an enchantment, but he found himself shrugging the shield from his left arm, setting it down on the table, picking up the mirror, not wanting to look into the glass, but unable to prevent himself from so doing, studying his reflection in the glass, bearded and bloody, and remembering that he had seen himself like this before – exactly like this.

Then his face seemed to dissolve, replaced by that of someone else, someone much younger but whose eyes were also of different colours: one green, one gold.

And Konrad realized that he was staring at himself as he had once been, seeing his younger self on the day that he had first gazed into a mirror – this very mirror.

He sensed someone behind him and he spun around.

It was Skullface!

He was sitting at one of the tables, quaffing a tankard of ale.

'A drink?' he offered, sliding another stein towards Konrad. 'You look as though you need one.'

Konrad sprang forward, his blood-streaked blade aimed at the seated figure. Skullface did not move. His pale figure was still preternaturally thin, his cadaverous face and head completely without hair. He was clad in the outfit of a courtier: green cloak, embroidered tunic, fancy breeches, shiny boots; but he seemed to have no weapon, no elaborately hilted rapier at his hip.

He glanced down at the tip of the sword which was poised a few inches from his torso, and he sipped at his ale.

'Even when I was human I had no heart,' he said, and he smiled ironically.

There could be no doubting what he meant. He was referring to the time when Konrad had shot an arrow into his chest – and drawn not even a drop of blood.

Konrad had been waiting this moment for so long, for the time when he had a chance to kill Skullface. But how could he slay an immortal?

He had believed that he would be terrified of Skullface, but he felt very calm. So much had happened in the years since he had first encountered the gaunt figure which stepped unharmed from the inferno of the Kastring manor house.

Konrad had seen far stranger deeds, witnessed even more unbelievable events.

They stared at each other, and the inhuman's unblinking gaze seemed very familiar. Pupil and iris were both jet black; his eyes were exactly like those of Elyssa.

'Where's Elyssa?' Konrad asked. 'What have you done to her? If you've harmed her...'

'I would never harm my own daughter.'

'Your daughter!'

'I told you – I used to be human. Why shouldn't I have a daughter?'

'But...' Konrad shook his head. His mind was a maelstrom of conflicting thoughts and memories, ideas and suspicions.

He had come to believe every part of his life was connected, that all the people he had ever encountered were linked by some invisible web which held him inextricably trapped. And it was Skullface who had spun the intricate network of threads in which Konrad had been entangled for so long.

He was the spider drawing him towards the centre of his lethal web, and here was his lair.

'Put down your sword, Konrad,' said Skullface. 'You can't kill me with steel, not even with warpdust welded into the blade.'

Konrad continued to stare at the spectral figure who had haunted his life for so long.

'I know everything,' replied Skullface, answering the unasked question. 'Drink,' he added, his bony fingers pushing the tankard towards Konrad again.

Konrad kept his sword levelled at his eternal enemy, but he put the mirror down on the table and reached for the ale with his left hand. He raised the tankard to his lips, sniffing at the liquid, then tasting it.

'Who are you?' he asked, and he drank deeply.

'Elyssa's father.'

'Who are you?' Konrad repeated. 'What debased Chaos god do you serve? Whoever it is, your evil plan did not succeed. Karl-Franz lives, he's still the Emperor. The skaven plot failed.'

'The skaven!' Skullface laughed without humour. He took another mouthful of beer and looked up at Konrad again. 'The Emperor is of little consequence, Konrad. You are far more important to the future of the Empire. That is why you have to die. And I've tried to bring about your death several times.'

'The village?' said Konrad.

'It was wiped out so you would be killed. Then the mine.' Skullface shrugged, a gesture which seemed almost human. 'A few other times. You are very resilient. That is why you were brought here, beneath Altdorf, so that you could be destroyed. The plot against the Emperor was merely a ruse to ensure your destruction. But perhaps I shouldn't have left it to the skaven to finish you off.'

Konrad shook his head in total disbelief as he tried to absorb what he had been told. He was more important than the Emperor…?

'They would have succeeded,' Skullface added, 'if it weren't for those other two, the wizard and the mercenary. They sacrificed themselves so that you could survive. Only humans willingly surrender their lives for the sake of one of their own.' He sipped at his beer. 'It makes me almost proud that I used to be one of your kind.'

'You could never have been one of my kind,' said Konrad, defiantly.

'But I was, until I became...' He broke off.

'Became what?' Konrad demanded.

Skullface still seemed more human than not. He showed no real signs of mutation, and he did not wear the insignia of any of the Chaos powers. He was one of the damned, and his master had rewarded him with the skills to walk through fire, to survive what would be a fatal wound to any other living creature. Far more than a mere benighted servant, Skullface must have been a champion of one of the malevolent deities.

'Are you going to kill me?' Konrad asked, when there was no reply.

'I could have killed you in your village had I wished,' replied Skullface, 'but I do not kill.'

'No – you get others to do that for you.'

The skeletal figure raised his tankard in acknowledgment of Konrad's perception.

And Konrad knew then which of the Chaos lords Skullface served.

There was only one who made an art of deceit and treachery, who manipulated every other being for its own debased purposes. Sometimes he was known as the Changer of the Ways, or else as the Great Conspirator; others referred to him as the Architect of Fate or Master of Fortune.

'Tzeentch!' hissed Konrad.

'You could also serve my master, Konrad,' said Skullface.

'What?'

He was still standing over the inhuman, his new blade aimed at the champion's chest.

'You have a great part to play in the future of the Empire, of the Old World. Why not play that role for your own benefit? There is no need for us to be enemies, Konrad, not when we can be allies.'

'What kind of trick is this?'

'A trick? Me?' Skullface laughed. He looked past Konrad, towards the triangular shield. 'I thought that would interest you.'

Konrad had believed that the shield originally belonged to an elf, and that the same elf was Elyssa's real father. But now he was sure that Skullface was telling the truth; it was he who was Elyssa's father.

Their eyes were the same, and she must have inherited her magical skills from him.

'Why should it interest me?' asked Konrad.

'The crest. It was the same as the one on the arrow you fired at me. That's why I gave the shield to Gaxar's bodyguard, so you would see it, pursue it.'

'You gave the shield to him? And where did you get it?'

'From your father.'

'What?'

Konrad stared deep into Skullface's black eyes. Totally confused, he glanced down for a moment, and his eyes focused on the oval mirror.

Skullface should have been reflected in the glass, but instead the image revealed another figure seated at the table.

Elyssa!

Skullface was gone. Elyssa was sitting in his place. Perhaps he had never been there, and the girl had disguised herself as her father – or possibly the Champion of Tzeentch was now masking his appearance with the image of his daughter.

Elyssa's jet black hair hung to her waist, and she wore a woollen dress, white and unadorned. She had aged since Konrad knew her, and her face stared back at him with a malevolent glare. It was a look he had seen before, and he remembered what his talent had foreseen that same long ago time: how Elyssa would become changed, and how she would one day cause his death.

This was that day.

They gazed at each other, and he could see himself reflected in her jet black eyes.

'I gave you your name,' she said. 'I gave you everything. I made you, Konrad.'

'And I loved you,' he replied.

Elyssa was a creature of Chaos, possibly she always had been, and perhaps it was true that the only way to fight Chaos was with Chaos.

He gripped the hilt of his sword even tighter.

This was no longer Elyssa, he told himself. This was not the girl he had loved, not the girl who he still loved.

He swung the sword, arcing the blade towards her neck, and he closed his eyes an instant before the metal sliced through the girl's flesh, decapitating her.

'We shall meet again, Konrad,' said a soft voice – a voice Konrad was not sure whether he truly heard or only imagined, a voice which could have been that of Elyssa or Skullface.

He gazed at the severed head which lay upon the ground, trying to ignore the blood mingling with the dirt. Elyssa's eyes were open and they seemed to be staring directly up at Konrad, but there was no hatred in her expression. She appeared young again, her features relaxed and peaceful. Perhaps in death she had been saved, her soul redeemed.

Konrad closed his eyes for another moment and said a silent prayer. This was something else which he remembered from that same momentous day over half a decade ago, a future memory of this very event; he had imagined Elyssa being dead.

He had only succeeded in reaching this far because of the power within his new sword, but warpsteel was not sufficient to slay a champion of Chaos.

Although Elyssa may have died, Skullface had not.

The tavern began to dissolve, the deception over. The walls and floor and ceiling once more became part of the underground cave which they always had been.

Konrad picked up the triangular shield, sliding his left arm through the handle, gripping it with his fist. Already it felt a part of him, as once had the bow and the arrows which Elyssa first gave him.

All had originally belonged to an elf – and was that elf really his own father...?

There was no reason why Skullface should have been telling the truth; it was in his nature to lie.

As the hallucination faded, Konrad realized that he had conquered the destiny which had condemned him to death.

It was Elyssa who had died. Her severed head and lifeless corpse lay on the floor of the tunnel, the only evidence of Skullface's duplicity.

There could be no such thing as fate. Konrad's future lay entirely within himself, with his own mind and in his own hands.

He gazed ahead, and saw countless pairs of red feral eyes staring back at him through the darkness.

He was the master of his own life, nothing was pre-ordained – but he had many other battles to fight, other opponents to kill, other conquests to make.

Konrad kissed the crosspiece of his warblade, raised the weapon in a silent tribute to Sigmar, and then advanced along the tunnel and into the midst of his waiting enemies.

His warpsword hacked through their bestial shapes.

The shield which may have been his father's fended off their deadly blows.

And Konrad fought his way through the benighted swarms of Chaos, up and beyond and towards the light.